GET UNDRESSED WITH ME

AYLA CHANDLER

For the quiet ones

GET UNDRESSED WITH ME

PROLOGUE

BRITTANY

It turned out breaking and entering was actually pretty easy. Brittany didn't even have to pick any locks since she already had a key to Robbie's apartment. He had given it to her after six months of dating because he was, quote, "tired of walking downstairs to let her in."

So romantic.

And since Robbie insisted on posting absolutely everything he was doing on social media, even though she had warned him several times not to tell strangers when he was going to be out of town, she knew for a fact he was spending the weekend in Vegas with his latest girlfriend.

Which meant he wasn't home to stop her.

Brittany tugged on her skirt. She was dressed in her "too sexy for you" outfit–a low-cut tank top paired with her favorite bra and with her favorite black leather jacket, finished with a short skirt so tight that underwear wasn't an option. Robbie hated this skirt, so Brittany felt right wearing it tonight.

She let herself into the complex with the code Robbie had given her, sipping on the largest fountain soda known to man that she had purchased from the convenience store down the street. The mixture of sugar and caffeine rushed through her, exhilarating her.

Brittany had plans tonight. And those plans involved revenge.

She approached the door to Robbie's apartment, noting that the windows were dark, confirming that the idiot was indeed out of town. Brittany approached as casually as she could, keeping an eye out for neighbors to avoid. Luckily, it was late enough in LA that either people were in bed or they were still out at the club, leaving the coast clear. At the door, she slid the key into the lock and let herself inside.

The familiar scent of Robbie hit her immediately, flooding her with anger and the slightest twinge of grief, which she would never admit if anyone asked her. Doing her best to breathe through her mouth, Brittany scanned the room. It was almost exactly how she had left it that night when he had told her their relationship wasn't working. That he wanted to move on. At the time, Brittany had accepted his decision, had even agreed. Robbie was outgoing and charming and good for a laugh, making every situation feel new and exciting—wonderful at the outset but exhausting in the long run. After almost a year of dating, Brittany knew they were pulling apart, outgrowing each other. She had been grateful he had felt the same way, that they could part as friends and not have any drama.

But after some recent revelations, Brittany was ready to break shit.

Ignoring the black and chrome-themed decor that she hated, Brittany headed straight to Robbie's extra bedroom, the one he used for streaming. His gear was all there, perfectly organized and arranged in a way that made the rest of his place look like a college dorm. The equipment was top of the line, everything from computer processing to microphone to control deck, some of the best money could buy.

Brittany should know. She bought it for him.

There was a bed on the other side of the bookshelf Robbie used as a room divider, the bed his brother Gus would use when he would visit, which was often. But Gus was safely in his home over in Kimball, and Brittany didn't want to think about him. Gus was level-headed, logical, reasonable. If he knew what Brittany was up to, he'd probably pull out a PowerPoint presentation to prove how insane she was acting, and she frankly wasn't in the mood to be talked out of her anger. When Brittany was angry, she refused to stop until everyone understood exactly how she felt.

She sank into Robbie's chair, the one she had bought him for his birthday, the one designed specifically for gamers with adjustable everything because he had complained about back pain. It was comfortable. Maybe not worth the amount she had paid, but she could see the appeal of it. Hitting the button to start the equipment, she sat back and listened to the familiar sounds of the fans blowing, watching the LEDs light up and blink cheerfully at her as she took a long sip of her soda.

Robbie was a gaming streamer, and Brittany had to admit he was pretty good at it. He had only begun in the last few months but had already amassed a solid following. He wasn't particularly good at the games he chose to play, but his charm and humor got him far with his audience. He had worked diligently for hundreds of hours to build his characters and levels in the various games he played, and because of the needs of his job, he required a lot of data storage for the saved games. Over the time they had been dating, Robbie had gone from amateur streamer to one of the better-known names, landing a sponsorship and launching a line of merchandise to his fans.

Once the computer booted up, Brittany typed in Robbie's password—K1ngR0bbie, the same password he used for everything—another thing she had warned him about doing. His desktop loaded, and she went straight to his game files, the ones he had spent hours and hours cultivating and grinding for.

One by one, Brittany deleted them.

Once she was certain the digital trash had been emptied, she took one more sip of her overly large, super sugary soda, letting the caffeine and other mystery chemicals flood her system. Then, taking off the lid of the drink, Brittany poured the entire thing all over his rig. Into the tower. The monitor. On the keyboard. She double checked that all the equipment was still on, not wanting to risk him being able to clean it. There were damn good IT people out there, and Brittany didn't want them ruining her revenge by doing their jobs.

There was something satisfying about watching the set up slowly glitch out. The screen pixelated beyond recognition. Noises were coming from the tower that it really shouldn't have been able to make, and Brittany absorbed them like a symphony.

And then she pulled out her new favorite lipstick, the aptly named "Dirty Talk." A dark red that advertised it was made to leave marks on whoever you kissed. Brittany thought it was nicely ironic, considering how much Robbie hated any talking during sex and got uncomfortable if she ever deviated from their usual routine.

She applied the red liberally, making sure to layer it. Robbie had always complained when Brittany wore red lipstick, said it made her look "cheap." And he hadn't been amused when Brittany laughed in his face and told him the lipstick was anything but cheap. That red flag should really have been enough to send her running. And honestly, Brittany didn't know why it didn't, other than he had said it in his usual joking manner and she hadn't realized at the time he was being serious. Now, knowing what she knows, she would kick herself if she could.

Once she was satisfied with her lipstick application, Brittany took out the gift card Robbie had gotten her for her birthday, the one to the local seafood restaurant famous for its fresh crab, the one that sponsored Robbie. The one she knew for a fact he got for free. And the one she would never, ever use because of her deathly allergy to shellfish.

Very carefully, Brittany kissed the center of the gift card. She admired the perfect shape of her lip print, congratulating herself again on the purchase, and then placed it on the keyboard, right in the center so Robbie wouldn't miss it.

"Brittany?"

She spun to find Gus staring at her, his eyes hard as he scanned the room and the destruction she had caused in the last few minutes.

Fuck.

Gus wasn't supposed to be here. He didn't even live in LA,

but Brittany knew he would often visit Robbie. She just didn't think this would be one of those weekends. Robbie hadn't posted about it, and Gus didn't have social media, but Brittany still felt like she should have known. They were friends, after all. Or, at least, they had been.

His eyes traveled to the rig, where the electronics were losing the war against the soda. The whirring noise from the tower must have drowned out Gus coming into the apartment. The plan had been to get in and get out, no witnesses, and now she had to deal with Robbie's brother, the one person who could probably fix all of this before Robbie got back just by sheer force of will.

His eyes met hers, much colder than she was used to. Gus spent his time being the quiet but amiable companion. He had joined her and Robbie on many nights out, and Brittany had never minded having him along. Sometimes, he was the only one who could keep Robbie from causing a scene or pissing someone off, and Brittany was often relieved he was there. Now, however, she wished he had just stayed home.

"Killer, what the fuck are you doing?"

She frowned at the nickname. They had done a day of paintball for Robbie's birthday last year, a tradition the Lozano family had done since they were kids. Robbie had bragged about his skills for a straight week before the match, which meant when Brittany had smoked him over and over again, he had left the facility as pissed off as a child denied candy, and Gus had bestowed her with a new nickname. The fight her and Robbie had that night had been epic, and she hated being reminded of it.

She focused on the present day, shutting him down.

"Don't worry about it, Gus."

"You're trespassing. Destroying his property. What the hell are you thinking?"

"I'm thinking your brother is a bag of douches, and I'm tired of it."

Gus pinched the bridge of his nose, something she had only seen him do when he was dealing with Robbie's bullshit. There was some slight satisfaction in seeing his demeanor crack when she was the one causing it.

"I thought you guys had a friendly break."

Brittany snorted. "Yeah, well, turns out that wasn't the case."

"Do I want to know?"

"Do you ever?"

They glared at each other, and Brittany felt the thrill of victory that she had managed to rile him up. Gus was always so calm, so cool, so collected in the face of almost any situation. He worked for a security company, offering personal security to people rich enough to afford it. He was used to dealing with assholes, and with having to take charge in stressful situations. And apparently, Brittany now qualified as a stressful situation.

She might get a T-shirt made. Her followers would love it.

"You need to go. Robbie's coming home tomorrow. He won't be happy to find you here."

"I wasn't planning on staying."

Just then, a spark sizzled from the computer's tower, flying up into the air before dissipating into nothing. Gus strode toward the wall, brushing past her.

"Hey, don't—"

Ignoring her, he pulled the cord out of the wall, dropping it on the ground. When he turned back, she couldn't help but notice how tall he was, how straight his shoulders were, how solid he seemed. It was unfair that men got to be big and strong, especially when they were being jerks.

"You've made your point, Brittany. He broke up with you and moved on, and you're pissed about it. Not sure why you needed to destroy his stuff, but it's past time for you to leave."

Brittany burned at the implications.

"Is that the story he told you? That I'm pissed he moved on?"

"That, and something about how you only dated him for clout. And honestly, I'm not really seeing any evidence here to refute that."

Brittany flattened her mouth into a line. In all the time they had been hanging out, she had known she and Gus weren't close. When they had first met, she had set out to get to know him, wanting to be friends. But even from that first meeting, he had always seemed to keep her at a distance. Gus was Robbie's older brother, older than Brittany's twenty-seven by about four years, although if you knew the brothers, the age difference felt like more. Robbie was impulsive and outgoing and loud, whereas Gus was quiet, steady, solid. Something about him thinking she was jealous of Robbie dating a new woman was rubbing her the wrong way, but she refused to show Gus that. So instead, she flipped her hair, a practiced move that had gotten her a number of free drinks at bars and gave him her best smile.

"That's me. Just your run-of-the-mill bitter ex-girlfriend."

His eyes narrowed with suspicion. "Okay, killer, time to go."

Gus took her arm in a grip that was firm but not bruising and pulled her out of the room toward the door. Brittany made a weak attempt to get away, tripping to keep up with his longer stride.

"Hey, hands off. Us bitter women don't like men grabbing us."

He dropped her arm, opened the front door, and gestured for her to leave.

"Have a good night. Don't come back."

She sniffed, not happy about his attitude, but he wasn't calling the cops. Brittany was smart enough to take the wins when they came.

When she stepped out of the apartment, his hand gripped her arm again, stopping her.

"Leave the key."

They stood like that for a moment, staring at each other, and for some reason, Brittany could feel herself breathing hard, like she had just gone for a run. Her arm where he held it was warm, sparks zapping from the contact. It must be rage. She hated being touched by people she hadn't given express permission to, and though she had never minded a casual touch from Gus in the past, their relationship was so different now. That must be why she was reacting so strongly.

Keeping her eyes locked to his, she reached into her bra cup and extracted the key. To Gus's credit, he kept his eyes on hers, never dropping them to where her low-cut top was currently advertising the goods. He simply took the key from her and let her arm go.

"It didn't have to be this way, Britt."

"It sure as fuck didn't. Ask your brother why it is."

She was stomping toward the exit before he shut the door.

Outside the building, she spent the walk to her car fuming at Gus's attitude, his dismissal of her. Although she should've anticipated it. Gus and Robbie were tight, with Gus very protective over his younger brother. If Robbie told him Brittany was a crazy, bitter ex, there was no reason for Gus to think otherwise. Even if he knew Brittany. Even if they had once been friends. Or at least friendly.

It's fine. Brittany was used to not being top priority. There was no reason to think Gus would view her differently.

She forced her thoughts to Robbie and how he would react when he heard about what she did. He would definitely freak out. As controlled and rational as Gus was, Robbie was the opposite, a live wire of reaction and emotion that could get exhausting to those around him. He was going to lose it, which Brittany looked forward to. She had been the one to buy everything for him, and it was all insured under her name. And as far as she was concerned, Robbie deserved it, especially after hearing what he told Gus about their breakup.

Clout. As if it raised her profile even one follower that she had dated some lame streamer with the emotional maturity of a zucchini. Brittany was a fashion influencer who spent her days helping her followers put together outfits from underwear to outerwear, find deals, and dress their very best. None of them gave a shit about Robbie the gamer.

Robbie hadn't been anyone when Brittany had started dating him. Just a cute guy who liked to have fun and slept on a futon in a studio apartment. But he had gained popularity over the last year, propelling him into the 'professional streamer' category. And Brittany had been the proud and supportive girlfriend every step of the way.

And then Robbie started pulling away. Said he felt like she was crowding him. He was suddenly busier and busier, often too busy to meet up with her. Robbie had started dating shortly after they broke up, which stung but wasn't unexpected. After all, Brittany knew he was a man who liked to be taken care of, and it was only a matter of time before he found someone willing to do so. And Brittany was resolved to be the bigger person.

But then Devery had texted her…

Brittany tried to shake it off, not willing to go back into her rage when there was no outlet for it. Gus was at Robbie's, and he had caught her. Gus was hard to read, but Brittany had thought they had a good rapport. She thought he knew her well enough to know she didn't go off like this without a good reason. But here he was, just another one of the Lozano boys who only pretended to give a shit about her.

Well, fuck Gus. And fuck Robbie. Brittany was entering her villain era, and she was done with mediocre men playing a role in her life.

CHAPTER 1

ONE MONTH LATER

"Absolutely not."

Gus banged through his condo, looking for his damn keys. Everything in his place was normally organized and clean, a fact that his best friend, Val, often gave him shit about. But now his brother, Robbie, was in town, a few days earlier than normal for Kickoff, and wasn't able to check into his hotel room yet. Though Gus always told him he was welcome to crash on his couch, he was secretly glad Robbie preferred to stay closer to the convention center where the event was held. Robbie was his brother and he loved him, but Robbie was also… a lot.

Case in point, Robbie had been staying at the condo for only one night and had somehow managed to move almost everything in Gus's living room, and now the spot where Gus hung his keys was empty. Gus deeply hated when things weren't in their proper place, and now he had no fucking idea where the keys were.

"You didn't even let me ask the question."

Gus rolled his eyes, thankful he was only talking with Val on the phone and not FaceTiming her.

"I already know what you're calling about. You call every year. I told you, I don't want to work Kickoff."

Gus was willing to work most any day, even holidays, but he loved Kickoff. It was the one weekend where he got to immerse himself in the pop culture he enjoyed. The games, the comics, the movies, everything he loved quietly during the year he let himself love out loud for Kickoff. The weekend was crazy and chaotic and he looked forward to it every year.

Of course, this year was going to be different, what with Robbie and Brittany broken up, but still. Gus was determined to have fun.

But now Val, his best friend and boss and all-around pain in the ass, was calling for a favor. Val ran a local security company, and she was often hired to work Kickoff for the various high-profile people who came. But Daryl's wife had gone into labor early, which left her short on security for her Kickoff clients.

"Gus, come on, I'd owe you one."

"You owe me about forty at this point, Val."

"It's one client. One of the celebs has a stalker and their team is asking for security for her meet and greet line. You babysit someone while they smile for the camera. Make sure people don't get too handsy. It'll be over before you realize."

"No way."

"Time and a half, and I'll add a week to your vacation time this year."

Gus took a deep breath, willing himself to say no even though he knew he was going to say yes. He had a thing for helping people, and friends like Val didn't come around every day.

Unfortunately, Val knew that.

"Gus, you're a lifesaver."

"I didn't say yes."

"Your silence says everything. The client needs a ride from the train to her hotel room. I'll send you all the info."

"Wait, you never said—"

Val hung up before Gus could get a word in edgewise, which was probably the smartest thing she could do.

Gus shook himself, realizing he still needed to find his keys and get the fuck out of there. But once again, the universe was against him as Robbie came slamming out of the bathroom. He was still in his boxers, his hair a mess in the way that Gus knew for a fact his online fans loved. He threw his signature grin at Gus.

"Hey, you're up early. Is there breakfast?"

Annoyance flared as Robbie flopped himself onto the couch. Though Robbie was twenty-six, he perpetually acted like he was still in college. This didn't usually bother Gus, but right now, when he was late and couldn't find his keys, Gus was annoyed.

Not that Robbie noticed.

"Where did you leave my keys?" Robbie had borrowed Gus's SUV last night for some late-night club party that gaming streamers were invited to. He had tried to convince Gus to come, but the club scene wasn't for Gus, and the gaming streamers were never interested in talking with Gus. Robbie's friends had dubbed him "the boring one" for the way he would cut them off from drinking more, would make sure they weren't making asses out of themselves, and basically would smooth over whatever trouble they would get into. Gus knew he wasn't the fun brother, that Robbie was universally liked, was charming, could talk his way into anything, but it bothered him how easily Robbie's friends classified him as "boring." So Gus had stayed home last night, read a book and watched the news in what he was sure was the most uninteresting Tuesday night a person had ever lived.

And he had liked it.

Robbie had his arm over his eyes, blocking the light.

"On the table."

Gus glanced at the empty kitchen table. "Which table?"

"I don't know, they're there somewhere."

"Robbie, please don't tell me you lost my keys."

"Of course I didn't lose them. I'm here, right?"

"Then where are they?"

Annoyed, Robbie sat up and walked to the kitchen, scanning everywhere Gus had already looked.

"I don't know, did you move them?"

"If I had moved them, they would be in their proper place."

Robbie rolled his eyes at that. He had heard Gus's lectures on putting things away for his whole life, and it had made zero impression on him. Bored with searching, Robbie climbed on to a stool at the kitchen counter.

"You should've come out with us last night. There were so many women at the club just hunting for a hookup."

Gus opened drawers, opened the fridge, trying to think like Robbie.

"I thought you were dating Diamond."

"She dumped me."

Gus looked up at that.

"When did that happen?"

"Last month. Someone told her some lies about me. She believed them and dumped me."

"What lies?"

"Does it really matter?"

Robbie ran his hands through his hair, quick, clearly frustrated with the conversation. But at this point, Gus was mostly immune to Robbie's moods.

"It matters if you want her back."

Robbie looked up at him at that.

"You think I can?"

"Not if you're going out picking up women at clubs, no. But if you can sit down with her to talk to try to prove she heard lies, then maybe. Diamond's a smart woman."

Gus liked Diamond. She was no Brittany, but she was intelligent and funny and ran her own streaming page with makeup tips, including the occasional wild art piece. Because of her popularity, she was often hired to do the makeup at various magazine shoots, worked with other influencers, etc. She was solid, and someone he had thought could make Robbie wake up and start acting like a grown man.

But if she had dumped him…

"What lies, Robbie?"

Robbie just shook his head.

"I think Brittany got to her with some nonsense. That girl is batshit. No idea why I dated her so long."

"She's not batshit."

Gus had spoken automatically but knew in the moment it was a mistake. Proven true when Robbie spun his gaze to him.

"What the hell are you talking about? She broke into my apartment and ruined my rig. I lost over a thousand hours of gameplay because of her and had to replace all my equipment."

Okay, that was a fair point.

But Gus's mind went back to that night, to Brittany in a miniskirt so short it haunted him, handing him the key she had still warm from her bra. Her eyes had flashed when he accused her of being angry about Robbie dating. There was a hint of disappointment in her look that Gus couldn't get out of his thoughts.

His mind a thousand miles away, it took Gus a moment to realize he had opened the freezer and was now staring at his keys. He grabbed them.

"The freezer, Robbie?"

Robbie nodded as if it made sense.

"Oh, right, I was going for a popsicle and must have dropped them."

Gus didn't have time to lecture Robbie on how stupid that was. He headed to the door.

"Don't break anything, don't steal anything, don't throw a party."

Robbie called after him just as he was shutting the door.

"Booooring."

The door firmly shut, Gus took a breath to center himself just as his phone dinged with a text message. He glanced at it, seeing it was Val sending him the client information... and his gut dropped at the name.

Kickoff just got a lot more chaotic.

CHAPTER 2

BRITTANY

The morning Brittany left for Kickoff really should've been the indication that the day was going to be a shit-hole of a dumpster fire.

She'd had a morning meeting with Champagne, a high-end fashion design company that was looking to start doing capsule collections with popular fashion influencers. Which, on the surface, was Brittany's dream, the one she had been working toward since college when she posted her first outfit of the day to social media.

However, this meeting had quickly devolved from a dream into a nightmare.

Her first sketches had been cocktail dresses based around different facets of her personality. Brittany was known for mood dressing, and for her first real collection she wanted to capture the feeling of that for her buyers.

Champagne hated it.

Now she was dodging phone calls from her mom, not

wanting to feel even worse than she already did. So she was distractedly sending yet another call to voice mail when she stopped short at the sight of the package outside her apartment door.

He'd left another one.

When the DMs had first come through, the ones promising love and affection from a nameless, faceless social media account, Brittany hadn't really paid them any attention. As a fashion influencer, she often posted pictures of herself in various states of dress, nothing salacious, but enough to show her followers what undergarments worked with what outfits. Brittany was a firm believer in the underwear making the outfit, and so had never shied away from talking about it or showing what worked for her. But Brittany was a public figure on the internet, so no matter what, any skin showing got her attention from the wrong crowd. As a result, she got marriage proposals every other week from both fans and creepers. When she had gotten the first message it wasn't out of the normal, just some compliments with an abundance of rose emojis. But slowly, the DMs had gotten more and more explicit and disturbing. Brittany had eventually blocked the account and reported them. But, of course, it didn't stop there. Whoever sent the messages simply created a new account, sending Brittany more aggressive attacks and threats. It had gotten so bad she had reported them to the police, several times. But the police weren't able to track the messages, and there wasn't much they could do in the meantime other than to warn her to be careful and to keep everything for evidence in a possible future case.

Then Brittany had started getting gifts left at her apartment in Los Angeles. Flowers—always red roses. Some candies. The hair ties she liked to wear on her stream.

And then he had started drawing her. The art was objectively terrible, ranging from something as mundane as drawing an Instagram post of hers, to explicit paintings of whatever the creep was currently imagining about her. Brittany hated them, wanted to burn them, but the police had warned her to keep them, just in case. They were currently collecting dust in the very back of her hall closet, waiting for the day Brittany was finally allowed to stage a bonfire.

Now, here was another package, wrapped in fancy gift wrap and a ribbon in a way that would make Martha Stewart jealous. She looked up and down the hall, knowing it was futile, knowing the guy was long gone, but it was still unnerving. Brittany slowly approached the package and opened her door, kicking it inside.

She let it sit on her floor while she went through her other chores for the morning. There was a lot of prep involved in going to Kickoff, and she couldn't get distracted and forget something. She spent an hour going through her packing checklist, making sure everything was ready until she couldn't pretend the package wasn't sitting there anymore. Finally, Brittany grit her teeth and opened the box.

The note was inside, in a red envelope of high-quality cardstock, just like it always was. Brittany saved it for last, knowing whatever he had written was going to be disgusting and make her spiral. She pulled back the layers of carefully folded tissue paper to find what she had already known was there.

A red rose, the stalker's signature. And a painting. Of Brittany, to be exact, splayed out on a bed without a stitch of clothing on, her legs spread and her mouth open in what Brittany could only assume was meant to be a moan. Brittany did her best to examine the painting dispassionately, trying not to let the image unnerve her. Whoever the guy was, he would never make it as a professional artist, but Brittany could see enough of herself in the painting to be creeped out.

And then she noticed the dried substance caked onto the small canvas.

She dropped the painting immediately, going to wash her hands twice before she picked up the card the creep had included. And immediately regretted it.

Can't wait to see you this weekend. Hoping you'll spread just for me while I pound your—

Brittany threw down the note before she could read any more. His notes had slowly gotten more and more graphic. The last one she read all the way through had made her nauseous for the rest of the day, and frankly she had too much to do to put herself through that. Instead, she took a few photos of the package and sent the pics to her mom, remembering too late that she had been avoiding her call.

Immediately, her phone rang. Brittany, accepting the inevitable, answered.

"Were you avoiding me?"

Leave it to Kathleen to react to a picture of her stalker's latest 'gifts' with only thoughts of herself.

"I have a lot to do today, that's all. I wasn't avoiding you."

"Can we talk about your complete disaster of a meeting?"

Britt's jaw clenched at her mother's words, the gaping feeling of failure expanding in her chest. Kathleen Jenssen had a lot of expectations. She'd been amassing them since Brittany was old enough to enter pre-school, and she had slowly moved down her list as Brittany aged. Spelling Bee champion. Honor student. Captain of the volleyball team. Prom queen. Top of her class for her business degree.

And it was there that it all went to shit.

Because college was where Brittany met Min. Min, whose mother encouraged her to follow her dreams. Min, who discovered she could stream herself playing video games. Min, who showed Brittany how to monetize something she naturally did every day—showing her friends how to dress for various life events.

From there, BrittKneeSocks had taken off, her streaming channel where she shared fashion tips, her outfit choice of the day, and her sock choices for her chronically cold feet. Somehow, her content led to a large online following, people asking her advice on what to wear, how to wear a piece, or just wanting to see what she put together for the day. Brittany loved it, loved the sense of community and the feeling of actually helping people with a small aspect of their day.

Kathleen had hated her streaming at first, calling it a "useless hobby" that took time away from Brittany pursuing a real business career. Brittany somewhat understood her point. Growing up, Brittany had often heard the story about how Kathleen had wasted her youth waiting for Brittany's father to leave his wife. It wasn't until Brittany was a teenager that Kathleen finally saw the reality, that she was simply a side piece to Brittany's absent father and that he would never break up his home for her. After a brief depression, Kathleen had bounced back and completely focused on making sure Brittany didn't make the same mistakes she did.

Which is why the streaming thing wasn't ideal to Kathleen, who thought Brittany was wasting her time. But after the first sponsorship with a sock company, a small bit of income but still exciting, Kathleen changed her tune and threw herself into managing Brittany's career as a fashion influencer. It had been Kathleen who had brokered the deal with Champagne, and this post-meeting call was just as terrible as Brittany had known it would be.

"You're overreacting, Mom." Brittany tried to keep her tone light, professional. She glared down at her manicure, the gel nails making it impossible for her to bite through. Yet another thing in her life keeping her from what she wanted.

"You're not designing for your college friends anymore, Brittany. This is the real deal. Champagne wants high-end luxury, not your usual cheap clubwear."

Brittany couldn't distinguish which part of the conversation was making her angrier—her mother speaking to her like a child, her calling Brittany's designs cheap, or the fact that she hadn't even commented on the photo she had sent. But Kathleen was right, Champagne wanted high-end, and Brittany wanted to deliver. This deal would make her career, propel her from just another online influencer to her dream of actually designing and creating fashion.

She just had to figure out what they wanted from her.

"Okay, Mom. I'll rework the designs and get some new ideas in the next couple weeks."

"Weeks? Why not tomorrow?"

Brittany blew out an impatient breath. "Because I'm heading to Kickoff, Mom. My train leaves tonight. You know this."

The silence over the phone told Brittany that, while her

mother had definitely known this, she had put it aside and pretended it didn't exist like she did with everything she didn't approve of.

"I still can't believe you're wasting time at that fan convention." Her voice was cold, and Brittany braced herself for the passive-aggressive argument that was about to follow. Brittany hated when her mother was like this. If Brittany argued with someone, she wanted it to be loud, she wanted to get everything out in the open and not hide behind expectations or proper words.

But her mother was built different. As she liked to constantly remind Brittany.

"It's great exposure. And it's fun. I have several big meet-and-greets planned, I have panels I'm speaking on. Min's here—"

The sound Kathleen made on the other side of the phone line could only be described as a derisive grunt. But if you asked Kathleen, women never grunted, so instead it was a sound that existed for her with no name and no intention other than for Brittany to feel judged. And while Brittany was willing to take a lot of her mother's passive-aggressive comments, she felt her spine straighten at the thought of Kathleen judging her best friend.

Kathleen just couldn't help herself. "I find it hard to believe you're still friendly with that woman after what she did."

And that's all it took. Brittany saw red, and there was no putting her temper back on leash.

"She didn't 'do' anything, Mom. Her asshole ex took a video of them together against her consent and posted it. She's the victim, and it's crap that you don't recognize that, especially considering your history with men."

Okay, the last part was definitely out of line, and Brittany braced herself for Kathleen's reaction.

Her mother's long-suffering sigh could've powered the sun.

"Have you even once considered that my 'history with men' as you call it, is perhaps why I am worried about you. I don't want you to fall for the same traps I did at your age."

Brittany's mouth gaped open at that.

"Mom, it's a stalker, not a married guy who strung me along for years."

The silence on the other end of the phone was deafening, and Brittany was suddenly happy she wasn't having this conversation in person. Brittany had a volatile temper, but her mother could go nuclear at the drop of a hat. And the subject of Brittany's sperm donor was something that could trigger an attack.

Luckily, Kathleen was already focused on something else.

"All I'm saying is that if you want to be taken seriously in the fashion world, you need to pay closer attention to the people in your life that you associate with. Minerva is a nice girl, but even without those pictures, she doesn't really fit the brand you're creating. I'm trying to elevate you, and this deal with Champagne will do just that. I wish you would get on board with your own success, especially now that you don't have to worry about that man anymore."

"That man" was Robbie, who since the incident at his apartment had continued his whirlwind of dating in an attempt to stick his dick in as many people as possible, with his current date of choice being a popular cosmetic influencer Brittany admired. But Brittany hadn't been lying to Gus when she said destroying Robbie's equipment was the end of it. Her temper had flared out shortly after arriving home that night, and while she wasn't exactly remorseful, she also wasn't satisfied. She'd been left feeling empty and slightly worried she had disappointed Gus, which was annoying. Gus was a good guy, had always been, and him thinking poorly of her was rubbing her the wrong way for some reason.

Not that she wanted to think about that.

An alarm went off on Brittany's phone, telling her it was time to leave to catch her train, thank god.

"Mom, I gotta go. I have to make my train."

Kathleen sighed but shared Brittany's hatred with being late. "Okay, your security should be meeting you when you arrive tonight."

Brittany froze.

"Security?"

"Yes, I hired someone because of your problem."

Brittany bit back her irritation, reminding herself that she loved her mother.

"Don't you think that's a little overblown?"

"Well, he just sent you another disgusting package, so no, nothing is overblown when it comes to your safety. A man is stalking you, and you're about to be in a public situation. This is to give both you and me peace of mind while you're at this convention you insist on attending."

"Mom—"

She wasn't listening, already on to whatever new thing she had deemed important.

"Accept the security, Brittany. I'll text you later about the designs. Don't ignore me."

Brittany shoved her phone into her back pocket, trying not to be irritated. Kathleen loved her, and this was how she showed it. Brittany just had to accept that. Besides, it would bring Brittany peace of mind to have some burly guy following her around and watching her back, even if it felt like she was getting saddled with a babysitter.

Of course, having some bodyguard following her around was going to get in the way of one thing Brittany had been planning on doing while she was in Kimball.

Getting laid.

It was time to get back on the horse, so to speak, and Kickoff was a great time to find some convention fling and work out her built-up tension. But if she was going to be saddled with some meathead, she was going to have to talk with him about not scaring off the guys she wanted to talk to.

Brittany grabbed her bag and left, heading for the train station, finally letting herself feel the excitement about attending Kickoff.

The Kimball International Convention for Fans was an event Brittany looked forward to all year. Sure, she was a fashion influencer, but there was no better place to see how clever and creative people could be with their outfits than at Kickoff, where creators could invent entire looks to mimic their favorite characters, jokes, memes, all of it. The joy of the convention invigorated Brittany, and the majority of her followers loved her Kickoff content. And yes, while Brittany wanted to design and be recognized, she didn't know that she agreed with her mother that she had to give up this nerdy, geeky side of herself in order to succeed.

The train ride to Kimball was thankfully uneventful, although by the time she arrived, Brittany was ready to curl up and fall asleep. As she exited the train, Brittany sent a text to her roommates who were already checked into the hotel.

Since Brittany wasn't with Robbie anymore, Brittany had agreed to share a room with five other influencers she was friendly with in order to stay at a more expensive hotel closer to the convention center. It wasn't ideal, but the alternative was taking Min up on her offer to split a room. Brittany knew this weekend was also Min and her boyfriend Hayden's anniversary. Brittany was a lot of things, but she wasn't a cockblocker. Especially since Hayden was launching his first game this weekend and would most likely want to celebrate with Min. In a loud, sexy way that would probably get complaints from the other guests at the hotel.

Brittany braced herself for sleeping on the floor of a crowded hotel room. It would be fine.

She hoped.

"Brittany?"

She spun, the sound of her name pulling her out of her reverie and froze at the sight of the man waiting for her. His dark hair had grown since she last saw him, a curl hanging over his eyes in a way that would make him the perfect Clark Kent cosplay. His hands were shoved into his pockets as if he were completely at ease. But she knew him too well. The set of his jaw was clenched, which he only did when he didn't like what he was about to say. And though he was filling out his T-shirt well, she could see the tension in his body from here, probably uncertain how she was going to react to seeing him, especially considering their last interaction all those months ago.

Unluckily for him, Brittany's entire shit of a day had put her in a terrible mood. She crossed her arms in front of her and planted her feet for the fight she knew was coming.

"What the fuck are you doing here, Gus?"

CHAPTER 3

GUS

Gus had known this would be a bad idea. Fucking Val.

"Hey, killer," he said, keeping his voice casual. Brittany was a small woman, but she had a temper big enough to fill the train. She rarely unleashed it unprovoked, but Gus wasn't willing to take any chances. Currently, her arms were crossed, which wasn't a good sign, and her signature glare was definitely in her eyes. But as he studied her, he could also see how tired she was. Something about the tense set of her shoulders made it clear that she was approaching the end of her rope and would rather be anywhere but here. Gus tried not to take that personally.

She waited, her rolling bag tucked next to her as she stared him down. Some women would've just walked away, but Brittany always confronted problems head-on. It was one of the traits he admired. And it meant he wouldn't be chasing her down the street in the middle of the night just to talk to her, which was a bonus.

Brittany tossed her hair with practiced ease. "If you're here to get me to replace Robbie's equipment, the answer is no. I bought it, it was all registered under my name, I get to decide what to do with it."

"You also ruined the carpet and caused some damage to the wall which had to be repaired."

She hesitated, and Gus silently berated himself. He wasn't here to argue with her. She just brought it out of him.

"I can send you money for the repairs."

Fuck, this wasn't what he was going for. He shook his head.

"I'm not here for money."

"Well, whatever this is, I'm not in the mood. Just spit it out so I can tell you no, and we can move on with our lives."

She had a point. But he had no intention of letting her go anywhere.

"Can we move this to the car?" He pointed down the street to his hybrid. "I'd prefer not to have someone live stream us arguing."

"So you admit we're going to argue," she deadpanned.

Gus sighed. If there was one thing to know about Brittany, it's that she wasn't afraid to cause a scene, especially when she was angry. And she had clearly decided to be angry at Gus.

He sent a significant glance toward the other people exiting the train station, some throwing the two of them curious glances. Gus wasn't a face that most people would know, but Brittany was a popular influencer, and her thousands of followers knew she was here. Gus had done his homework since getting the text from Val. Brittany documented a lot of her life online. And even though she was careful not to post about personal details, such as travel arrangements, she had been promoting her upcoming panels and appearances at Kickoff. Which meant her stalker could already be here, waiting.

Gus didn't like that.

She followed his gaze around, suddenly uneasy, her eyes flitted across the people exiting the train, and he could see her internal debate, which was when he made his move. She may not want him there right now, but if she was doubting her safety in the public space, it was time to relocate her somewhere she would feel secure.

With a swift grab, he took her suitcase with one hand and planted the other on her back, ushering her toward his SUV, never pausing. If you paused with Brittany, she would sense your hesitation and react accordingly.

"Hey, asshole, hands off."

Gus immediately lifted his hand from her back but still kept it hovering as he led her steadily toward his vehicle, listening to the familiar click of her heels. Which was ridiculous because she had just been on a train, and normal people didn't wear those fuck-me heels to travel. But that was Brittany.

When he got to the SUV, he stowed her bag in the back and shut the door before turning to face her. Gus was glad to see that, while she was clearly irritated, she didn't seem angry. That was good.

Their eyes locked in a staring contest, and Gus refused to lose. Gus knew she wanted to tell him to fuck off, but she also didn't want drama to leak online, and the street had just enough people to be wary of someone filming them. She was caught and she knew it. He could see it in her cold, ice-blue eyes, and he felt the sensation of her gaze run down his spine. Brittany had a way of being the sexiest woman in the room while also making you feel like she was the most dangerous predator you'd ever met.

"Gus, I'm not going anywhere with you. My security detail will be here any moment."

"I am your security detail."

She paused at that, surprised, no doubt making the exact same face Gus had made when he read the file.

"Is this some kind of joke?"

He shook his head. "I wouldn't joke about that."

She glanced around, thinking fast, and Gus braced himself. She knew what he did for a living, even if he didn't share too many details with her or Robbie. And for all that they weren't really friends anymore, they had been once, so she knew him. He wouldn't lie about something like safety.

Finally, she nodded. "Let's get this over with, then," she tossed over her shoulder as she headed to his passenger door. He just managed to beat her there with his longer stride, opening the door for her before her hand could even reach for the handle. When he shut her door and walked around to the driver's side, he tried to control his sigh of relief. This was going to be a long weekend for both of them.

Brittany was quiet, watching as he climbed in, buckled up, and, after checking that her seat belt was on, started driving.

"I'll call the company in the morning and request a different detail," she finally said, breaking her silence.

"We're short-staffed. Daryl's wife went into labor."

"It's you or nothing?"

"Basically."

She drummed her fingers on the door, and Gus could feel the rhythm on his skin. He scanned the mostly empty streets for activity, but it was still the day before Kickoff, and the town was quiet. But then Gus thought about what he had read in her file, and he felt his blood heat just a bit.

"Why didn't you tell me?"

She looked away from him then, out her window. "Tell you what?"

"You know what."

Brittany blew out a breath that felt long and deep.

"Why would I tell you about my stalker? It's not like we were friends. You made that crystal clear the last time I saw you."

"I'm always your friend, Brittany. Even when you're ruining the carpet."

"That carpet was ugly. I did Robbie a favor."

She was deflecting, but Gus couldn't let her. She was his client now, and he needed to know everything to keep her safe.

"The file says you've been dealing with this for a year. As long as you were with Robbie. You never mentioned anything."

"There was nothing you could've done. I went to the police. They made it clear that without real evidence or the guy escalating, I had to wait and hope he lost interest."

Red. That's what Gus saw at her words, the idea that she finally worked herself up to go to the police and they just sent her away. And gnawing in the back of his mind was the knowledge that she had never, not once, mentioned this to him.

"Did Robbie know?"

"Yeah. He was at my place when one of the packages was dropped off."

Robbie knew and never told Gus. Which probably made sense, since Robbie was the one dating Brittany, but still. Gus should've known she was going through this.

"What did he do?"

"What do you think Robbie did?"

Gus thought about it. "Probably was worried out of his mind. Wanted to install security cameras and new locks to keep you safe. I'm surprised he didn't call me to help."

She was quiet for so long that Gus glanced over at her. She was staring at him again, her expression hard to read.

Finally, Brittany answered. "Well, then you don't know your brother very well."

There was something about that statement that rubbed Gus the wrong way, but he didn't know how to respond. Because it was true. Whenever he thought he knew Robbie, Robbie went and did something completely out of left field and often made a huge mess that Gus would end up having to clean up. And if he hadn't even bothered to tell Gus that Brittany had a stalker…

"You might be right."

Brittany rubbed her temples. "How the hell are we going to get through this weekend? This is awkward as fuck, I'm already stressed about work, and I'm not sure how much more I can handle."

"I'm only here to watch your back. I stay in the background, out of the way. You'll barely notice I'm there."

She snorted at that. "Gus, you're a lot of things, but you don't fade into the background."

Gus didn't know what to say to that. He had made a career

of being able to blend, to not be noticed. And when Robbie was around, it was even easier, since Robbie liked to soak up attention. But now Brittany was saying otherwise, and he wasn't sure how he felt about it.

Which meant it was time to change the subject.

"I have your schedule for Kickoff. I'll pick you up at your hotel in the morning, and we'll make our way to the center together. You're not to be out of my sight."

"That sounds like a lot of fun."

"More fun than the possible alternative."

"And what about Robbie?"

Gus's gut clenched. "What about him?"

"What are you going to tell him when he wants to hang out? That you can't because you're busy hanging out with his ex-girlfriend? The one who went ballistic on his gaming equipment?"

"I'll tell him I'm busy working. Which I am. He'll understand that."

"He won't, and you know it."

"Then he'll get over it. I'm not leaving you unprotected with some stalker out there just because it might hurt Robbie's feelings. I'm already annoyed you didn't tell me about this in the first place. I thought we were friends."

She gave Gus a funny look, like she was trying to figure him out.

"Yes," she said slowly. "I would consider us friends. I'm just surprised you feel the same way."

He looked at her then, surprised. "I never stopped."

And it was true. Robbie had introduced him to a few girlfriends over the years, but Brittany had been his favorite. They had spent time together, talking, hanging out, always friendly. When Robbie had broken it off with her, Gus had been disappointed at the thought of not seeing her regularly. But he had never stopped thinking of her as a friend.

Until she broke into Robbie's apartment and destroyed his equipment. And then treated him like the bad guy because he caught her.

She didn't know what to say to that, and so they fell into silence for the rest of the trip.

Gus finally pulled up to her hotel, parking in the drop-off area out front. And then he turned to her, their eyes locking.

"Come on. I'll walk you to your door."

Brittany rolled her eyes. "The hotel has security and cameras everywhere. I think I'm safe."

"Humor me."

He stepped out of the car and went to the back, grabbing her bag. She was out of the SUV by the time he stepped around toward her. With a glance around, he led her into the hotel, this time having his hand hover over her back. Brittany wasn't a fan of people touching her without permission. He wasn't going to piss her off any more than was necessary.

At the front desk, a man brightened at the sight of her. Gus couldn't blame him. When Brittany was in the room, it was hard to look away. Gus, however, focused on scanning the lobby, searching for anyone who might seem too interested in them. Fortunately, the place was empty.

"Good evening, miss. How can I help you?"

"I'm staying here. Someone should've left me a key."

She gave her name, and the attendant looked her up, flashing her a wide smile the whole time as if Gus wasn't standing right next to her. Not that she was his, but this guy didn't know that. Gus glared at him just to get his point across, and the guy visibly gulped and typed faster.

Once Brittany had her key, she turned to Gus, holding out her hand for her bag.

"To the door, killer."

With a sigh, she headed to the elevators, Gus on her heels. Her hips swayed with that rhythm only she seemed to hear, and he was once again grateful the place was mostly empty. Brittany could draw a crowd just by being herself.

The elevator was thankfully empty, so they settled on opposite sides.

"Was he pissed?"

He knew exactly what Brittany was asking, and what she was digging for. And, considering the night they had, and the long weekend they were about to have, he decided to give her what she clearly wanted… the truth.

"Robbie was livid. He wasn't able to retrieve any data or any of his saves. Had to buy new equipment and start fresh."

If he thought she'd look happy at that, he was wrong. She simply took it in with a nod.

"Good."

The elevator dinged, and Gus followed her down the quiet hall to her door, where she turned and blinked at him, clearly not expecting him to be so close behind her. She looked up at him, those long dark lashes framing those sky-blue eyes that Gus could easily drown in, and for a second, he could feel himself start to sweat. It was one thing to be around Brittany when she was dating his brother. It was another to be around her, standing this close, when she was unattached.

As if reading his mind, she cleared her throat.

"My roommates are asleep, so I don't think it's a good idea for you to come in."

Gus ran through a list of possibilities of what she could find in that room, but also sensed she wouldn't budge on this. He had to trust the room would be safe. He handed over her bag.

"I'll be here tomorrow morning. Eight sharp. We'll walk to the center together."

"I'm supposed to meet Min and Hayden in line."

"Then we'll meet them in line. But I'll be with you."

She nodded at that, even though she clearly didn't like it. Gus stayed close, looking down at her. Even as tired as she was, Brittany was still the most beautiful woman Gus ever laid eyes on. Objectively speaking.

"Who are you staying with?"

Brittany grimaced. "About six other influencers. The bathroom's gonna be a nightmare."

Gus frowned. "But you know them? They're friends?"

"Some of them more than others. But I needed a deal, and they had space."

"Britt…"

"Gus, don't. I can't do this right now."

Brittany turned, opened the door, and headed inside her room, ending the conversation. She turned to shut the door, pausing when they locked eyes again.

"I'll see you tomorrow," Gus told her, a warning. He didn't like leaving her here when he couldn't check the room, but she wasn't budging.

She nodded and very gently shut the door in his face.

As Gus waited, listening through the door to make sure she didn't scream or suddenly need him, he thought for the thousandth time about what an idiot Robbie was to let Brittany go. Sure, she had a temper. Sure, she streamed her life to an uncomfortable degree. But there was no one like her.

Shaking his head, Gus headed back down to the lobby and climbed in his vehicle. He had a lot to do before meeting Brittany the next morning, and he didn't want to get distracted.

Even though, let's be honest, he already was.

CHAPTER 4

The last straw was the snoring. Brittany could take a lot, could handle drama and all of it. But if she couldn't get the sleep she needed, she turned into Raging Bitch Brittany (TM), and she couldn't spend the first day of Kickoff in that mood.

She opened her eyes, the stiffness of her entire body hitting her at once. She was sleeping on the hard carpet of the hotel room, the only space left available when she got in so late and the rest of her roommates had already claimed the beds and were fast asleep. Exhausted, Brittany had only enough energy to quickly wash up, put on her pajamas, and curl up in her tiny corner of the room.

Of course, now that she was awake, she realized she wasn't the only one assigned the floor. And that her floormate was apparently a cuddler.

The hard hand that was currently wrapped around her middle gave her a squeeze. A sleepy voice rumbled in her ear.

"Brittany, that you?"

"Get your fucking hands off me, Kyle."

A chuckle hit her, but the hand moved, along with the arm it was attached to, and Kyle turned over on his back.

"Sorry, babe. You know I'm a sleep snuggler."

Brittany rolled her eyes as she jumped out of her makeshift bed, eyeing the room to gauge the chances of her getting the bathroom to herself. Six people in one hotel room didn't give her great odds.

"Then pick yourself up a teddy bear, asshole."

Kyle stretched, putting his ridiculous muscles on display since he refused to ever wear a shirt, for all Brittany could tell. Kyle was a fitness influencer and was a big fan of "giving the people what they want" as he put it. From the floor, he put his hands behind his head and threw her a grin.

"I'm working on it."

"Work faster because next time you're getting a nut punch."

Brittany grabbed her toiletry bag and went into the bathroom, only to find Sam already there, in the middle of filming a makeup application, their ring light blinding Brittany in the mirror. Sam's eyes narrowed.

"A little busy here."

Brittany rolled her eyes and wedged herself in front of the mirror next to them.

"There's six of us and your videos take hours. You can't really expect to hog the bathroom this whole time."

Sam smiled. "Okay, but that means you're cameo-ing."

Brittany shrugged and then made sure to smile and banter for the video before turning to her own makeup. Sam talked through their application, doing take after take to get it right, but Brittany barely heard them as she thought about last night. She had been shocked to find Gus waiting for her at the train station, looking stubborn and frownier than she had ever seen him, which was saying a lot since he had caught her destroying computer equipment. When he had informed her that he was the security detail her mother had hired, she almost turned right around and took the next train back to Los Angeles. Her entire Kickoff was now going to be spent with her ex's judgmental older brother glued to her side. What the fuck was her mother thinking?

But Brittany loved Kickoff. It was really the only time during the year she let her nerdy side shine. For the most part, being a fashion influencer meant following trends, looking her best, setting high expectations for the fashion world. But Kickoff was for fun, for exploring fashion that otherwise her mother wouldn't allow her to stream. And Brittany got to meet her fans, something that was tiring but that she loved doing because it reminded her why she put together outfits online—it made people feel a little more confident about putting together their own outfits. And would change their moods for the day.

Telling Kathleen to cancel the bodyguard was a no-go. The latest "present" from her stalker had creeped her out more than the others. So far the guy had limited himself to the presents, but everything Brittany had researched online said that he could turn at any moment, so if Brittany wanted to enjoy Kickoff, it meant she had a babysitter whether she wanted one or not.

Even if that babysitter was Gus.

She was stuck with Gus, for better or worse. They were both at the very least professional, so Brittany felt like they could get through the weekend without drama. After all, Gus was the calm, cool-headed one. He was the one who always handled whatever trouble Robbie found himself in, so he was clearly used to the situation. Maybe it was why he got into personal security.

Glancing at her phone's clock, Brittany hurried through her usual morning routine. Gus the bodyguard was probably already downstairs waiting for her, and she was eager to get her day started.

Once finished, she snapped a quick picture of her outfit to post, grabbed the small backpack she was using for the day, and quietly stepped over a few other sleeping influencers to leave the room…only to stop short at the sight of Gus, leaning against the wall opposite her door. In a well-worn T-shirt and old jeans that clung to his thighs, he looked tall and strong and capable, and suddenly Brittany, who always dated the wild child bad boys, found the sight to be a relief.

Not that she'd let him know that.

"I thought we were meeting in the lobby," she said.

He gave her a mild look, like he had been expecting her surprise.

"The hotel has cameras, but there's also hundreds of people going in and out of this place every day. Remember what happened to Min last year?"

Brittany did, of course. Min had come back to her hotel room to find it completely trashed. Her asshole ex had broken in and torn up the place, writing derogatory insults on the walls. More worrisome was that he hadn't been caught until he outed himself days later.

"Am I paying you enough for the door-to-door service?"

"You're paying me plenty, killer."

She narrowed her eyes at the nickname. "I've told you not to call me that."

"It's how I remind myself to be careful when you're around."

Feeling her temper flare, Brittany closed her eyes and breathed in deep. It was going to be a long day if Gus was going to insist on being this annoying.

Before she finished breathing, the door behind her opened and Kyle practically walked into her. On instinct, he grabbed her around the waist to steady himself, pulling her back against his carefully sculpted hard body, and her temper flared again.

"What the fuck, Kyle?"

Kyle, the idiot, flashed her a grin.

"If you want to press that hot bod up against me, you just gotta ask, babe."

Brittany was opening her mouth to tell Kyle exactly how much she wanted to slice him with razors when suddenly he was yanked several feet away from her. Gus's towering form was now between her and Kyle, and even though Brittany had on the heels she was currently hired to sponsor, she was still too short to see over Gus's back.

"You don't touch her," Gus said, the steel in his voice cutting deep through Brittany's psyche. Kyle held his hands up in supplication.

"Whoa, bro, I didn't mean to try anything, she was just in the way."

Gus must not have liked that answer because he took a step forward. Brittany, already seeing where this was going and knowing in her bones that Kyle wasn't worth the drama, grabbed Gus's arm and pulled him back.

"It's fine, Gus. Let's go, we're late."

For a second, Brittany wondered if he even heard her, he was so focused on Kyle. To his credit, Kyle had landed on the "maybe if I freeze, he'll just sniff me and go away" method of dealing with danger and was determined not to make any sudden moves. Brittany tightened her grip on Gus's arm, squeezing until he turned his head and looked at her, his body still tense.

"He's one of my roommates," she told him in a quiet voice. "He didn't mean anything, he's just handsy and doesn't think."

Gus kept his eyes on her, but his body was still tense. "You don't like being touched without permission."

Brittany blinked. It was true, she wasn't a hugger, didn't like to be randomly touched by people she wasn't close with. But she never really talked about it, so she was surprised Gus had even noticed.

"It was an accident, he won't do it again. Right, Kyle?"

Kyle nodded emphatically.

"Great. Can we go now?"

Gus just looked at her, and in that moment Brittany felt more seen than she had ever been, which was saying something since she regularly streamed her life to thousands of people online. His gaze seared through her, looking for what she may be hiding from him, and she found suddenly herself feeling exposed, that he could see her secrets and was weighing him in that Gus way.

Whatever he was seeing calmed him down, and the arm she was holding finally relaxed. Kyle must have sensed the change because in the next instant, he was slipping away and heading for the stairs.

"Brittany, next time warn me when you get a new boyfriend. I don't need this drama in my life."

He was gone before Brittany could correct his assumption, but it didn't matter. Kyle was a doofus and not worth explaining things to. Brittany squeezed Gus's arm one more time before releasing it.

"Can we go now?" she asked.

Gus threw one more glance toward where Kyle had disappeared and then nodded at her.

Breathing in a sigh of relief, Brittany headed to the elevator. She had never seen Gus act like that before, so protective and riled up, but she wasn't surprised. Gus was a guy who liked to take care of his things, and for better or worse, Brittany fell into that category for the weekend. Gus had effectively claimed her, which was going to hurt her plan to find a guy to give her an orgasm this weekend. But Brittany was crafty, and Gus wasn't going to be on the clock twenty-four/seven, so she felt like she could manage. And he had said he could blend into the background. Brittany didn't believe it, but maybe if he disappeared long enough, she could find a cute guy for a night of fun. It had been too fucking long since someone other than herself had given her an orgasm.

They rode the elevator without a word, Gus clearly a master of the silent treatment, and then walked out the door together. Her hotel was close enough to the convention center to walk there, a must considering her crazy schedule. When they stepped outside, they were immediately surrounded by other convention-goers, all heading in the same direction as them. Gus moved closer to her, his eyes scanning the crowd.

"Stay close."

They slowly made their way up the street, Gus using his

size to knock people away when they got too close. His hand hovered behind her, not touching but close enough that she could feel his heat through her thin blouse, which was comforting in a way she didn't want to think about.

They crossed the street to the convention center, Gus not saying a word but keeping his eyes moving constantly looking for threats. They easily spotted the long line to enter, and Brittany stopped, going on her tiptoes to scan the line.

"She's over there."

Brittany followed his arm to see her friend Min wildly waving in her direction. Her boyfriend, Hayden, stood with his hand on her hip, looking around them as if someone was going to pop out of the crowd and attack Min with an autograph request.

It wouldn't be the first time. Hayden had built his streaming platform as DeathsHead with only his voice and his love of games—but never had actually shown his face. Until trouble went down at a gaming tournament last year, and he outed himself publicly to show his commitment to Min. Previously rivals, FlameThrower and DeathsHead were now considered a celebrity couple in the streaming circles, and so events like Kickoff meant they were often recognized. Especially since they were usually together because they were disgustingly in love.

Brittany tried not to hold it against them. Mostly because it was nice to see Min so happy. She had had a rough time last year when her asshole ex posted racy pictures of her online without her consent. Hayden was a good man, for all that he was an idiot for a hot second before they got together. But now he was committed, and Brittany could appreciate his obvious devotion.

Once Brittany got near, she threw herself at Min, who gladly caught her in a hug with a laugh.

"You bitch, where have you been hiding?"

Min squeezed her tighter. "Me? You're the one locking down uber-important design deals and having meetings with fashion houses. No time for your lame gamer friend."

Brittany pulled back in time to catch her grin and immediately smacked Min on her shoulder.

"Excuse me, which of us has been working non-stop on an exclusive sponsorship, as well as helping our boyfriend with his game release. Hi, Hayden."

Hayden threw her an easy grin.

"Hey, Britt."

Min looked over Brittany's shoulder, and her eyebrows shot up.

"Gus, hi. Didn't expect to see you here. Together."

Min's eyes went to Brittany's, silently demanding an explanation for why Brittany was hanging out with her ex's brother. Brittany glanced at him, seeing her own reflection in his aviator sunglasses, before turning her full attention on Min.

"Gus is working. Mom hired me security for the convention, and it turns out Gus was the only one available."

Honestly, if Brittany wasn't so annoyed by the whole situation, she would've enjoyed Min's mouth dropping open in shock.

"I have so many questions," Min finally got out. "Does this mean you're attached at the hip all weekend? What was asshole Robbie's reaction when you told him? Why do you need security?"

Brittany slid her arm through Min's, nudging her forward with the line.

"Gus has worked freelance for a local security company for a few years. Hopefully not attached at the hip, because I have plans for this weekend." Brittany let her eyebrows wiggle for Min, who laughed at the implication. Min knew all about Operation: Get Laid, and she fully supported it.

A deep voice behind her interrupted them.

"Robbie doesn't know yet. But once he understands the situation, I'm sure he'll be fine."

Min turned innocent eyes on Gus. "Yep, when I think of Robbie, I always think of well-thought-out complex emotions and reactions."

Gus didn't react, which had Brittany biting back a laugh.

"Leave him alone. He's working, and Robbie's his brother so he's not going to talk shit about him. Weren't you supposed to bring me breakfast?"

Min handed her a small breakfast sandwich as they shuffled forward with the line. Brittany bit into it, moaning at the delicious bacon, cheese, and egg biscuit.

"I love you so much."

"Are you talking to me or the sandwich?"

"Don't make me choose."

Brittany took another bite, practically inhaling the thing before she noticed Min looking at her with anticipation.

"What?"

"You didn't say why you needed security."

Brittany took another bite before answering. She could feel Gus's eyes on her, as if he was waiting to see what she would actually say.

"My stalker left me another gift. Said he would see me at

Kickoff. My mom freaked out and hired security, and somehow through a chain of kooky events hired Gus's company."

Min's smile faded. "He's still sending you stuff?"

Brittany shrugged, trying to be casual. No one liked to hear people complain a lot, and Brittany didn't want to drag Min into her mess when she was already stressed about the game launch.

"Just some drawings, a painting, and the odd note every now and then. But this is the first time he said he'd be somewhere specific, so Mom thought we should be cautious."

Min eyed Gus from where he had stationed himself behind Brittany.

"And you're ready for this guy?"

"Absolutely." He said it with a conviction that Brittany felt in her bones, and she was hit with the flash of her almost-year with Robbie. Whenever Robbie had a problem, the response was always to call Gus. And now she had Gus on her side, protecting her, and it felt...

...nice.

"So what's the plan for this Kickoff? Anything special?"

Brittany shrugged. "The usual. Heading to Randall's booth now for a live stream. A couple meet-and-greets through the weekend."

Min eyed her. "And the sexy plans?"

"Still on. Assuming I find a willing participant."

Min huffed. "Any man would be so lucky."

"Not according to the last one."

Brittany had been aiming for a self-deprecating joke, but it had come out sounding a little more serious that she expected. Which had Min and Hayden turning sympathetic eyes on her. Christ, it was one thing for Min to look at her like that, but Hayden too?

"He was a jerk and didn't deserve you, Brittany," Min told her. "His actions made that abundantly clear. Tell me you're not broken up over him."

Brittany could feel Gus's eyes on her, but she ignored him. He only knew Robbie's side of the story, and whatever she had let slip that night in Robbie's apartment. And he was Robbie's brother. There was nothing Brittany could say that would move his opinion in her direction.

Brittany rolled her eyes, trying to lighten the mood she had inadvertently brought down. "Hell no. Pissed, yes, because I feel like an idiot that I stayed so long."

"Have you dated anyone since?"

"No."

"Brittany." The way Min said her name, so full of sympathy, had Brittany feeling a suspicious burning behind her eyes, which she quickly pushed down, very aware of Gus's eyes on her.

"It's not a big deal."

Min looked at her with sympathy. "He really got to you, didn't he?"

"I think it was more that he opened my eyes to how little I was demanding from a romantic partner. And then he stomped all over me."

"Don't let him turn you bitter."

Brittany snorted. "He doesn't have that power."

Min nodded, looking relieved. "You don't actually have to be around him, right? Just because…" her voice trailed off as she looked at Gus, who was purposefully looking in the other direction even though he had clearly been eavesdropping on the entire conversation.

"No," Brittany said, tapping Gus's arm. "Just the big guy."

"Is Robbie here?" Hayden asked. His eyes had gone narrow, focused, even as he put his arm around Min and pulled her away from the guy behind them in line who wasn't respecting the idea of personal bubbles.

"Yes." Brittany almost jumped at the sound of Gus's voice.

There was a silent pause. A tense pause. Mostly from Min. Brittany had known Min since college, when they made a pact to fucking hate each other's exes no matter what. And if Robbie was here at Kickoff, Min was ready to either pretend he didn't exist or cause a big scene, depending on what Brittany wanted.

If the situation was reversed, Brittany would've done far worse to Hayden. In fact, she'd had a whole car barbeque planned before the idiot fixed his ways.

Brittany rolled her eyes. "He's here, but unless he's dying to come to one of my meet-and-greets, we won't see each other. Kickoff is a huge event, and we sure don't run in the same circles anymore. It'll be fine."

They had finally reached the front of the line, so Britt, exhausted from the conversation and from dodging questions, scooted toward the far scanner for her badge, throwing a wave behind her.

"Running late, gotta go, love you, bye!"

She heard Min's exasperated laugh from across the room but didn't hesitate in her exit. Min was the best of friends, but when she got protective, there was no stopping her until you were figuratively swaddled in bubble wrap. And sometimes, like in college, literally.

Trusting Gus to be able to follow, Brittany quickly slipped through the crowds, using her height disadvantage to avoid being trapped in the mob of people pushing their way into the Exhibit Hall. Once there, she stopped in the aisle, trying to orient herself.

"Over there."

Gus, a head taller than her, nodded down an aisle, his hand still hovering over her back to stop the crowd from pushing into her. Seeing where he indicated, she headed in that direction.

This year, Randall's booth was one of the bigger ones in Retailer's Row, where designers of everything nerdy could come and sell their wares to the Kickoff attendees. She saw the booth before she finally saw Randall. Never accused of being subtle, her over six foot, Black, male-identifying friend was in his full FlameThrower cosplay—hot pink wig, some sort of glittering unicorn corset layered over one of his own designed t-shirts, a miniskirt that showed off his legs, heels that made him almost seven feet tall, and FlameThrower's signature bright pink lipstick. Randall had built an online following because of his immaculate cosplay and had often been featured on websites and news stories. When he spotted her, she could see his shoulders sag in relief as he handed a customer their change and a bag.

"You're late."

She grinned at his grouchiness. "I'm making an entrance."

"Your entrance is useless if you're not live-streaming."

He was right, but Brittany still flipped him off before turning her back to him and pulling out her phone. She had a few missed calls, all from her mother, and she was ready to spend the day ignoring every single one. Kathleen could wait.

"I'm going to walk around and get the lay of the land. You're good here?"

She looked up at Gus, who was the picture of professionalism and concern and felt her stomach flip a little. Probably just the weird circumstances they were in.

"I'll be here for a couple hours, so yeah, I should be good."

He nodded. "Yell if you need me, but I'll be close. Do you still have my number?"

"I do."

Gus gave the booth another once-over and then stepped back.

"Stay safe."

And then he disappeared into the crowd, leaving Brittany to her morning with Randall. Grateful for the space, she turned back to Randall, who was dying of curiosity.

"Want to tell me why Rambo is here attached to your hip?"

"Not particularly."

"Do it anyway."

Brittany sighed. If today was any indication, she was going to spend a lot of her weekend explaining Gus.

"Mom hired me security for the weekend."

Randall's eyes narrowed. "Because of that creepy stalker?"

"Yes."

"Kathleen hired your ex's brother to be your security this weekend?" Randall had met Brittany's mother a few months ago when he had been in town. He had read her immediately and had easily become Kathleen's favorite of Brittany's friends. But he also had recognized Kathleen for the committed momager that she was and showed nothing but respect for the work and hustle. Kathleen loved him.

"She didn't know it would be Gus. She just hired the best."

Randall let his eyes wander to where Gus was slowly walking down the aisle, large and looming, his eyes scanning the crowd for any threats.

"He single?"

"Randall!" Something flared in her stomach. Randall must have picked up something because he threw her a wink, his over-the-top fake lashes making the move extra dramatic.

"That's a yes. I say go for it. He looks like he could throw you around."

"We're not like that. Besides, he's Robbie's brother."

"Who cares about that?"

"Well, Robbie, for one."

"Fuck that guy."

A customer grabbed Randall's attention, so he turned and left Brittany with her jaw hanging open. She couldn't even look at Gus, Randall's words ringing in her ears.

He looks like he could throw you around.

Fuck, she was not going to think about how true that statement was.

Brittany focused on opening her streaming app, fluffing her hair for only a moment before going live. She had posted her schedule that morning, so more than a few followers were already waiting for her.

"Hail and well met, friends! As you know, I'm here at Kickoff ready to consume all things nerd and pop culture. My first stop is at Randall's Riveting Designs, booth 713E, owned by none other than my friend Randall, who is rocking some killer FlameThrower cosplay. I'll be here all morning, so if you're nearby, come and say 'Hi!' Randall's also just revealed he's currently running a deal for his first hundred customers. Randall, can you tell us about your deal?"

Randall launched into his spiel, delighting her loyal followers who always loved when he guest-starred. Brittany settled in for a long morning, letting the energy of the convention fill her up. She met several fans who had seen her live and come over, she rang up Randall's customers, and all around was busy enough to almost forget Gus was watching her from somewhere nearby.

Almost.

A couple hours later, Britt's feet were as sore as her face from smiling all morning. Randall's booth had been swarmed, and she could see even he was starting to fade a little. She handed him a bottle of water from the cooler under the table, which he took and guzzled in almost one gulp. He nodded to the crowds of people pushing their way down the aisle.

"I think it's easing up."

"How can you tell?"

"We actually have time to talk."

He had a point. Randall eyed her over his water bottle.

"What's going on with you?"

"What do you mean?"

"You're very melancholy. Usually you're so peppy I fantasize about hitting a mute button."

"Hey, I'm peppy."

He shook his head. "Not to your usual standards. Plus you got a morose gargoyle hanging around you. He could give Hayden a run for his money in the silent game."

Brittany glanced over at Gus, who had stationed himself on the outskirts of the booth, eyes on the crowd. More than a few of the convention-goers eyed him with interest, and Brittany couldn't blame them. Gus wasn't one to demand attention, but once you looked, it was hard to look away.

Before Brittany could think of a reply, a small, bright redhead popped into the booth. She was in jeans and a walking medical boot, her smile was huge and genuine.

"Hey, Britt, you're still here!"

Brittany couldn't help but smile. As Min's little sister, Devery presented as the more wholesome version of Min. Where Min swore like a sailor, Dev always avoided it, although Brittany had heard her mutter a "fudge" once or twice in the years she had known her. She was only twenty-three, but Devery was cute as a button. If ever there was a woman who fit the description of "girl next door" it was Dev.

"Hey, Carrot, how's the leg?"

Dev grimaced at the admittedly not-too-original nickname she had been graced with her entire life.

"Good. Doctor says a few more weeks in this bad boy and I'll be ready to fly solo."

"Amazing. Next up, a marathon."

"You know it."

They grinned at each other. Once, the two of them had ganged up on Min and bullied her to join them in training for a marathon. They had lasted about three pathetic runs before giving up and declaring marathons for the birds.

"Hey, I don't pay you to chat with the help."

Devery rolled her big brown eyes at Randall's mock sternness. "You don't pay me at all, wiseacre."

Still, she took the tablet Randall handed her and walked over to a customer that had entered a booth, waving to Brittany as she went.

"Catch you at Hayden's thing!"

"Hayden's thing" was the release party he was throwing for his game. It was a huge deal and would be hosted at his brother's fancy restaurant the following night. It was invite-only. Though he was considered more of a recluse, Hayden was going all out for the party, and it was shaping up to be the gaming event of the year.

Brittany waved back, then blew Randall a kiss. "Gotta jet, babe, duty calls."

He waved her away, already working his magic on a new group of customers, and Brittany turned to Gus, who had appeared almost from nowhere.

"Leaving?" he asked.

"Unless you have some shopping to do?"

"Not while I'm on the clock."

"Then come on, big guy, I got places to be."

She turned into the crowd to head for the exit just as her phone rang again. The caller ID showed her mother, and with a sigh, Brittany answered.

"Mom, I'm in the middle of a crowd."

"How are the new designs going?"

Brittany stopped abruptly, causing Gus to bump into her back, his hands coming to her shoulders to steady her, but she barely noticed.

"It hasn't even been twenty-four hours since you told me."

"So you haven't done anything? Brittany, I thought you were going to take this seriously."

"I am, but you gotta give me time. I told you I had a full schedule this weekend."

There was a pause at the other end, and then Kathleen cleared her throat in a way that made it clear how disappointed she was in Brittany's lack of progress.

"Fine. Send the new designs when you have them."

She hung up before Brittany could respond, which was

just fine since Brittany was certain she would've said something terrible in response. Something not productive. Something that would've felt so, so good.

"Everything alright?"

Gus spoke low in her ear, and Brittany was made suddenly aware that he still had his hands on her shoulders and that he was leaning over her, almost tucking her into his body to shield her from the crowd.

"You hold a lot of clients this way?" Brittany asked instead of answering his question, hoping the white noise of the crowd hid how breathless she sounded.

Gus let his hands slip away and stepped back. Brittany felt a flicker of regret and then pushed it aside. She wasn't going to feel bad about keeping space between her and Gus. It was for the best.

She kept walking to the door, thinking about the conversation with her mom. Leave it to Kathleen to make her feel guilty about doing what was already on her schedule, that had been on her schedule for weeks, and not dropping everything to do exactly what she was told.

Shrugging off her melancholy, Brittany made her way out of the Exhibition Hall, pausing to take a deep breath when she was out of the crowd. She loved Kickoff, but damn if constantly being surrounded by people didn't wear her patience.

Gus came to stand in front of her, scanning her from head to toe.

"What?" she asked, a little annoyed.

"I'm sorry I put my hands on you without permission."

Brittany looked away, suddenly uncomfortable.

"It's fine."

"It's not fine."

"You were doing your job."

"That doesn't excuse it."

Something about the sincerity in his voice when he said it, as if he was making a vow only for her, had her turning back toward him.

"Gus, you're here to protect me. You have permission to put your hands on me if you need to for my safety. I trust you."

She watched him exhale and realized how much it bothered him that he had touched her without permission. Amazing. Robbie was a touchy-feely guy, a hugger who made instant friends with everyone he met. Brittany hadn't liked the instant familiarity he had shown with her when they first met, but she had grown used to his need for physical touch and his lack of boundaries.

But here was Gus, concerned he had made her uncomfortable just because he had steadied her in the crowd. And something about her telling him she trusted him felt… important. Like it had shifted their relationship in a way she was unprepared for. But it was the truth. She did trust Gus.

She just didn't want to think too hard about why.

Finally, he nodded and surveyed the area, always keeping an eye out.

"Thank you. Should we get going?"

Brittany nodded and turned.

"Let's do it."

They made their way through the convention center, Brittany pausing every now and then to pose for pictures with fans while Gus watched silently from the sidelines. Finally, Brittany found the autograph and meet-and-greet area and approached a woman with a headset and a tablet who looked official and stressed. She brightened when she saw Brittany and immediately started typing something on her tablet.

"Ms. Jenssen, let's get you checked in and settled into the green room. Can I get the name of your guest?"

Gus stepped forward. "Gus Lozano, Ms. Jenssen's security detail."

The woman kept typing, nodding at Gus. Brittany realized she must not be the first person to show up with security that day, which made her feel a little better. Like it was normal.

"Right this way."

She walked at a clip quick enough to have Brittany skipping to catch up. Gus was beside her as they were led to the back area, where a portion of the large room had been curtained off. A few chairs and several mirrors filled the space. One table boasted a beautiful arrangement of red roses, the sight of which had Brittany freezing in her tracks.

"Anything you see is for your use if you need it," the woman told her. "There's water in the fridge in the corner for you and your guest. I'll come get you when we're ready. The line is going to be allowed in shortly."

With an efficient nod, the woman was gone, all without actually introducing herself. But Brittany barely heard anything that was said, her gaze so focused on the flowers. She felt herself go cold.

"What is it?"

Gus's voice was soft, and closer than she expected, coming from behind her. She heard the concern there and swallowed hard, willing herself to act normal, to not care, or at least to not show that she cared. She felt Gus's hand on her back, light but steady, like he was ready to catch her if he needed to. She looked up at him, a little off guard. Was this how Robbie felt about his brother? Was this why he always called Gus when something was wrong?

Because Brittany, a woman who was used to taking care of herself in more ways than one, very suddenly saw the appeal.

"He likes to send me roses." She didn't have to say who 'he' was for Gus to understand. His jaw went hard, his eyes turning back to study the roses more closely.

"Don't move."

Like that was an option. Brittany counted her breaths while Gus strode over to the curtain and stuck his head out. After a moment, the woman with the tablet came in, still stressed but chipper.

"What can I do for you?"

Gus took over. "Where did the flowers come from?"

The woman—Barbara, from her name tag—checked her tablet.

"They were delivered this morning for Ms. Jenssen."

"I'll need the name and contact for the delivery company."

Barbara bit her lip, suddenly worried. "Is... is there a problem?"

Gus ignored her question. "No one else is to come in or out of this curtain except for us."

She nodded at the sound of steel in Gus's voice. "Of course."

"And get me the name of that company."

Barbara, clearly dismissed, headed out, and Gus turned to Brittany, who realized she hadn't said a word since they walked in.

"There's a note," Gus told her, his voice now gentle. "Do you want me to open it for you?"

Brittany cleared her throat, then cleared it again, willing herself to act normal.

"If you could. Please."

Gus immediately reached out and plucked the small note from the middle of the arrangement. He kept his eyes on her until he had the envelope open and then glanced down. After a moment, he put the note in his pocket.

"I will deal with this. Stay here."

He started to move to the curtain, and Brittany couldn't help but panic.

"You're leaving?"

"I'm only going to make a few calls. I won't be far, and you're safe in here."

"Could you…" Brittany bit her lip, wondering if she was being crazy, and then decided she didn't care. "Could you take the flowers out of here?"

Gus didn't hesitate, just grabbed the flowers and walked out, leaving Brittany alone in the dressing area. She went to a vanity set up and sat down, staring at her reflection.

"Get it together, Jenssen." After a moment of deep breathing, she pulled out her makeup bag and her change of clothes and went to work. She still had a meet-and-greet to attend. Fans had spent money to see her, and she sure as fuck wasn't going to disappoint them. She set up her phone to live stream her getting ready and put on her influencer smile as she went live.

"Hey everyone! I'm getting ready to see you all today and thought you should join me!"

CHAPTER 5

Gus was burning.

He had known about the stalker thanks to the brief, but seeing both the evidence of it and Brittany's reaction to the latest 'gift' left Gus wanting to slam his fist through a wall. The note alone was something he never wanted Brittany to read, and knowing that she had been getting notes like that from some creep for a year…

Gus gritted his teeth and turned his focus back to the situation at hand. The note had mentioned Brittany's new 'boy toy' which meant the guy had been watching her and seen her with Gus. Not the best circumstance, but Gus didn't mind. He'd prefer the asshole to know Brittany had someone watching her back. Maybe he'd think twice about whatever sick plans he was harboring.

Brittany was on hour two of her meet and greet and gave no sign of slowing down. Her smile was big and genuine, and she freely hugged the fans who came up to her for their turn, listening patiently at whatever they were saying and making sure to get a smile out of them. She was good at this, Gus realized. No wonder she had such a strong following.

Against his will, his gaze trailed down to Brittany's legs. She had put on her signature knee-highs, this time made of some sort of glittering nylon material. Gus couldn't remember paying that much attention to what women wore on their legs, but Brittany, well. She was hard to ignore.

The latest group approached her, a couple of men who said something to make Brittany laugh, a welcome sight after the drama of the green room. Gus had the number for the delivery service in his pocket, and he was waiting for the event to end so he could go ask them some questions, see what kind of trail this guy left behind. According to Brittany, previous packages and gifts had all arrived at her apartment with no mailing address, and not by her mailman. Which meant her stalker usually hand-delivered things. Him using a delivery service this time was a unique deviation, one that Gus was hoping would give him a clue to who this guy was.

Brittany jumped away from the two men, reacting to something, and Gus snapped out of his reverie, already moving toward her.

In the seconds it took Gus to reach her side, the men had moved closer to Brittany, talking fast... faster than an innocent person would need to talk.

"We paid for the meet and greet. Just relax."

He shrugged his shoulders like whatever happened wasn't a big deal, but Brittany looked ready to shove dynamite in his mouth. She stood her full height—which was taller in heels, but probably only up to Gus's shoulder, and pushed herself into the guy's space, her outrage clear.

"A meet-and-greet is just that—meeting and greeting, and a picture. That does not give you permission to put your gross hands on my ass."

Gus glanced around, noticing the cameras out already, filming the scene, and decided to wait until Brittany said her piece. She was a hothead, but she tended to have a point, even when her temper took over like it had in this moment. Sometimes, people needed to be yelled at.

Still, the guy tried to play it off, reaching his hand for Brittany's shoulder in a move he probably thought would calm her down.

"Baby, look, you're blowing this way out of proportion."

"I said don't put your fucking hands on me." In the blink of an eye, Brittany grabbed the guy's hand and twisted it in a way that Gus knew would hurt like hell but not cause permanent damage. "Consider your meet-and-greet canceled. Get the fuck out of my face before I make you bleed in front of the whole internet."

Gus was impressed. Brittany angry was always a sight, but she must have extra fuel in her engine from the flowers. And right now, in her knee highs and heels, she looked like an avenging goddess ready to smite those who would oppose her.

Unfortunately, the guy was an idiot. His face screwed up with the rage of unrequited lust, and he attempted once again to grab Brittany.

"Listen, you bitch—"

Gus was moving before he could finish, grabbing the guy and hauling him away from Brittany in a move he learned during his old bouncing days. He shoved the guy into the arms of the waiting security guards at the door.

"Get this guy out and revoke his pass."

The guards nodded, taking the asswipe away, his face contorting as he realized his time at Kickoff was completely over. Gus turned back to Brittany to make sure she was doing alright and then realized he shouldn't have worried. She was already smiling with the next group, posing for a picture while one of the women told her what a hero she was. Gus shook his head at the sight. Brittany was a scrapper, and he couldn't help but admire her for her ability to bounce back.

Her eyes wandered to him just then, and Gus felt a shock through his entire system. The kind of feeling when you're falling asleep and suddenly jolt awake—like your body was slowly dying without you realizing, and now you finally had what you needed to survive. The air practically crackled with tension and Gus couldn't look away, drawn into her in a way that he didn't want to end.

The whole moment was maybe a second long before Brittany snapped back to the people she was talking to. Gus found himself shaking his head, trying to make sense of it without actually thinking too hard.

His sugar was low. Or maybe he was dehydrated. That must be it. He sure as hell wasn't finding himself attracted to his brother's ex, who had only dated him for clout. The one who had used Robbie for followers and then sabotaged his game system when he called her on it.

Gus shook his head again, trying to clear out the cobwebs that were forming around his thoughts of Brittany. He was there to do a job, so he would do it. Keep her safe and whole and then get the hell out of her sphere. Because if this weekend had taught him anything so far, it was that he sure didn't belong there.

When the meet-and-greet was finally over, Gus was waiting for Brittany outside the curtained-off green room while she changed back into her sneakers. When she emerged, she looked all the levels of tired she hadn't wanted to show to her fans. He held up her water bottle.

"I filled it up."

She nodded, taking the bottle without saying much, tapping her fingers on the side in a distracted way. Clearly gearing herself up for a question.

"What did you find out about the flowers?" she finally asked.

"They were sent from a local florist. I've already left a message saying I wanted to meet about a private matter. I'll go talk to them after I drop you off at your hotel room."

Brittany was already shaking her head, lifting her chin with the stubborn tilt that he knew spelled trouble.

"I want to come with you."

"You just spent three hours putting on a show for people. You're exhausted. I'm going to walk you to your hotel room, you're going to rest, and then I'm going to check the florist."

"I'll let you know when I need to rest, Gus. You don't get to tell me what to do."

"On the contrary, killer," he said, leaning toward her, purposefully getting in her space. "As long as some asshole is sending you notes saying he wants to fuck your throat raw, I'm calling the shots. When your safety is on the line, I'm not going to cater to your ego. Yell all you want, but the guy could be hanging around the shop waiting to see if you show up. Fuck, he could be one of the employees there. And you'd do nothing but feed his obsession in those short-shorts and bite-me lips. So I'm going to walk you to your hotel room, and you're going to rest while I go ask some questions."

They were in a standoff, Brittany's arms crossed over her chest, pushing her breasts up in a way that Gus wished to god he didn't notice. She was pissed, but there was a flicker of heat in her eyes that was making his breath come faster than usual.

Finally, she relaxed, and he could sense victory.

"Fine," she said. "But you have to tell me if you find anything. Don't keep me in the dark because you don't want to worry me or scare me. He's been sending me shit for a year now, I can handle whatever you find."

"Fine by me. It's better you're informed and cautious than stupid and reckless."

He bent down, scooping up the backpack she had dropped on the floor when they started arguing. He threw it over his own shoulder before gesturing toward her.

"Stay close."

That was the last they spoke as they made slow progress back to Brittany's hotel. The crowds of the convention were still present as everyone settled into a weekend of lines and exclusives and parties. At one point, the crowd outside the convention center was thick, pressing them in, and Gus felt a hand take his. Glancing over his shoulder, he met Brittany's eyes.

"Don't make it weird. I don't want to lose you in all the people."

He gave her hand an involuntary squeeze.

"Never."

After that, he kept a solid grip on her hand, not wanting her to move too far from him. When they finally emerged, they were across the street walking past several shops and restaurants. The area wasn't as packed with people as the convention center was, but still Gus kept her hand in his, the memory of the graphic note from the flowers flashing through his mind. There was no way he was letting her go.

When they finally reached her hotel, Gus reluctantly dropped her hand and followed her into the elevator, pushing back into the space when more people joined them. He grabbed Brittany by the hips and pulled her to stand in front of him as more and more people piled in. Her back was pressed into his chest, and Gus realized his mistake too late. He wanted Brittany close but being this close to her meant he could smell the floral scent she wore, light and breezy in the otherwise stuffy elevator. He could sense the heat from her skin, could see how soft it looked, and all those things combined were enough to make his cock stir to life. If one more person pushed into the elevator, she was going to be able to feel exactly how hard he was.

And since Gus had the absolute worst luck, one last person shoved onto the elevator, holding a large bag of whatever loot he had purchased that day. The elevator shuffled, and Brittany was firmly pressed against Gus, her back to his front, his hard-on right above her ass. She shifted a little before freezing, realizing what she was feeling. She shot a sly glance back at him, her eyes wider than normal, filled with shock and something else that Gus couldn't identify.

"Really?" she asked, keeping her voice as quiet as possible in the elevator as it started to rise.

"Proximity, killer. Just stay still until some people get off."

His hands were still on her hips so when she shifted slightly, he felt it everywhere, his body responding in such an eager way that Gus would be embarrassed if he wasn't so turned on. He gripped her tighter, letting the loud conversation from the other people in the elevator cover his voice.

"What did I just say?"

She fucking smirked, and Gus almost lost his mind.

"The elevator is rocking, I can't help it."

He leaned closer to whisper in her ear.

"Don't start something you can't finish."

"Worried you can't get me to finish?"

They stared at each other, both realizing at the same moment the line they were about to cross, the one Gus could've sworn was never a possibility before today. She was his brother's ex and should be off limits. But she was sexy and warm, and her softness was pressed against him in a way that was making him forget exactly why this couldn't happen.

The elevator dinged as it opened, and almost everyone stepped out, leaving Brittany and Gus alone with two other people who were quietly talking to each other. There was plenty of space to stand, but Brittany made no move to leave, so Gus left his hands on her hips, both of them silently agreeing to stay where they were. They stood pressed together for the next few floors, Gus soaking in her heat, the floral smell of her hair, the catch of her breath when the elevator made an abrupt stop on their floor, all while his brain screamed at him, trying to understand what the fuck he was doing.

And then the elevator opened on their floor. With a small squeeze, he let her go, leading her off the elevator and down the hallway toward her room, keeping an eye out for anyone that might be lurking in the hall.

Without a word, Brittany stepped forward to unlock her

door, holding the handle open as she turned back to look at him, the air between them still charged since the elevator.

"Thank you. For today."

Gus nodded. "Stay inside. Call or text if you need anything."

She nodded and slipped through the door. A cacophony of hellos came through, and Gus remembered suddenly she had a number of roommates in the hotel room with her, one of them the asshole that had put his hands on her earlier, and that bothered him. A lot.

Brittany gave him a small smile, then shut the door, leaving Gus alone in the hall wondering why he was suddenly torn in leaving her there.

Shaking off the moment, Gus headed to the florist shop that delivered the flowers, only to learn from the owners that they take online orders and can't share any personal information about customers with him. He explained in simple terms the situation, and they promised to notify him if it happened again.

Left with no other lead to follow, Gus headed out, only to hear his phone chime with a text.

Val: Update needed. Coffee in ten.

He smiled. Val must have surfaced enough from the constant chaos that was Kickoff. He sent her a quick text—an emoji of a hand flipping the bird—and made his way the few blocks to the coffee shop he knew she loved.

The smell of espresso and sugar assaulted him the minute he stepped through the door. Polka Dot was the newest café in town and already a hit with the locals. Clearly the Kickoff crowd had also easily discovered the place because the entire café was packed with nerdy shirts and a few cosplays, some Gus recognized and some he didn't. He stood at the back of the long line, not seeing Val, and was about to send a text when a foot kicked in his left calf, making his knee buckle. He turned to find his boss sipping some disgusting sugar concoction.

"What is this, junior high?"

"Of course not. I was way too popular to talk to you in junior high."

Val was practically an Amazon—Chinese, almost six feet tall, with short dark hair and eyes that could cut a man's genitalia from across the room. She was in a slim-cut suit, the hint of one of her tattoos spilling out from the open collar of her button-up shirt. She handed him his standard drink—cold brew with some foam milk that he had to admit tasted like heaven—and they pushed their way to the table she had managed to snag. Her laptop was set up, along with a small plate with the remains of a muffin. She glanced at the plate as they settled in.

"The coffee here is amazing, but their baked goods taste like dirt water."

He chuckled. "You say that every time but you keep buying the damn muffins."

"Hope springs eternal."

She took a sip of whatever blended sugar monstrosity she ordered and then leveled him with a look.

"So. Update?"

Gus shrugged. "It's been mostly quiet, except for an incident at her meet-and-greet. Our stalker left her some flowers and a pretty graphic note."

He pulled it out of his pocket, handing it over to her for her to scan. He already had it memorized.

You've been ignoring me, you naughty girl. I can't wait to punish you this weekend, to watch your tears stream down your cheeks when I face fuck you so hard your throat is raw. Your new boy toy won't be able to keep you from me. You're mine, and it's time I branded you as such.

Val finished reading and then filed the note away in a folder, nodding.

"On par with what he's sent her before."

It was, but that only made Gus burn more. Gus could feel his chest tighten with the idea that Brittany had been receiving those damn notes for almost a year now, never letting on how much they disturbed her. He should've known she was having problems.

"It's an escalation. He's going to try something this weekend. I can feel it."

Val gave him a measured look.

"That's why she hired us. To make sure that doesn't happen."

Gus didn't say anything for a moment, and Val very deliberately put her drink down.

"We got a problem here, Gus?"

"Not sure what you mean."

"I mean, if you're getting personally involved—"

"She's my brother's ex. I was personally involved before you called me begging for help."

"That was when I thought you were just acquaintances. You're acting like..." She stopped, rethinking whatever she had been about to say, but Gus was annoyed enough to push her on it.

"What? What am I acting like?"

"Honestly, you're acting like an overprotective boyfriend."

Gus looked out the window, not able to meet her gaze. Was that really how he was acting? He couldn't tell anymore. His brain was too fogged up with Brittany, with the worry about her being in trouble.

Unfortunately, Val loved to belabor a point to death. "You can't protect her if your feelings are wrapped up in this."

"That may be so, but there's no one else to do the work. That's why you called me, remember?"

Val shook her head.

"You're right, I'm an idiot. I'll switch you out with Doug. He's got a nice, happily married actor that you'll hate."

"No."

The word came out before Gus could think about it, but he wouldn't take it back. Brittany needed someone to watch her back right now, and the truth was that Gus didn't trust anyone else to do it.

Val threw him an exasperated look.

"Gus, it's for the best. I shouldn't have put you in this position."

"No, you shouldn't have. But we're here, and I'm not leaving her alone."

"She wouldn't be alone, she'd have Doug."

"I said no."

They stared at each other for a moment, Val squinting at whatever she saw in his expression before she sighed.

"Fine. But if she breaks your heart, I'm going to want words."

Gus grinned at that. Val was a ball-buster, but she was also loyal as fuck.

"I should warn you. She has a temper."

Val smirked. "So do I."

"She also has a slight tendency to start fires when she's angry."

Val quirked an eyebrow. "Just my type."

Gus laughed just as he heard a voice behind him.

"Gus?"

He turned to find a young, cute redhead smiling at him.

"Hey, Dev. Good to see you."

"Good to see you, too. Heard this place was as delicious as it was caffeinated."

"The rumors are true, but you'll probably want to avoid the pastries until they get their chef sorted out."

She nodded, looking a little disappointed.

"Thanks for that warning."

It was then Dev glanced over at Val and froze, her eyes widening as if in shock. When Gus turned to follow her gaze, he found Val staring at the young woman with a calculated look, her expression carefully blank.

Suddenly nervous, Dev pushed a strand of hair behind her ear, her eyes darting away.

"Anyway, I'll let you get back to… okay, bye!"

She waved, leaving the café without buying anything that Gus noticed, and Gus turned to Val, who was focused on her laptop. Avoiding his gaze.

"Do I want to know what just happened?"

"You ran into a friend and slandered the local bakery."

"Why did she look like you were going to eat her?"

"I have predator energy. Focus, Lozano, there's paperwork to fill out."

She pushed a stack toward him, and he took it, letting the subject drop. Val was a vault when she didn't want to talk about something, and whatever was going on between her and Dev was clearly on Val's 'no talking' list. Gus settled in for the familiar routine of the paperwork, grateful to be distracted from thinking about Brittany.

And how good she felt in that damn elevator.

CHAPTER 6

BRITTANY

Since Brittany had gotten back to her hotel room pretty early and was too tired and freaked out by the roses to do any exploring on her own, she settled into her corner of the hotel room to work on her new designs. A few quick sketches later, she had sent them off to her mom for her thoughts and notes and then began to get ready for her dinner with Min and Hayden that night at Hayden's brother's restaurant.

While she was washing her face, Kyle came back into the room and cornered her in the bathroom.

"So that guy this morning. He your boyfriend?"

Brittany didn't hesitate. "None of your fucking business, Kyle."

"It's my business if some rando is going to be hanging out in our room, threatening me."

She sighed. Kyle was a prick, but he had a point. However,

they weren't close enough for Brittany to feel comfortable explaining why she needed security.

"He's overprotective is all. I'll ask him to chill when we're here."

"So he _is_ your boyfriend?"

"Again, not your fucking business."

He leaned over her then, putting his hands on either side of her at the sink and leaning in to smell her hair in a way that instantly made Brittany's skin crawl.

"If you need someone to treat you right, baby, I'm here and willing."

Not hesitating, she elbowed him, hard, in his gut. He doubled over, moving away from her to try to catch his breath. She immediately shoved him out of the bathroom and locked the door behind her.

"Brittany, what the fuck was that about?" He was yelling through the door, but his breath was still wheezing, which made sense. Brittany had hit him pretty hard.

"You've lost bathroom privileges."

"Is this how you react when a guy hits on you?"

"Only the sleazy ones."

She could hear him grumbling at that and tried to focus on her makeup. Kyle was an ass, but he was mostly harmless. He just didn't know how to take a hint unless it literally slammed into him.

An hour later, Brittany stepped out of the bathroom, relieved to find that Kyle had already headed out to his evening plans, most likely involving impressionable women with lower standards than they deserved.

She headed out to the lobby. Brittany hadn't mentioned

this dinner to Gus, mostly because she wanted a night with her best friend where they could talk freely without worrying about him overhearing whatever tea she felt like privately spilling about his brother. She rationalized to herself that she would use a rideshare both ways, not talk to strangers, and not be alone if she wasn't in the car.

As she climbed into her rideshare, Brittany's phone rang, showing it was Kathleen. Thinking that she was just calling to confirm she received the designs, Brittany answered… which turned out to be a big mistake.

"Brittany, what is this?"

"What is what, Mom?"

"These sketches you sent me. These aren't serious, right?"

Brittany steeled herself for the rest of the phone call, biting back a sigh. Kathleen was in a mood and was apparently going to take it out on Brittany like she always did.

"They are serious, Mom. You said you weren't happy with the last round, so I attempted something new."

"And you think these are high-end?"

Of course she did, but she sure wasn't going to admit that now.

"I guess I'm not certain what your definition of 'high-end' is," she said carefully.

"Lux fabrics. Fresh perspective for the person with money ready-to-wear art."

"Mom, that's not really my brand. I show people how to repurpose clothes they already have, or gently used clothes they can buy second-hand. My audience isn't the one percent, it's the everyday."

"That may be true now, but this partnership is a chance to

elevate your brand. This is the time, Brittany. You have to take this seriously."

Brittany knew, deep in her heart, that everything her mother was saying was coming from love and support. But it sounded really shitty. Kathleen had a way of cutting you to the core with words that felt like afterthoughts to her.

Her rideshare pulled up outside the restaurant, and Brittany exited, hovering near the entrance. She didn't want to be out in the open in the street, but she also didn't want to be having this terrible conversation in a restaurant where anyone could overhear.

"And we also need to talk about your attire for that convention, Brittany," she continued. "What were you thinking? Shorts and a T-shirt? You're an influencer. How are you supposed to influence in clothes like that?"

"I'm at a fan convention, Mom," Brittany said, sure her exhaustion was showing through her voice. "My followers know I go to Kickoff every year. They like seeing the casual, nerdy version of me. The people at the meet-and-greet loved it."

Brittany didn't add that she preferred this casual, nerdy version of herself. Brittany was a woman of contrasts, who was either completely made up or completely dressed down. Kathleen didn't like hearing things like that, not when she worked so hard finding Brittany designer brand deals. As far as Kathleen was concerned, Brittany should be in cocktail attire at all times.

"Your fans are paying for pictures with BrittKneeSocks. Dress your brand, or else they're going to be disappointed and you'll start to lose followers. Understand?" Kathleen's voice had taken on an edge, which meant that she was ramping up for round two of the lecture. But Brittany didn't have time for it.

"Yes, Mom, I have tomorrow's outfit picked out, and it will be so on brand no one will complain and post bad things, okay?"

"You don't have to say it with that kind of tone."

Sometimes Brittany daydreamed about doing literally anything else for her job, something that her mother wouldn't want to be involved in. A schoolteacher. A lawyer. Some sort of accountant. But Brittany also knew she had wanted to design clothes since she was little, and for whatever fateful reasons this was the path that was getting her there. With Champagne.

With her mother.

"Mom, I gotta go, I'm running late for dinner."

"Who are you having dinner with?"

Brittany tried not to get frustrated at her mother, but she knew she was going to fail if the call wasn't over soon. Her patience, already at a low thanks to the day and dealing with her stalker sending her flowers, and then whatever the hell that was in the elevator with Gus, was about to break.

"Min and Hayden."

The silence on the other end of the line said a lot, as well as the deep sigh Kathleen heaved into the phone.

"Very well. Tomorrow, make sure to post more pictures with your socks. Your viewers are asking for it."

"I will, Mom. Gotta go, love you." Brittany hung up before her mom could ask her another question, and took a deep breath, trying to cleanse Kathleen from her energy. As she breathed, she reminded herself that she loved her mother very much, even when she was being difficult.

"Hey, sorry we're late!" Brittany spun around to find Min and Hayden walking toward her, looking just flushed and out of breath enough for Brittany to suspect they hadn't been power walking. Once they were near, Brittany pulled Min in for a hug, taking a big inhale.

"You smell like sex," she teased.

"Why are you smelling me, weirdo?"

"Because it's been so long I have to live through you."

Min pushed her away, and, laughing, Brittany turned and waved at Hayden.

"How did your meet-and-greet go?" he asked, casually pulling Min toward him as a few people walked near them on the sidewalk.

Not wanting to ruin the mood, Brittany deflected.

"As expected."

Min's eyes narrowed, but she didn't say anything they entered and Hayden approached the hostess. She immediately led them to a table in the far back, away from the crowds.

"I'm so glad you're here, Hayden." The hostess was practically whispering, which was new.

"Why? What's going on?"

"He's fighting with Rosa again. It's been… tense."

Hayden nodded with a deep sigh, leaning toward Min. "I'm going to go check on him. Be right back."

He kissed her quickly and left, walking to the kitchen. Brittany threw Min a skeptical look.

"What's that about?"

Min rolled her eyes. "Theo is going to be opening his second restaurant soon and has been trying to hire a new executive chef for this place. But he keeps firing people for stupid reasons, and Hayden's about ready to strangle him."

"Rosa's a new chef?"

Min nodded. "Yep. She's been doing really well, and her food is amazing, Brittany, just as good as Theo's, although don't tell him that. But they fight. Constantly."

"About what?"

"Whatever it is chefs fight about. Something about blanching. The best pans. Cook times versus temperature. Japanese knives versus German. From what Hayden's told me, all chefs are insane, and in order to work together you need to find a mutual insanity."

"And their insanity doesn't match?"

"Not even a little bit."

Just then, there was a crashing noise that came from the kitchen that made the whole restaurant jump. Her eyes wide, she met Min's eyes. At the same time, they both burst into laughter.

Min said. "Last night Theo sent Hayden a dozen pictures of the walk-in freezer, all annotated to show exactly what Rosa had moved. Theo thinks it's a conspiracy."

"Like, she's using the walk-in to send a code to others?"

"Probably."

Just then the server came over, giving Min a relieved smile. "Min, thank god."

"I heard, I'm sorry. Hayden's trying to talk him down now."

With a nod, the server took their drink order and left to the bar just as Hayden dropped into the seat next to her, looking annoyed and amused all at once.

"Everything okay?" Brittany asked.

Hayden nodded, taking a deep drink of his whiskey.

"Theo's insane, but calmer. I managed to convince Rosa not to quit, but they've split the kitchen down the middle in an attempt to finish the night while not talking to each other."

Brittany blinked. "Being a chef is a lot more intense than I thought."

Hayden grimaced. "Huge egos mixed with sharp knives and actual fire. It's a wonder he hasn't gone to jail yet."

They settled into their dinner, with Hayden and Min going over the last-minute details for Hayden's release party the following night. Brittany was feeling happy and mellow, the wine doing its work as well as watching her best friend be so clearly in love with her guy.

It was during an after-dinner coffee that Brittany's phone beeped with a text message. Thinking it was her mother, she checked her screen… and felt her blood run cold.

> BLOCKED: Don't think you can ignore me, my love. I'm closer than you think.

"Britt, you okay?"

Numbly, Brittany glanced up at Min, who was looking at her with concern. Not wanting to dive into the explanation of the crazy day, not when Min was so clearly having a lovely evening, Brittany deflected.

"Yeah. Just a text message."

"Is it Gus?"

"No, it's… wait, why would you think it's Gus?"

Min gave her a look that reminded Brittany they had been friends for a long time. "Well, you're spending a lot of time together. You and him always seemed to… get along really well."

"I get along with everyone."

Hayden snorted at that, and Brittany glared at him.

"I don't need commentary from the guy who almost ditched my friend over a stupid photo."

He immediately sobered up. "Fair enough."

Min rolled her eyes but wasn't ready to let go of the subject. "It's just that you and Gus always seemed to click. And now he's acting like a bodyguard, and I was just wondering if you two were getting, you know… friendly."

"We were always friends, Min."

Min nodded, sitting back. "Yup, of course. You'll talk when you're ready, got it."

Brittany narrowed her eyes, knowing her friend was placating her. It was extremely annoying when people knew you this well.

"Shut up, I have to send a text."

Min laughed and turned to Hayden while Brittany took a screenshot of the text and sent it to Gus. She paused when she opened Gus's contact, seeing the last text he sent her, months ago, right before she and Robbie had broken up, something about the store having the drinks she liked in stock, and should he grab her some?

That was Gus for you. Taking care of people.

Shaking off her thoughts, she sent Gus the screenshot.

> Brittany: Just got this.

It took less than a moment for him to write back.

> Gus: Where are you?

> Brittany: Dinner with Min and Hayden.

Gus: Stay there, I'll come get you.

She was shaking her head even as she typed.

Brittany: NO! That's not why I'm telling you. I just thought you should know the asshole has my phone number now.

There was a moment of no response, and then the three dots appeared.

Gus: Have Hayden and Min ride back with you to the hotel. NO EXCUSES. I'll see what I can do about the text.

Brittany already knew there was nothing to do. The message came from a blocked number, and she had been through this multiple times with the police.

It was late by the time they wrapped up the dinner. They left the restaurant, with Hayden stopping to say goodnight to Theo and threatening him not to piss off the new chef. Min and Hayden were more than willing to grab a rideshare together, and soon they were all tucked into a warm SUV. Min yawned.

"Are you sure you're okay in that room with all those people?"

Brittany laughed. "It's the life, Min. I'll be fine. It's only for the weekend."

The SUV pulled up to Brittany's hotel, and so with many hugs, Brittany left them to walk into the lobby. Once inside, she turned around to watch their car drive off, noting that Hayden moved to sit next to Min and pull her close.

Something twinged in Brittany's chest at that. She wanted a partner to pull close, who would go with her to follow her friend to make sure she was safe. Someone who was crazy about her.

After a moment, she shook off her melancholy and headed to her room. She wasn't one to sit around and wish for a man, she was a woman who made her own dreams come true. And she apparently had some designs to work on tonight.

CHAPTER 7

GUS

Gus had still been at the coffee shop when he got the text from Brittany. He had immediately sent the screenshot to Val, who said she would do her best to track the number, but blocked numbers were often impossible to trace. When Brittany had insisted he not meet her to walk her home, Gus had to breathe deeply to control the sudden protectiveness that overcame him when he got Brittany's text. Brittany was a small woman, but Gus knew she hit hard, and was no stranger to yelling at the top of her lungs when the situation called for it. Hell, sometimes when it didn't call for it. Brittany liked yelling.

It was… endearing.

Attempting to put aside thoughts of his brother's ex-girlfriend, Gus was deep in thought when he let himself into his condo, which is why he stopped short at the sight of Robbie, standing near the front door, looking mad as hell.

"Are you out of your fucking mind?" Robbie asked in that pissy voice he always used when he didn't get his way.

Gus hung his keys on the hook by the door, counting in his head to control his temper. Robbie must have used his key to let himself in. And while this is usually not a big deal, for some reason today, it bothered Gus. A lot.

"You'll have to be more specific," Gus told him in a dry voice. "There are a lot of reasons I could be out of my mind. Currently I'm wondering why I gave you a key."

"You're hanging out with Brittany? Walking around with her, showing up at her meet-and-greet? Are you purposefully trying to piss me off, or is there actually something going on there?"

Gus leaned against his kitchen counter, his arms crossed. Usually, Robbie was best dealt with by keeping your voice even and not letting him get a rise out of you. Still, this reaction was over the top, and Gus wasn't having it.

"I wasn't aware that hanging out with a friend was about you."

"She's my ex, of course it's about me."

Gus blinked at that. Sometimes Robbie's narcissism was truly astounding.

"So when you went to Disneyland with Annabelle after we broke up, that was about me?"

It had been about a month after the amicable break up, when Annabelle had confessed she no longer felt a spark with Gus and wanted to move on. At the time, he hadn't even been mad. He and Annabelle had dated for about six months, and at most when he thought of the relationship, he considered it 'fine.' When she had gone out with Robbie a month later, it had stung, but Gus had spent his life being the less interesting brother and didn't hold it against either of them. Robbie couldn't help being charming, and Gus couldn't help being the boring one.

But still, if he was going to pull this shit with Gus now, Gus was going to say something.

Robbie pointed a large finger at him, his color heightening.

"This is different, and you know it."

It wasn't, not even remotely. But Robbie apparently still viewed Brittany as his and was determined to throw a tantrum about it.

"She's a client. I'm her security for the weekend."

Robbie laughed in disbelief.

"Is that what you're calling it?"

"That's what Val was calling it when she begged me to take the case."

"What could Brittany possibly need security for?"

"Her stalker. The one you apparently knew about."

Robbie had the nerve to roll his eyes.

"She's really worried about some creep in a basement stroking off to her photos? The guy is harmless."

Rage. A burning rage had been kindled in Gus's chest.

"He's not harmless. He's been escalating for a while now. And I can't believe you knew about this and didn't tell me."

"Why would I tell you?"

"Because I work in security, Robbie. I do this shit for my job. If Brittany was having issues, I could've helped."

The sound that came out of Robbie just then could only be described as a snort.

"You know why I didn't tell you. I was doing you a favor."

Gus's head spun with confusion.

"A favor? What fucking favor? Why wouldn't I want to help?"

"You would want to help. That's why I didn't tell you."

They stood there, staring at each other. Robbie clearly thought he had the upper hand, some knowledge that he believed Gus had, but for the life of him, Gus couldn't figure it out. And it was pissing him off. Immensely.

Robbie gave him a look.

"Gus, I saw your face."

"What face?"

"I saw your face when I first brought Brittany home. You looked like you had been hit by a bus."

Gus froze, ice in his veins as he tried to compute what Robbie was telling him.

"What the actual fuck are you talking about?"

"I had never seen you react that way to a girl before. It was like you forgot how to breathe."

Gus turned to go into his kitchen, needing to get away from the words because they absolutely weren't true.

"You're out of your mind."

"I'm not," Robbie said. "You like her. You've always liked her. I just had her first. And now she's single and you think there's a chance for you."

"That's not what I'm doing."

Robbie was on a roll, and definitely not listening. "And it's fucked up, Gus. She's my ex-girlfriend."

Gus gripped the counter, counting in his head even though he knew it was futile. His chest was tight, like it was trying to expand and was stuck. There's no way what Robbie was saying was true. Gus had been nothing but polite to Brittany. They had never once had a moment of heat or chemistry between them before this weekend. Gus had always, always only seen her as Robbie's girlfriend before the breakup.

But maybe, just maybe, there had been a moment when he first saw her. Before he knew she was Robbie's. When he had looked at her and thought she was the most beautiful woman he had ever seen in his life.

Only a moment. But apparently Robbie had noticed. Fuck.

"You're wrong about a lot of things," Gus ground out. "But I'm also going to again point out that you didn't seem bothered by dating ex-girlfriends when you dated Annabelle."

Robbie rolled his eyes. "That was a completely different situation."

"How is that different from this? Other than the fact that I'm not sleeping with Brittany?"

Even as he said the words, images flashed in his mind. Brittany's lips. Her long legs wrapped around his waist, holding him tight. Her lipstick smeared from kissing him, her skirt rucked up from his hands.

"It's different."

They stared at each other a moment, both pissed and tense and angry and a thousand adjectives in between.

Finally, Gus grunted. "I told you, we're not hanging out. Her mom hired the company for protection. She has a stalker."

"Seems like a pretty flimsy excuse to hire security over some guy."

Gus studied his brother, wondering. "It never seemed like a big deal that your girlfriend was scared of some creep sending her dirty paintings and explicit notes?"

Robbie scoffed, showing what a dumbass he was.

"Brittany doesn't get scared. She's the one people are scared of."

Brittany's face from earlier that day flashed through Gus's mind, her eyes wide with worry, how her entire body froze at the sight of the flowers. Robbie really was an idiot.

"I guess that answers that."

"What the fuck does that mean?"

"It means she was scared, Robbie, and she clearly didn't feel like she could show that to you."

Robbie immediately tensed.

"Don't tell me about my relationship with Brittany. It was none of your fucking business."

"From the sounds of it, it was barely your business."

"Fuck you."

Robbie stormed to the door, steam practically billowing off his head, but he paused before he left, not turning around.

"Just… don't sleep with her."

Gus sighed, suddenly very tired. "Nothing's happened."

"But you want it to."

Gus was ready to deny it, but the words were somehow stuck in his throat. And Robbie immediately sensed his hesitation.

Robbie's face fell into a scowl. "Fucking great."

He stormed toward the door, about to make a classic Robbie exit, but stopped and threw Gus a look over his shoulder.

"She likes the spotlight, Gus. It's the only thing she cares about. Likes and profiles and followers. She's not going to be happy with some regular guy. Don't let her hurt you."

He was gone before Gus could react, the door slamming behind him. Gus was left alone with his second thoughts and third thoughts all fighting for supremacy. But the one thing that held him by the throat was the possibility Robbie was right.

Gus liked Brittany as a person. She was funny and strong and charming and extremely easy to be around. But he couldn't like her more than that, or want her as more than just a friend, because Robbie was right. Because besides being his brother's ex, he was just regular guy Gus. He liked his job. He liked living in his condo, in a quiet town that got loud once a year with his favorite convention. He didn't like paying attention to his social media. He was nothing like Robbie, which meant he wasn't Brittany's type. Brittany lived her life in front of the camera. She had a million fans. Hell, hundreds of people had shown up for a meet-and-greet today just to spend time with her. She needed someone who could meet her on her level.

And that wasn't Gus.

For all that Robbie was a shithead, he had still given Gus a great reminder that he needed to not get attached to Brittany, because she wouldn't be getting attached to him.

The next morning, Gus was determined to keep everything with Brittany professional, and pretend the elevator never happened. He was hired to protect her, and he was damn good at his job. Time to focus on that. Whatever he had been thinking the night before, the nonsense Robbie had brought up, he was wrong. Gus only saw Brittany as a friend, and he was lucky to call her that.

While he was brushing his teeth, he got a notification that Brittany was going live. When he clicked over to her page, his phone screen filled with Brittany as she got dressed for the day. He had watched a few of her live streams in the past, mostly out of curiosity about the woman who was dating his brother. This one was obviously catered to the Kickoff crowd, a more casual version of what she would normally put together, but even with that difference Gus couldn't get over how natural she was in front of the camera. She had an ease to her that pulled the viewer in, making you feel like her best friend instead of a voyeur. She answered questions on chat about her bra, where she got her shoes, the deals she was able to find for the whole wardrobe. She sat on the bed and pulled on her signature knee socks, one by one, keeping up her banter with her chat as she did, and Gus felt himself start to sweat. Brittany was short, but she was all leg, and watching her slowly encase those calves was going to kill him. Or make him combust.

She finished getting dressed and signed off with a kiss, the screen going dark, and Gus realized he was standing alone in his condo smiling like an idiot.

Shaking it off, he finished getting dressed and headed to the coffee shop, eager for caffeine and a distraction that didn't have him thinking about Brittany's legs. He placed an order, including a chocolate scone against his own better judgment, and headed over to Brittany's hotel room.

By the time Gus knocked on her hotel door, he had gone through an entire speech to himself in his head about how professional he was going to be today. Brittany was a client, and she needed protection. That's it.

The door swung open, revealing Brittany in those damn

socks and her heels, her skirt short enough to make Gus's heart stop just for a moment.

"Here," he said before she could say anything. Gus handed her an iced coffee and a small pastry bag, which she took automatically. She looked in the bag, curious.

"What's this?"

"Treats to butter you up."

She glared at him with suspicion even as she took a sip on the straw of her new drink.

"I don't know what's more suspicious, that you need to butter me up or that you know my drink order by heart."

"Think of it as a personalized service available to clients."

She continued eyeing him, then peeked inside the pastry bag.

"Chocolate croissant?"

"You know it."

She sighed. "Lecture me on the way. I'm already running late."

She took another sip of her drink, relaxing as the caffeine and copious amounts of sugar hit her at once. Gus smiled at the sight of her, then glanced up when he sensed movement in the corner of his eye. It was one of her roommates, the shirtless guy from before, who swiftly put down the phone he was holding and walked out of Gus's sight. Weird. Gus narrowed his eyes, his mouth opening to start asking questions, when Brittany grabbed his arm and stepped through the door, closing it behind her.

"Let's go. I've got a big day, and I don't have time for you to yell at Kyle."

She was already speed walking down the hall, so Gus

settled for throwing a glance at the door before hurrying to follow her.

Once they were out on the street, Brittany smiled at the sunlight beaming down at them, then turned to Gus.

"Okay, hit me."

"Stay close and do what I say."

"That's your lecture?"

"I prefer getting to the point."

Shaking her head, Brittany sashayed down the sidewalk, in a good mood that Gus couldn't help but admire. He watched as she walked ahead of him, her tight ass swinging with the confidence she always felt. Gus had a brief vision of those legs, encased in those socks, wrapped around his waist, his hands running up the silk until he reached the skin of her thighs. Fuck, it was going to be a long day.

Shaking his head and very specifically looking away, Gus caught up with her, pulling her toward him on the sidewalk and out of the way of the sign spinner who had taken one look at Brittany and dropped his sign. She was laughing and waving while Gus glared, pulling her away.

"Gus, chill. He's not chasing us."

"Not at this moment, but you never know. You can't just flash that smile of yours and expect men not to act like idiots."

"Of course I can. You resist me all the time."

"I'm a special case."

"More like you're a head case, but I'm not judging. You're fun to be around."

Gus snorted. He had been called a lot of things in his life. Dependable. Trustworthy. All the boring adjectives that made women fall asleep once they started dating. He had never been called fun in his life.

Brittany heard him snort and eyed him, curious. "Do you not think you're fun?"

"I've been told on numerous occasions that I'm pretty boring."

"By who, Robbie?"

She was laughing when she said it, but when Gus didn't respond, she sobered up. He kept walking, eyes scanning the streets for anything out of the normal.

"Gus, wait."

He turned to find Brittany had stopped walking. She had her hands on her hips, her ponytail and her socks making her look more cute than fierce. But her eyes were showing the beginning of her temper.

"Robbie's an idiot," she said. Gus opened his mouth, but Brittany held up her hand, stopping him. "Just listen. Robbie is loud and extroverted and thinks everyone has to be like him in order to have a good time. But he's wrong. You're kind and funny and sexy and a hell of a lot more fun to be around than him. Don't let him and his bullshit convince you otherwise."

Gus stared at her a moment, not sure what to say, not sure what to do about this weird feeling blooming in his chest.

"Did you just call me sexy?"

She rolled her eyes at him, moving past him toward the convention center.

"Moderately attractive if I squint in the sun and am feeling slightly nauseous. Now hurry up, buttercup. I got a full day of panels to get to."

Shaking his head, Gus could only follow.

BRITTANY

Brittany was completely exhausted. She had been on a number of panels all day, answering questions, bantering with her fellow influencers and panelists, and interacting with fans, all while moving from one end of the convention center to the other. Brittany wasn't really a big name, not compared to some, but her fans had come out in force, and she could only be grateful.

All during the day, Brittany's mom had been calling and leaving messages for her. After the last panel, Brittany finally plopped herself onto a chair in relief just in time for her phone to ring, yet again, with her mom. With a sigh, Brittany answered, Kathleen somehow already mid-conversation with her.

"Finally, Brittany, I swear you're purposefully ignoring me."

"Mom, I was in panels all day. You know this. I sent you my schedule. This is my first break."

"Champagne called, they moved up the deadline."

Brittany froze. "Moved it up?"

"They want to see designs on Monday."

Brittany's jaw dropped. "Monday?! Did you tell them I'm out of town this weekend for work?"

There was a pause on the other side of the conversation and Brittany knew, without a doubt, that her mother absolutely did not mention it. She groaned.

"Mom, I'm already swamped here."

"This is a big opportunity. Champagne is high end, this is everything we've been waiting for, so no, I wasn't going to tell them that you were too busy for them. I thought this was what you wanted."

It was what she wanted. But Brittany was also tired and feeling uncreative after her mother had hated yet another round of designs. Impostor syndrome was drifting in, making her feel like a fraud. And that made her angry. But getting angry with Kathleen was never productive.

"Of course it's what I want, Mom. I'm just out of town, and you've hated everything I've sent you so far. I don't see how I can meet this new deadline."

"You'll figure it out."

She hung up before Brittany could answer, which was for the best, considering the only words on the tip of Brittany's tongue had started with 'f.'

"Rough call?"

His voice was right in her ear, which was why her pulse raced. At least, that's what Brittany told herself as she turned her head and looked up into Gus's dark eyes, losing her breath a little at how he was leaning over her. She tried not to inhale his scent, some sort of woodsy cologne he wore, and smiled up at him.

"Just the normal with my mom."

"Ah. How's Queen Kathleen doing?"

She did her best not to laugh at his nickname for her mom, but she wasn't sure she pulled it off. Gus was the only person she knew who had not been impressed with her mother when they met. Granted, it was a meeting in passing, they hadn't said more than hello to each other since she had focused on Robbie at the time to grill him about his follower count and ambitions, but still. Maybe it was because he spent his time saving lives instead of worrying about his next social media post that he didn't understand how scary Kathleen was.

It was refreshing.

"She just wanted to tell me a deadline got pushed up." Brittany knew she was lucky to have her mom, that she worked hard to make sure that Brittany succeeded and had what she needed, so she did her best not to complain. But something in her face must have shown, because now Gus was frowning at her.

"She's mad about you being here at Kickoff, isn't she?"

How he guessed, Brittany had no idea, so she turned her attention to her feet, and the gorgeous heels she loved desperately that she needed to get off her feet as soon as possible.

"She might not be thrilled with it. She's not a fan of these conventions. She thinks when I dress down for them, I'm cheapening my brand."

"You're hot as hell, Britt. Don't let her make you feel that way." He sounded genuine and Brittany relaxed a little. A glance up at him told her he was completely focused on her, something she was still getting used to. Gus was in the background, the periphery for so long, and now he was right here, in front of her, demanding her attention in that quiet way of his. They stared at each other for a moment, and Brittany felt her temperature rise a little, which meant it was definitely time to look somewhere else. Like her shoes.

Finally getting the little straps undone, Brittany pulled off the four-inch heels, a moment that felt better than the last three orgasms she had had put together. She moaned, rubbing the arch of one aching foot, and at the sound she saw Gus swallow, hard, and look away from her.

"Why do you wear them if you don't like them?"

"My stream is about how to make fashion work for you in the everyday. I sure can't recommend wearing heels to my fans if I can't handle wearing them."

"But you can't handle wearing them."

She immediately froze what she was doing and glared up at him.

"Excuse me?"

He really should have known something was horribly wrong, and maybe he did, but still, he went on.

"You collapsed in the chair. You're rubbing your feet like they were about to fall off. Brittany, you're on your feet all day, you don't need to be in heels."

The look on his face was one of sincere concern, but still. Brittany didn't like being told what to do, and she certainly didn't like being told what to wear.

"Gus, I'm going to need you to mind your own fucking business. Women don't always have the option for what kind of shoes they have to wear during the day, and I'm here to give them recommendations on how to help their life be just a little bit easier. You don't understand that, fine, but don't fucking tell me what to do."

Her blood was up, and her glare could've set the table on fire, but Gus looked from her to her feet and back.

"I'm sorry, you're right. I just don't like seeing you in pain."

And just like that, her temper fell back to a simmer.

"Just keep your opinions about what I'm wearing to yourself, and we're good."

He nodded, and she took a moment to wonder at how easy it was to argue with Gus. Robbie would've thrown a tantrum about how she was twisting his words, would've accused her of trying to purposely start fights for attention. Gus just... listened and acted. Which was really the bare minimum when Brittany thought about it, but still.

"Noted," he said. "Ready to go?"

She nodded, pulling her sneakers on and carefully placing her heels in her bag, trying not to grimace while he was watching. "Yes. I need something to eat and someplace quiet to sit away from people."

"Coming right up, killer."

The green room they were in was on the opposite end of the Exhibition Hall, so they had to cut through the crowds to get to the exit. Gus hovered nearby, towering over people while glaring at everyone if they got too close. For some reason that glare comforted Brittany. With Gus's help, they slowly made their way across the expansive space.

"Is it more crowded than usual?" She couldn't believe how packed in everyone was. There were way more people than yesterday, to an alarming degree.

"Stay close," was Gus's only answer, which was silly since she had no plans to go anywhere, and there certainly wasn't room for her to make a break for it. Still, she stayed right next to Gus, trying to tamp down her anxiety at the overwhelming amount of people.

Which is when the fire alarm went off.

Thousands of people jumped, staring up at the now flashing red lights, cringing at the loud whooping sound of the alarm. From across the way, Brittany could see volunteers waving people toward the exit. Gus reached back and grabbed her hand, pulling her toward him.

But it wasn't working. They were suddenly in a crush, pressed bodily up against several strangers who were just as caught as they were. The tide of the crowd pulled Brittany away from Gus, her hand slipping out of his.

"Gus!"

His head whipped in her direction, but she lost sight of him, her feet stumbling over the small space she occupied as the crowd pushed her further and further away. She felt panic rising in her chest as she realized she had no control. She turned to the guy pressed against her right side.

"I need to get to my friend."

He just looked at her. "Girl, the best you can do is follow the crowd and stay calm."

She knew he was right, but there were too many people, they were too close, and Brittany's panic was rising.

Which is when someone behind her pushed too hard, and she went down.

Her ankle twisted in pain as she hit the ground. She immediately curled into a ball, covering her head as best she could as the crowd surged around her, over her.

"Help!" Brittany yelled, but between the people and the alarm, she could barely hear her own voice. She settled in, praying that people would be able to move around her until she could move again.

And then she heard shouting.

The movement around her seemed to slow down, but she wouldn't look up from the protective position she had put herself in. After a few moments, there was a rush of air on one side of her, and then strong hands were gripping her arms.

"Brittany, it's me."

She had never felt such relief as she did in that moment. Gus was here, and he had her, and that meant everything was going to be okay. She let him haul her up but found she wasn't able to put weight on her ankle, collapsing against Gus's hard chest. The crowd was still around them, but it didn't matter to her as she wrapped her arms around his waist and held him tight. She felt his strong arms go around her, locking her against him, and his head drop near hers so he could speak in her ear.

"Are you hurt?"

"My ankle," she whispered.

"Fuck." He held her tighter and then shifted his arms, moving to scoop her up against him. Instantly, she wrapped her legs around his waist and buried her face in his neck.

"Hold tight, killer," he said. "We're about to piss some people off."

She felt them moving but didn't care. He had one arm locked under her butt, holding her up, and must have been using the other to push people out of his way because she suddenly felt a hard surface against her back. She looked up to find he had managed to get them over to the side, against the wall, and was now shielding her from the crowd with his body. He was so close, looking down at her, ignoring the massive amount of people pushing to get past him.

"We're gonna be smart and just wait this out, okay?"

She nodded, her voice sounding weak even to her own ears. "Okay."

He leaned even more into her space, and instead of it panicking her she welcomed it. One of her hands around his neck sunk into his hair, clutching him to her, but he didn't seem to notice, his eyes a little wild.

"Christ, Britt, I thought I lost you." He leaned his head against her temple, and she heard him inhale deeply.

"The crowd pulled me away. It was so fucking scary, Gus."

"I got you now. You're safe. I got you."

Brittany wasn't sure how long they stood like that, holding each other so tight their breathing synced, ignoring the crowd of pissed-off convention-goers trying to get by them. Brittany felt safe and calm and taken care of and she was ready to revel in it.

There would be time later to wonder why it was Gus who made her feel that way.

CHAPTER 9

GUS

Gus had nearly lost his mind when he felt Brittany's hand slip out of his. The fear on her face when the crowd took her away would be in his nightmares for years.

He braced himself in front of her, holding her to him. Her legs were still around his waist, but with her back firmly against the wall, he could keep her mostly blocked from the crowd. They were as safe here as they were going to get, so Gus figured they could ride it out until the space cleared enough to move around safely. And then the convention center was going to get an earful about fire codes and letting people in the Exhibition Hall when they're already past capacity.

Gus hadn't been able to get a good look at Brittany when he pulled her off the floor, and his heart was in his throat as he wondered if she was okay. From the way she gripped him, he knew she was terrified, and he hated it, hated that he hadn't been able to stop any of this from happening. Her broken admission of being scared would haunt him.

Finally, he felt the pressure of the crowd ease a little. Not willing to let her go yet, Gus pushed himself more firmly against Brittany and freed one of his hands, sliding it down her thigh.

"Are you groping me right now?"

Gus could almost laugh, he was so relieved she sounded more like herself.

"I'm trying to feel your ankle to see how bad it is."

He kept sliding his hand around her leg until he had a gentle grip on her foot at his back. He felt more than heard her hiss of pain.

"Sorry, killer, I gotta check it."

He probed as gently as he could, not feeling anything more terrible than some swelling, and let himself relax for a moment. Gus released her foot and resettled his hand on her thigh to support her weight, enjoying the feeling of her pressed up against his chest, of her wrapped completely around him.

"Brittany, show me your face."

She lifted her head from where she had buried it against his neck, and the vulnerability in those big blue eyes shot straight to his gut. His grip tightened on her before he made himself relax. Scanning her face, he frowned.

"You've got a bruise on your forehead."

"I may have gotten stepped on a little while I was down there."

Gus cursed, glancing around. The crowd was finally thinning.

"We need to get you to the first aid station. You need medical attention."

Her grip tightened around his neck.

"No, Gus, I just want to leave. Can we go back to the hotel? Please?"

Something about that word made Gus's cock jump, and he suddenly realized exactly how close they were, how soft she was against him. He needed to move before his body decided to do something about it that he'd regret.

"If you can make it to the street, I'll order a ride share. We're not walking anywhere after this."

She was already nodding. "I can. I definitely can."

Gus pulled away from the wall, slowly lowering her to the ground and watching as she tried to hide how painful her ankle was. She shot him a weak smile.

"See?"

"You're not fooling anyone, killer."

He turned his back to her, going to his knees.

"Climb on."

"Are you serious right now?"

He glanced back at her, impatient and exasperated and so fucking grateful she was feeling enough like herself to argue.

"Your choices are to climb on and let me carry you or stay here while I get you a medic."

"Fuck."

With some awkwardness, she grabbed him and climbed on his back, once again wrapping her legs around him as he stood up, bouncing her to settle their combined weight. He had hoped this position would let his cock calm down but had underestimated the feeling of her breath in his ear, her breasts pressed against his back, and her nails digging slightly into his shoulder.

"Don't drop me," she told him, her voice unsteady with what he told himself was stress.

"Never."

He slowly carried her to the exit, dodging around the remaining stragglers as the fire alarm was finally shut off, the relief of the silence echoing through the center. Once they were outside, he waved over a waiting taxi, and carefully placed her in the back seat. She gave him a wry grin.

"Gus, I got it. I'm not a toddler."

He tapped her nose lightly. "Let me do it, it'll make me feel better."

Gus reached across her, clicking in the seat belt, their faces no closer than they had been before but for some reason, this was different. The energy between them was charged, heated. Almost volatile. With a shaky breath, he stood, closing her door and walking around to the other side to slide in next to her.

He gave the driver the address, and they were moving.

"Gus, that's not the hotel address. Where are we going?"

He looked out the window, already knowing she was going to want to argue, and already over it. "My place."

"Gus."

"Brittany, don't. You're hurt, you need medical attention, and you won't let me take you to the medic. I have a first aid kit and a quiet condo. I don't want to hear it."

She was quiet, so Gus dared to shoot her a look. She was shaking her head.

"You're really overbearing. You know that?"

It was then he noticed she was shivering, her body

jumping a little as the adrenaline wore off and the shakes took over. Without thinking about it, he slid an arm around her shoulders, pulling her to him, and was surprised when she let him, even sinking into his side.

"Humor me," he told her. "My heart stopped back there. I'm still recovering."

They sat like that for the duration of the ride, neither of them acknowledging how close they were sitting, how well they fit together. And when the taxi pulled up in front of Gus's building, he was out and at Brittany's door before she could touch the handle, scooping her out of the vehicle, hauling her up in his arms before striding inside.

"This feels excessive," she managed to say as they rode the elevator.

"Getting really tired of you complaining that I'm taking care of you, killer."

"I'm just saying. This is feeling like some real movie cinema shit. Also, how often do you work out to be able to carry me around all day?"

"As much as I need to in order to be certain I can carry you around all day."

He saw she didn't know what to do with that statement, which was good because he wasn't really certain how he would explain it. Instead, he carried her down the hall and managed to open his door without putting her down.

Once inside, he strode straight to his sofa, gently placing her down. He grabbed her ankle and worked on untying her shoe.

"Gus, I can do it."

Ignoring her, he placed her sneaker on the floor and then maneuvered her leg so she could stretch it out, putting a pillow underneath her foot to elevate it. When he was done, he stood, towering over her. She looked so small on his sofa, delicate in a way that was easy to miss when she was upright and yelling at you, stomping around in her heels and demanding her way.

Gus shook off the weird feeling of tenderness that was invading and went to the kitchen to get her an ice pack and grab the first aid kit. He took advantage of the moment alone to get a hold of himself. Brittany was Robbie's ex-girlfriend. Gus couldn't get involved with her. He couldn't betray Robbie that way. Which meant he had to get all these damn thoughts out of his head now.

After that quick pep talk, he went back into the living room, sitting at the end of the sofa with her ankle. He took a better look at it, poking and prodding gently, her ankle warm in his hands and her big blue eyes on him in a way that he knew she could see right through him.

"My guess is it's a bad sprain. Some ice, rest, and anti-inflammatories and you should be good in a few days."

Her mouth gaped open. "Days? Gus, I have a full schedule this weekend."

He shrugged. "We'll get you some crutches."

"Crutches?!" Her look was comical enough to make him laugh, but he bit down the urge, knowing she'd bite his head off and spit it back out at him if he tried.

"Luckily, you're not going anywhere tonight, so you can rest here on the couch, keep it elevated, and focus on healing."

"Gus, I can't stay here."

"Of course you can."

"Robbie would kill you if he knew I was here."

Gus paused. She was right, of course. Robbie wasn't

known for measured and mature responses, and he would shit a brick if he knew Brittany was on his couch, lounging, after a harrowing experience. Hell, now that he knew what it felt like to have her wrapped around him, he understood Robbie's position even more. Brittany was soft and strong and smelled like the promise of sex and Gus really needed space before he caved to any of these thoughts.

Standing up quickly, he brushed her concerns aside as he placed the ice pack on her now-wrapped ankle.

"My condo, my rules. Besides, you're a client. Robbie has no say in how I do my job."

Brittany was silent at that, and he glanced up, seeing her chew her lip, her eyes wary.

"Right. Your job."

Gus nodded, turning away before she saw what a fucking liar he was. "For now, you just need to relax and stay off that ankle. Pick a movie if you want."

He went to the kitchen, putting away the first aid kit and setting about making them a couple sandwiches, aware that she hadn't eaten in the rush of panel to panel. He had shoved a protein bar at her at some point, but she needed some real sustenance.

Sandwiches in hand, he headed back out to the living room, placing her plate within reach. She took it silently, staring at it.

"What?" he asked, annoyed for reasons he didn't understand.

"You made me food."

"It's a sandwich. You've barely eaten."

"Still."

He didn't know what to say, and she clearly wasn't going

to follow that comment up with anything, diving into her sandwich as she picked some asinine dating show to watch.

"This okay? I'm behind."

"Whatever you want, killer." He sat on the other end of the couch, gently pulling her feet into his lap and propping them on the pillow, making sure the ice pack was stable and not touching her skin directly. He settled in for the mindless show, knowing he was going to hate it but also knowing few things would keep Brittany still once she decided that she needed to move.

The show started, just as dumb as Gus was expecting.

"Gus?"

Her voice was quiet.

"Yeah?"

"Thank you. For today."

He looked at her then, and something in his look must have told her a little of what he was thinking because she was turning a delicious pink.

"You're welcome."

He said it with more gravity than he expected, but he meant it. After a weird, tense moment, she deliberately turned her attention back to the show, and Gus followed her lead, reminding himself of the list of reasons he needed to chill around her. The reasons that were getting harder and harder to remember.

CHAPTER 10

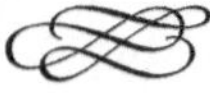

BRITTANY

Brittany woke suddenly, her vague dream of falling slamming her back into reality faster than her brain could compute. With a few blinks, she realized Gus was gone and her foot was now carefully propped up on a pillow with a Post-it Note stuck to it.

Grabbing food for dinner. Back later. Don't move from this couch. I mean it.

She smiled at the bossy note, imagining his frown as he was writing it. A glance at the coffee table also showed her he had piled various snacks and drinks there for her to easily reach, along with the bottle of anti-inflammatories. Gus may be grouchy as fuck, but he was a hell of a nurse.

Brittany slipped his note into the pocket of her shorts with a wiggle and then gingerly attempted to stand. She had no desire to leave the condo while he was gone and race around the city, but the bathroom was calling her.

She gently tested to make sure her ankle would hold weight and then did a combination of a limp and a hop to the bathroom. After taking care of her business, Brittany washed her hands and got her first glimpse of herself since that morning.

She looked like hell.

Her mascara was smudged under her eyes, with one fake lash coming away from her eyelid in an attempt at freedom. Her lipstick was long gone, and her foundation and careful contouring only a memory, allowing her faint freckles to show through.

She pulled out her phone and took a quick mirror selfie to post on her social media. While she was a fashion person, Brittany believed in showing her followers the real side of her life, the less than perfect moments that made her human and reminded all of them that they were in this world together. Her mom hated when she did it, but Brittany didn't care. She wanted to show the reality of herself as much as the online glam image.

She posted the photo just as she heard the front door to the condo open. Brittany yelled through the door.

"Don't be mad. I had to use your bathroom. It couldn't be helped. But I swear I'm going right back to the couch."

She opened the door and limped her way out of the bath-room... only to come face-to-face with Robbie. The shocked look he was giving her would've been priceless if she wasn't so certain it matched her own. It only took seconds for his expression to transform into the sneer she had become familiar with since they broke up.

"You sure don't waste any time, do you?" His tone was dripping with judgment, which sent Brittany's back up.

"You better watch your fucking tone, Robbie. Even with a bad ankle, I could still fuck you up."

She was barefoot, her five-foot-four inches barely coming to his shoulder because the stupid Lozano genes were tall, but she stuck her finger right in his face, her glare a palpable source of fierce energy.

He just shook his head. "I should've known. What is it? You needed a place to stay for the convention, so you conned him into letting you shack up here? Bat those baby blues at him and let him touch you? You're so fucking transparent, Brittany."

"Don't be disgusting. Your brother's been a gentleman, and you're acting like a jealous turd."

"Why would I be jealous? I'm the one that's moved on, remember."

"Yeah, I heard. You 'moved on' before we even broke up."

Brittany hadn't meant to bring his infidelity up, but her temper often got away from her, and to tell the truth, she wasn't sorry. From the way Robbie's eyes narrowed into a glare, they were apparently going to have the fight they should've had months ago when Brittany had gotten a message from Devery, Min's little sister. A message with a link to a social media page featuring a nutritionist and her latest boyfriend. That boyfriend? Robbie.

When Brittany did a deep dive into social media, she discovered Robbie had been cheating on her for months with several women, and she'd had no idea. Hell, there was actual photo evidence of it out in the world, photos that people all over had liked and shared and commented on while Brittany had blindly trusted him. Believed that he was as committed as she was.

"You left long before I did, Brittany."

The memory of that moment, of clicking on the link from Dev and seeing exactly what Robbie had been doing behind her back, hit Brittany like a truck. And she abruptly decided she was done being the nice guy.

"Is that bullshit what you tell yourself to justify cheating on me?"

"Maybe I'm finally telling you the truth about our relationship, which you seem keen on ignoring."

"That's some real gaslighting bullshit you got going on there, Robbie. And it's not going to work on me anymore, so how about trying an apology."

"An apology? That's rich coming from the girl who destroyed my hard drives."

She got closer to him, not backing down.

"You mean *my* hard drives, Robbie. I bought them, all their registration was in my name, all their warranties and repairs. My hard drives."

He rolled his eyes, crossing his arms in front of him in a classic defensive move.

"So, what? You pushed me into the arms of someone else, destroyed my work, and now you're going to fuck my brother in revenge?"

Brittany barely had time to gasp at the accusation before they both jumped at the sound of a door slamming shut. Brittany turned too fast, forgetting her bad ankle and wincing when the pain shot up her leg. There, in the doorway with a bag of groceries and a scowl on his face, was Gus.

Robbie immediately rounded on him, too fired up to give a shit about how pissed Gus was.

"And you. 'Nothing going on' my ass. How soon after you told me that did you sleep with her? Unbelievable, Gus."

Gus very carefully set down the groceries, placing his keys on the little hook by the door, and then turned to Robbie. His voice was quiet, especially in comparison to Robbie's yelling, his tone so cold Brittany shivered.

"First of all, I could hear you both yelling down the hall. If you don't have any respect for me, at least respect my neighbors and keep your voices down."

Robbie opened his mouth to reply, probably some asinine remark, but Gus sliced a hand through the air in front of him. His expression was thunder, fierce and protective, and Brittany couldn't take her eyes off of him.

But Gus only had eyes for Robbie.

"No. You've already said your piece, and it was some pretty horrible shit to say, Robbie. Nothing is going on between me and Brittany. She's a job, which I told you about. She hurt her ankle and she's hanging out here where I can keep an eye on her. For my job."

Brittany wasn't ready for how that statement stung. But Robbie just switched tactics, his voice lower as he leaned toward Gus, switching to supportive brother in a blink of a personality shift.

"She's playing you, Gus. Don't fall for this damsel routine. She's using you to get revenge against me."

Brittany snorted at that ridiculousness, leaning against the wall to take the weight off her ankle. Gus ignored her to focus on his brother.

"Why would she need revenge against you, Robbie?"

Gus asked the question in exactly the tone of a person who already knew the answer and was waiting for Robbie to fess up. And Robbie knew it. His face turned bright red.

"She pushed me away, Gus."

"Did she push you away, or did you get bored like you always do?"

This was news to Brittany, but she didn't want to interrupt for follow-up questions. Robbie was already shaking his head.

"It wasn't like that."

"Look, your relationships are none of my business. But when you look me in the eye and lie to my face like you did about your breakup, that makes me feel a certain kind of way. That makes me feel that I don't mean a lot to you, and that I'm not worthy of hearing your truth, no matter how ugly. We're brothers, man. I thought we were better than that."

Robbie looked chagrined, and Brittany had to admire Gus's ability to talk about things like this. She had never really known someone who could phrase hurt in a way that made it a tangible thing to talk through. She certainly could never talk to Kathleen like that. She'd get too mad and one of them would throw something.

"I'm sorry," Robbie said. "I should have told you the truth. But she did push me away. I was never good enough for her, and she let me know it."

"Stop lying, dipstick."

Brittany was talking before she realized her mouth was moving, but she was too mad, so fuck it. If Gus kicked her out, he kicked her out. But she wasn't going to listen to Robbie's lies one more fucking moment.

"I was a hundred percent in, Robbie. But I was never a priority for you, and you made that abundantly clear, so clear that I feel like an idiot for not seeing it sooner. So don't you blame me for you cheating. I won't fucking stand it."

Brittany could feel tears in her eyes, which surprised her. She hadn't cried when Robbie had ended their relationship and certainly hadn't cried when she found out he had been cheating. But here she was, in front of both Lozano brothers no less, with her eyes watering.

"You were the one who moved on without telling me," she continued. "You were the one that violated my trust over and over again. You were the one who made it clear through your every action how little you respected me."

Robbie had the grace to look ashamed, but he was still Robbie, which meant he wasn't ready to give up being the victim. Instead, he focused on Gus.

"Is this because of Annabelle?"

Brittany perked up. Who was Annabelle?

Gus was shaking his head. "From what I've heard, this is a completely different situation."

Robbie glared. "Fine. If that's true, if you both are really just here because of his job, then promise me there's nothing more."

Gus rolled his eyes. "Robbie, there's nothing more."

"Promise me there won't be."

Gus went silent at that, and when Robbie swung his eyes to Brittany, she found herself instinctively looking at Gus. Their eyes met in this moment, memories of the elevator, of him holding her in the crowd at the convention center, of her hand in his, and an impossible feeling bubbled to the surface, a thought suddenly so clear that Brittany wondered how she hadn't seen it before.

I can't.

Shaking off that revelation, Brittany turned to Robbie.

"You lost the privilege of telling me what to do when you cheated on me. Feel free to go fuck yourself hard with a hammer."

Betrayal and rage clouded Robbie's expression.

"Just fucking great." He stormed toward the door, getting close to Gus on his way out for one last blast of ire and sarcasm.

"Finally getting what you want, aren't you, big brother?"

He was out the door, slamming it shut behind him before either of them could react. The sound echoed in the suddenly quiet condo, leaving them both in the awkward aftermath of the fight.

Gus recovered faster than she did, seeming to shake off the tension and turn to where she was standing.

"You need to get off that ankle."

"It's fine," she said automatically.

"I can see you wincing from here. And you're leaning against the wall to stay off it."

He approached her, taking her arm to gently lead her back to the couch. He fussed over her ankle while she watched him, the gears in her head spinning.

"What did Robbie mean?" she finally asked, not being able to wait anymore. He didn't look at her.

"He didn't mean anything, he was just being Robbie."

"Seemed pretty pointed at the end there."

Gus finished with her ankle, finally happy with its position, then turned back to where he left the groceries. Clearly, he wasn't going to answer her question, and she kinda realized that was for the best. She wasn't certain she was ready to hear his answer. But she did feel Robbie had painted a picture of her she didn't want Gus to believe.

"For the record, I wanted it to work with him," she found herself confessing. "On paper, he was everything I was looking for. For a while, I thought he was the one."

"What changed for you?"

He still wasn't looking at her, instead focusing on slicing up vegetables and other surprises for dinner, but Brittany knew without a doubt she had his full attention. That's how Gus was—he listened.

"Min met Hayden."

The memories from last year flooded back, all the horrible things Min went through. But also her connection with Hayden, how quickly and utterly they had fallen for each other. After the tournament, Brittany watched Min become even more confident, more sure of herself with Hayden in her corner, their connection deep and real and unbreakable.

And Brittany had realized she wanted that. Pretty badly, if she was being honest. And that person, the one who would have her back and build her confidence, who she would love unconditionally through thick and thin... wasn't Robbie.

"They were it for each other," is what she told Gus. "And something in watching them fight tooth and nail to be together made me realize I wanted that. Maybe it's dumb, because I don't think everyone gets a love like that. But still. I wanted to try."

He paused in his chopping, finally looking up to where she was on the couch, and the burning in his eyes took Brittany's breath away.

"It's not dumb. You're intelligent and beautiful and caring and you deserve a man who's going to worship you. You deserve a man who's willing to earn you. And if that's not Robbie, then fuck him."

He went back to cooking while Brittany tried to remember a time when her heart wasn't beating like it was about to be a medical emergency. Because the way Gus had just said that…

Looking for a distraction, she glanced down at the floor near the kitchen and frowned.

"Is that my suitcase?"

"I stopped at your hotel room. You're staying here for the rest of Kickoff."

Her mouth dropped open, her mind racing with reasons this was a terrible idea.

"Gus, you don't have a guest room."

"You'll stay in my room. It's not a big deal."

Not a big deal? To stay in his room, in his bed, that's going to smell like him and be full of his things? Is he out of his mind?

"I can't take your bed."

"It's already settled. I'll couch it. Now be quiet, I'm trying to cook."

He turned his back on her to face the stove, effectively ending the conversation, and she was left floored with what the last hour had brought her, her mind racing as it tried to process her fight with Robbie and the new dynamic she had somehow slipped into with Gus.

Dinner was a quiet affair, both of them ignoring the small dining table and eating on the couch, watching Brittany's dating show that even she had to admit was dumb. She finished the last bite of the grilled salmon with vegetables he'd made, setting down her plate on the coffee table and then flopping down on the groan, a hand gripping her stomach.

"Too much. I've eaten too much. How could you do this to me?"

Gus chuckled softly, a sound that reverberated down Brittany's spine. He was also lying back on the couch, reclining, her feet once again in his lap to keep the bad ankle elevated. And Brittany realized that, even with the horrible confrontation with Robbie earlier, even with all the questions she had in the aftermath, she was having a really, really good time.

Which meant it was time to leave. She didn't want to get between brothers, even if Robbie was an idiot and Gus saw her as a job. While angry Brittany would seek revenge for some of the garbage Robbie had spewed out of his mouth today, well-fed and tired Brittany wasn't willing to do anything to ruin this moment with Gus.

"Look, I appreciate everything," she said softly, feeling a small zing of electricity as his eyes turned to meet hers. "But I should really go back to my hotel. Me staying here is only going to piss off Robbie more, and while I delight in it, it's unfair for you to be caught between us and our drama."

He never took his eyes from her face.

"You can't even walk to the bedroom by yourself on that ankle. You're currently a vulnerable target for this guy who's been after you, and with him ramping up his actions, it doesn't make sense for you to stay at that hotel. You have five roommates who are constantly throwing parties and making out with strangers in that room. Hell, the person who let me in barely blinked when I showed up to get your stuff. Your stalker could get in there, easy, and you'd have no defense and nowhere to hide. So no, you're not leaving. You're staying right here."

Damn, those were really good, logical points and Brittany would be an idiot not to listen. And from the half-smile on his face, he knew he had her. Still, she huffed, crossing her arms.

"Fine. You win. No hotel room."

Instead of gloating, Gus just nodded and turned his attention back to the dating show that he must hate but was still watching because it was what she wanted to watch.

"Who's Annabelle?"

The question was out before she could stop it. She knew it wasn't her place to pry, but she was so curious. Robbie had said the name before like she was someone important, but Brittany, for the life of her, couldn't remember ever meeting an Annabelle. Gus froze in taking a drink of his water, clearly unsure what to say, and Brittany immediately felt horrible. His dating life was none of her business.

"Don't answer that, I'm being nosey."

Gus sighed, staying quiet, and Brittany assumed he wasn't going to answer her. And then he spoke, his eyes still on the TV.

"It was a few years ago. I met Annabelle on vacation. I was up the coast in Big Sur, surfing, and she was at the beach with her friends. She called me over and asked me to take their picture. When I went to hand her phone back, she told me to put my number in it first."

Brittany couldn't help but think Annabelle was seeming like a smart, logical woman when faced with what must have been Gus's shirtless, wet body. She had to shoot her shot, and Brittany respected it.

Gus continued. "I called her that night, and we went out a

few times. She was fun. Always taking pictures and posting on her social media, but I'm used to that with Robbie and didn't think anything of it. She never asked to take pictures with me or to post them."

"Were you guys serious?"

Gus shrugged. "Serious enough, I guess. I took her to meet my mom."

Brittany's eyes widened. Gus's mom was a force of nature, loud and overwhelming and judgmental in all the best ways. Brittany adored her.

"What did Mama Lozano think?"

"She said she was reserving her judgment."

Brittany winced. Mama Lozano was proud of how easily she could read people and had declared Brittany a keeper within an hour of meeting her. If she had spent time with Annabelle and not loved her… it didn't look good.

"The problem was more what Robbie thought of her. Or rather, what she thought of Robbie. They spent that night huddled up comparing follower counts and evaluating each other's streams."

Brittany's jaw dropped. "While your mom was there?"

Gus nodded. "After that, we were hanging with Robbie more and more, and I realized I was feeling like the third wheel in my own relationship. I talked with her about it, and she admitted she didn't really like hanging out with me. I wasn't 'fun' when we were together. And she wasn't really interested in our relationship moving forward. We broke it off. And then a few days later, she and Robbie started dating."

Brittany couldn't help herself, struggling to sit up so she could see Gus's face more clearly. His tone of voice said he was over it, but there was something in the hard set of his jaw, the glint of his eyes, that said it hurt him. And after the conversation she had just heard between him and Robbie...

Finally upright, she leaned toward him, putting her hand on his arm.

"Gus, you know that's complete horseshit, right? What she told you, that has more to do with what a shitty person she is rather than how 'fun' you are."

He shrugged, not meeting Brittany's eyes.

"It had to partly be about me, considering we were at the height of our relationship, and she found it very easy to throw me away."

Gus said it lightly, but there was no way he felt it lightly. Brittany couldn't help herself, and before she knew it, she was pulling Gus toward her, wrapping her arms around his neck in a hug that was tight and firm. She turned her head to his ear.

"You're not easy to throw away, Gus. You're the one worth keeping. And sometimes, you meet and connect with someone who is wholly not ready for what you have to offer, and they panic. But that's on them, not you. If she couldn't see how superior you are to Robbie in every way, then she doesn't fucking deserve you."

His hair was soft as she pressed her face into his neck. She inhaled, not bothering to think about how weird it probably was, taking in his scent of laundry detergent and a hint of his woodsy aftershave. Brittany felt his arms go around her, pulling her even closer.

Finally, she gave him one last squeeze and pulled away just enough to look him in the eyes. They stared at each other, neither breathing, the air uncertain and able to tip in any direction. Even Brittany could feel the unpredictability in the moment.

Gus raised a hand and tucked a stray blonde lock behind her ear, his eyes locked on hers in concentration, and Brittany could feel them on the verge of something new, something she wasn't sure she was prepared for but that she secretly, desperately wanted.

And then Gus pulled away. "Let me make up the bed for you. Give me a few minutes."

Just like that, they were back in platonic friend territory. Or in client/bodyguard territory. It was hard for Brittany to tell exactly how Gus cataloged her, but she knew she was disappointed.

She let him go, shimmying back to her side of the couch, reaching for a light tone of voice she definitely didn't feel.

"I'm fine on the couch. You can sleep in your bed."

"You're taking the bed, killer. I'm done talking about it."

To emphasize his point, he strode into the bedroom, and Brittany took the time to center herself. Sure, they'd had a heart-to-heart about Gus's dating and trauma and what a shithead Robbie was. Sure, they had just had a moment where Brittany absolutely thought Gus was going to kiss her, had even, for a brief second, wanted him to kiss her.

And Gus had made it clear he wasn't interested in her that way.

Fine, she was a big girl. This wasn't the first time a guy Brittany liked wasn't into her, and it probably wouldn't be the last. And, really, it was for the best, considering how messy everything already was just with him acting as her bodyguard.

Brittany managed to psych herself up to being friendly and

professional when he walked back in and held out a hand to her.

"C'mon, let's get you to bed."

Her stomach fluttered at the words, and she thanked the stars she wasn't a blusher because otherwise she would be flaming right now. She grabbed his hand and let him pull her up, stumbling a little into him as her ankle screamed a reminder that it wasn't up for any walking around. She braced herself with a hand on his chest, then quickly snatched it away.

"Sorry."

Gus didn't say anything, just helped her to the room, then went and grabbed her bag and dropped it near the bed. He had turned down the covers already to make it easy to climb into, and it was so inviting she wanted to collapse into it immediately and sleep for days.

"I'll be out here if you need anything."

He turned to leave and Brittany called out to stop him.

"Gus?"

He paused at the door, turning back to her, looking so handsome it took her breath away..

"Thank you. For everything. Really."

He nodded, then ducked out the door, quietly shutting it behind him. Brittany sat on the bed, staring at her bag on the floor, completely thrown by everything that had just happened.

"Fuck."

With a deep breath, she managed to change into her pajamas and do her nightly skincare routine, gratefully sinking into the bed with the soft sheets and the perfect pillows. And while she was laying there, drifting into Gus's smell, the feel of his sheets on her skin, the memory of him so close to her, his arms around her, hell, the elevator with his hardness pressed into her, she realized that, as tired as she was, she wasn't going to be able to sleep unless she did something about this.

Brittany rolled to her back. Her mind wandered to Gus. His eyes, his smile, his hard jaw. The way the dark curl fell onto his forehead, making him look like a real Clark Kent. She thought of how tall he was, and how strong, how he carried her through the convention center on his back and didn't even seem to be out of breath.

And as she let her hand wander down her stomach, lightly stroking herself through her silky shorts and the light cotton underwear she was sporting, she let her imagination focus on how different tonight could've ended. How easy it would've been in the elevator for him to unzip himself. Her hand could've moved behind her, finding him hard and long and ready. His palm could've moved slowly under her skirt, feeling how wet she already was for him, and she could've guided him inside her. He would've entered her in one stroke, enough to make her gasp but not enough to draw attention to them, thrusting in micro movements that wouldn't be enough to finish her, but would be just what she needed to edge.

Brittany bit her lip, trying not to moan as she thought of Gus's heat surrounding her, his voice in her ear teasing her, asking if she wanted to come, telling her she had to wait wait wait, imagining his hand was the one moving on her clit in tight, fast circles, his fingers the ones plunging into her in that steady rhythm designed to drive her insane, and suddenly Brittany was coming, shuddering with her climax, letting her fingers feel her own body clench against them as even then she imagined they were Gus's.

She opened her eyes, blinking at the ceiling above her, her fingers slipping out of her body, and she tried not to think about how she just orgasmed from imagining her ex's brother.

CHAPTER 11

GUS

Gus was up at the gym for his usual morning routine and back before Brittany had even stirred from his room. He set about to get the coffee going and breakfast started. It was going to be yet another long day, assuming Brittany's ankle was up for her schedule. And considering how stubborn she was, even if her ankle was bad, she would still find some way to insist on keeping her commitments.

As he was cracking eggs, the door to his room opened, and Brittany limped out, looking adorably disheveled and sleepy-eyed as she stared at him.

"Morning, killer," he said. "Any requests for your omelet?"

She didn't answer, and he was reminded that she was definitely not a morning person. He grabbed a cup and prepared her coffee, setting it in front of her just as she reached the kitchen. He slid a stool toward her, putting his arm out to help her perch on it. Satisfied that she was set, he turned back to breakfast.

"Last chance before I make the decisions for you."

"Are you always like this in the morning?" Her voice was husky with sleep. Gus glanced at her, her coffee mug clutched in both hands near her face, her eyes still drooping.

"You mean a normal functioning human being as opposed to some sleep-deprived zombie?"

Her eyes narrowed at that, and she took a sip of her coffee. She sighed into it, her whole body seeming to unclench, and Gus paused just to admire her expression.

"I want to sass you back, but I'm so happy to have coffee I can't find it in myself to complain."

He smirked. "I'll remember that for next time. How's the ankle?"

She took another drink. "Not great, but not as bad as it was. I should be able to walk today, at least slowly, which is good. I've got more panels, and a livestream today that I have to be ready for."

"No heels. Your ankle needs a break."

She frowned at him. "Caffeine only lets you be a little bossy, Lozano."

He placed her omelet in front of her, steam still rising from it, the smell of the peppers and eggs mixing with the toast to warm anyone's heart. When Brittany reached for the plate, Gus pulled it back toward him, waiting.

She sagged. "Fine, no heels."

"Good."

He let her grab her plate and turned to slide his own omelet onto his plate, grabbed his juice, and plopped himself in the stool next to her. They both ate in comfortable silence for a moment.

"If you're okay with it, I'd like to do a stream before we leave for the day."

Surprised, he glanced around his condo. "Here?"

Brittany nodded. "You have great light, and your space is tidy. I can set myself up in a corner somewhere out of the way. And try to be the least annoying as possible. But only if you're okay with it."

"You're never annoying, killer. Feel free to do whatever you need to do."

After breakfast, Brittany went to get ready for her day while Gus cleaned up the kitchen, marveling at how natural and easy it felt to have her here. But Brittany had always been easy to be around, had always done her best to make others feel comfortable with her. Robbie, as outgoing and gregarious and likable as he was, wasn't good at sensing when others needed space or reassurance, so Gus had always thought Brittany was a nice counterbalance to him. But now, knowing what had really happened when they broke up, Gus was starting to remember all the times they had been out together, plans that Robbie had made for all three of them that clearly turned into what should've been a date night with Gus tagging along, feeling uncomfortable and in the way. And he remembered how Brittany had always adjusted the plans on the fly to accommodate, because she could sense how uncomfortable he was being the third wheel.

But now he wasn't a third wheel. He was practically the driver since he had to be certain Brittany was safe.

Gus cleared his head as he finished with the dishes, not needing to go down that path, and went over to the living room. He adjusted the furniture so that the comfortable chair was against the corner, with a few of his succulents framing the space on the wall. When Brittany emerged, she was holding a small tripod for her phone and a small ring light.

"Where would you like me to… oh."

She blinked at the space he had created, and he felt himself growing uncomfortable with her reaction.

"If it doesn't work, I can move stuff, but you should probably sit for the stream so your ankle can rest."

"No, this is great, Gus. Thank you."

She blinked those big blue eyes at him, and Gus felt like he was drowning. Which meant it was time to get the hell out of there.

"Gotta shower. Do what you need to do."

He made his way to the bathroom, grabbing clothes to change into so he wouldn't do something stupid like come out in a towel while she was live. Once he got the water hot and stepped into the stream, he scrubbed his face, giving himself a mental talking-to. Brittany was a client. She was Robbie's ex. He had no reason to be thinking about how much he liked having her in his space.

But his mind wasn't in the mood to listen, taking a nose-dive straight to the gutter. Images of Brittany's long legs wrapped around his waist when he carried her out of the convention center. Thinking about the elevator, her pushing her cute little backside against his erection, his dick practically dripping with the need to be inside her. Gus had always been attracted to a woman's confidence, but something about Brittany looking over her shoulder at him as the elevator rocked that sweet ass against his dick made his head explode with want.

His hand was on his cock before he knew it, stroking hard and fast as he thought about her hair in that fucking ponytail, the perfect height to yank toward him. About her sassy mouth and how beautiful it would look wrapped around his cock. When his brain presented him with the image of Brittany, spread out on his bed, naked, her pussy on display and dripping for him, he grunted as he shot his load onto the bathroom wall, his breath heavy, pressing his forehead against the cool tile of the shower.

Fuck. He had just jacked off to the thoughts of Robbie's ex-girlfriend. To Brittany, of all people. The woman he had walked in on vandalizing his brother's apartment. The woman with no impulse control, a terrible temper, a clout chaser, and a user.

But wait. Robbie had pretty much admitted last night that he had lied about a lot of details about their relationship. So it was hard to know what about Brittany was true and what wasn't.

Confused thoughts swirled in his head. Gus didn't know what was right to do in this situation, but he knew he had a job, and Brittany was the client. He had to focus on that and less on how fucking sexy she insisted on being at all times. Resolved, he finished his shower and dressed, steeling himself as he headed into the living room.

There he found Brittany in the middle of streaming. She had set herself up in the corner he had prepped for her, sitting in the armchair like a queen. She was dressed casually but nice in some sort of blouse with skinny jeans that he could see from across the room cupped her butt in illegal ways. She had gone a little bohemian with her look, light and airy and sunny in a way that made Gus want to bask in her energy.

Instead, he turned to the kitchen to grab some coffee,

stationing himself at the bar there, pretending to read the news on his phone while he eavesdropped on her stream.

"Hey, Cassie," Brittany said into her phone's camera. "For the wedding, I would suggest something simple, elegant, that won't outshine the bride but will definitely remind the groom that he lost something great when he dumped you. Pick your favorite asset and flaunt it. I know budget is an issue but check out the local thrift stores—a lot of women donate their old dresses after an event, and those are usually only worn a few times. And make sure your date is hot."

She leaned forward to scroll through the comments, laughing at some, continuing to give advice and talk about her experience at the convention. She was good at this. Fun and charming and light, soothing enough to make a viewer have a good day just because they joined her stream. Brittany spent a few more minutes answering the questions in the chat, talking about her favorite fashion shows from the last few months, her favorite outfits she'd seen at Kickoff, and generally just conversing with people through a camera, until she finally wrapped it up with a smile.

"Okay, everyone, I have to sign off. If you're here in Kimball, come join me for all my panels today! My schedule is posted on all my socials, and I'd love to see you."

She finished her goodbyes and ended the stream, ensuring the camera was off and everything was over. Then she sat back in the chair and took a deep breath.

"I never realized how much work went into what you did," Gus said.

Brittany shrugged. "The point is to make it feel like it's not work. People like to have conversations with friends, and that's the vibe I'm going for with my stream."

"And you're expanding, right?"

She had been talking on her stream about her upcoming collaboration with Champagne, some company Gus only heard of in songs or on red carpet coverage. She grimaced at the question.

"Yeah, I'm trying."

"Why the face?"

"They're not liking my designs so far. And they're asking me to redo them all by Monday."

"What did they say was wrong with your first designs?"

"They were aimed too much for my current audience and not enough toward the richer, more sophisticated buyer that Champagne usually aims for. I have no idea how I'm going to have time to sketch and swatch between now and Monday."

Gus had no idea, either, considering what he knew of her schedule for the rest of the convention. But he didn't mention it, since she already seemed to be stressed out. He glanced at the clock, calculating the times between her panels.

"If you want, there's a fabric store near the convention center. Hole in the wall, family owned, the guy is grouchy as fuck, but they have a lot of interesting things to sell. People send them their scraps from the cosplay outfits and everything, so they tend to have a variety of things."

Brittany blinked at him. "That would be perfect."

"It's not super close, but we may be able to slip away after your panels and hit it before it closes. Depends on the owner's mood."

"Gus, you're amazing, thank you."

He glanced away, not ready to make eye contact when she was complimenting him and checked the time on his phone.

"We should get going. The lines are going to be even longer today."

She grinned at him, knowing he was trying to deflect from himself.

"You really gotta learn to take a compliment, Gus."

He ignored her, pointing at the time on his phone. "Leaving in five. No heels."

In five minutes on the dot, they were out the door, Brittany moving slowly with her ankle but otherwise claiming to feel much better than the day before. On the street, Gus took her hand, telling himself it was only to make it easier to keep her close in the crowd. They made it through the entrance of the convention center and were pushing toward the panel rooms when they heard someone shout. Brittany yanked on Gus's hand to stop him, and they turned to find three women heading their way.

"Oh my god, it's you! BrittKneeSocks! We're huge fans!"

Brittany smiled at the women, who immediately asked for a picture, one of them stepping out of the way for the other two. Gus kept one eye on Brittany and scanned the room, keeping his senses alert. A crowded public area like this was the perfect place for a stalker to blend, and Gus was itching to get Brittany out of there.

"Are you her boyfriend?" He looked down to find the one woman who wasn't a fan had moved toward him, flipping her hair as her eyes scanned him up and down.

"No," was all he offered, checking on Brittany, who was still smiling through a photoshoot's amount of selfies.

"Are you enjoying your Kickoff so far?" she asked, clearly not getting the hint that he wasn't interested in a chat. Gus really looked at her. She was cute, with dark eyes and dark hair, olive skin. Her shirt proclaimed her love for super-heroes, and if this were a week ago, her cheek dimple and obvious interest would've intrigued him.

Gus glanced up at Brittany, catching her eye. She had been watching them, and she quickly turned away. He turned back to the brunette.

"It's going well. You?"

"It just got much better." She winced after she said it. "Sorry, that was a cheesy line. I'm terrible at this."

Gus couldn't help but laugh. "You're doing better than I usually do."

She brightened, and Gus wished he felt a flicker of anything for this woman. Even a hint of the fire he felt for Brittany and he would be done.

But he didn't.

"Ready when you are." Brittany's voice was light but was laced with tension. She had finished her photos with the other two women, who pulled the brunette to them and waved goodbye, the brunette giving Gus a regretful look.

Gus waved back and turned to find Brittany was already moving, faster than she had been before, and he strode to catch up.

"Whoa, where's the fire, killer?"

"There's no fire, but I have a schedule."

"And you have time. You shouldn't be pushing that ankle so hard so soon after hurting yourself."

"Not that much time. Not enough for you to finish flirting with some girl. You're technically at work, by the way."

Gus stopped in his tracks, pissed at her words but also immediately realizing.

"You're jealous."

She whirled on him, her eyes on fire in a way that heated his blood.

"I'm not jealous," she said, her voice dripping with acid. "I just have a schedule that I'd like to keep."

Gus moved forward, crowding into her space. So far no one was really paying them any attention, but that could change at any moment, and he had no desire to cause a scene. But there was no way he was going to let this slide.

"You're jealous," he stated, loving the flare of rage in her eyes. "I've spent this weekend watching men drool over you and take pictures of you and make jokes with you without being able to say a word about it, and now one woman flirted with me and you're pissed."

"I'm not pissed," she lied.

"Liar."

They glared at each other, and Gus had never been so turned on in his life. Brittany opened her mouth to retort, probably something sassy that would make him want to both smack her ass and worship her, when a voice interrupted them.

"Hey, Brittany! Gus!"

Gus reluctantly looked away from Brittney to find Devery heading toward them, her smile big and genuine until she got closer and could focus on the looks on their faces. It must have been clear they were arguing, because she stopped a few feet away.

"Um, sorry, I was just heading to your panel and saw you. Thought I'd keep you company on your way there."

Brittany was the first one to recover, plastering a smile to her face.

"Hey, Dev. Thanks for coming to the panel, you sure didn't have to."

Ignoring Gus, she walked with Dev, chatting away as if the last few minutes hadn't happened. Gus followed, allowing them the space that Brittany clearly needed. As far as he was concerned, they weren't done talking about this. Because Brittany had just revealed she was as affected by him as he was by her, and once his mind latched in

on to that idea, there was no way in hell he was going to let it go.

Brittany's first panel went well, and the rest of the day was a blur after that, filled with rushing to panels, quick makeup refreshers, some photo-ops for her page, and a thousand other tiny things. Gus was tired and couldn't believe Brittany was still standing since she had barely had a rest during the crazy day. At one point, he had shoved a protein bar at her with a bottle of water, just to be sure she wouldn't collapse, but still. She had been on her bad ankle almost the entire time, and he could feel it like a timer in his head that she needed to sit, and she needed to sit soon.

Now they were in her last panel, thank god. She was speaking eloquently on how newcomers could start their own streams and grow their numbers, and on the surface, she looked happy and engaged and full of never-ending energy. But Gus knew her, better than he should, and he could see the strain she was holding back, how tired she was, and how she kept subtly shifting her ankle around. Brittany needed a break. Luckily, this was the last panel for the day.

"How's it been going?"

Gus turned to find Val there, dressed in her form-fitting suit, looking like she walked out of a Dior ad, even as he knew she could throw him on the ground and make him regret his actions if he so much as looked at her funny.

"No word from the stalker since his last text message."

Val nodded, her own eyes scanning the crowd of people sitting at the panel.

"Heard you moved her into your place."

How the hell she knew that already was baffling, but Val had an ear to the ground. At this point, Gus was used to it.

"She got hurt yesterday in a fire alarm gone wrong. I didn't want her laid up in that not-even-a-little-secure hotel room she was crashing in."

"So she's at your place for the job, is what you're saying."

Gus heard the irony in her tone and chose to ignore it.

"She's at my place because she has a threat on her life, her mobility is compromised, and her situation is untenable. Are you here to tell me I made an error in judgment?"

Gus knew he had, but he dared Val to call him on it. Val, who broke up with a new girlfriend every other week, was the poster child for errors in judgment, and she knew it.

She rolled her eyes. "Don't snap at me. I'm on your side."

"Since when?"

"Since always. I just want to make sure you're doing okay. I know this woman messes with your head."

Gus certainly couldn't deny that. And, since this was Val, he knew he had to tell her about the previous evening.

"Robbie came over last night and stumbled on her there while I was out getting groceries."

Val's eyebrows shot up. "That must have been quite the scene."

"I came home part way through it. Turns out Robbie had been cheating on her."

"Ouch."

"For months."

"Damn, Robbie." Val had met with Robbie several times, and always commented on what a loose wire he was, not impressed with his insistence on hitting on her even though she had been out as a lesbian for several years now.

They watched Brittany for a moment as she answered an audience question that had people laughing and falling in love with her at the same time. Val sighed.

"Just be careful, Gus. This girl is bright and beautiful, and I know you got a weakness for her. She'll mess you up if you let her."

Gus nodded. Val was right. But he didn't think he was actually going to be able to stay away from Brittany. She was becoming essential in a way that had him scared.

BRITTANY

Brittany was in the worst mood. First, Gus had flirted with some girl right in front of her, which was absolutely his right to do since they weren't even dating, but her stupid hormones didn't know that and she spent the rest of the day angry and hurt. It didn't help that her ankle was sore as fuck. And while she was pissed at Gus, at the same time, she just wanted to go back to his place and sit on the couch with him while watching a stupid dating show.

Apparently, she had lost her mind. She was thinking about him constantly, thoughts of her orgasm last night filtering in when she was trying to concentrate on whatever the current moderator of the panel had asked her. She needed to stop, needed to exorcise him from her brain.

And the only cure she knew of was a night out.

Luckily, Kickoff was just as famous for its nightlife as it was for its fan stuff. Brittany had been invited by a streaming company to attend their party at the Waterfront, a notoriously wild affair filled with all kinds of streamers, influencers, and content creators that was always both fun and the cause of the worst hangovers she ever experienced. Brittany had been going to skip it, but with her new weird fixation on Gus, she decided she needed to go. This crush or whatever was getting in the way of her job, and she needed to blow off some steam before she did something stupid and made a move on Gus.

Brittany mentally went through her list of friends at Kickoff, trying to figure out who to go with. She had plans to flirt with cute guys, and that meant that she had to leave Gus at home. And the only way he wouldn't kill her when he found out was if she went with someone he trusted.

Finally, she texted Randall and Dev. Randall was always up for blowing off steam after spending his whole day on the floor making sales, and Min's little sister was in need of more hangout time after her accident and several surgeries. Brittany shot them a text, and Dev immediately answered with a number of excited emojis, while Randall sent a GIF of someone giving finger guns. They arranged to share a rideshare so they could arrive together and so Brittany wouldn't be alone.

Gus came to gather her after her last panel, handing her yet another bottle of water that she took gratefully. Without a word, he took her hand, keeping her close to him as they both turned to leave, slowly making their way out of the convention center.

One quick rideshare later, Brittany and Gus pulled up outside of what looked like a closed section of a small shopping mall. Only the window declared 'Fabrics' in faded paint. Otherwise, there was no indication the store was open.

Brittany took it in, confused.

"You sure this is the place? It looks like it's been abandoned for months."

"That's just Liam's style."

Gus reached for the door handle and shocked Brittany when it opened right up. He led her inside, where she immediately froze at the sight of floor-to-ceiling shelves of fabric. Everything that she could think of was there, well organized with poorly hand-written signs that you had to search to find. But it was a treasure trove.

Brittany knew she was gaping but didn't care.

"We're closed," a hard voice rang out from somewhere in the back.

"It's me, Liam."

A head poked out from around a shelf, an older Black gentleman with glasses and a disgruntled expression that could rival one of Gus's.

"What are you doing here?"

Gus didn't even blink at the rude question.

"I brought a friend who wants to shop."

"Do you like her?"

"Yes."

"Do you trust her?"

"Yes."

"Then look around. But don't let anyone else in. This Kickoff crowd is too rowdy."

The head disappeared, leaving Brittany staring at Gus, who quirked an eyebrow at her.

"What?"

"How exactly do you know him?"

"He had some trouble last year with an arsonist. I helped him out with the police reports and did some investigating for him. We managed to catch the guy, and now he has to put up with me."

Brittany thought about how that was just like Gus, to help someone just because he thought they needed it. She turned to a shelf of silks to sort through them, feeling their texture and weight as she thought about everything Gus had said since they walked in there.

"So… you trust me?"

He was looking at his phone, not making eye contact.

"Of course I do."

"I broke into your brother's apartment and destroyed his stuff."

Brittany didn't know why she was bringing it up. She liked Gus and was secretly glad to hear he trusted her. But when she looked back at her recent behavior, she had to admit that if their positions were reversed, she wouldn't have said the same thing.

Gus looked up at her question, surprise in his eyes.

"Killer, you have a temper, but you tend to only get sparked when there's a legitimate reason."

"Oh." She stared at the fabric in front of her, not seeing any of it as she replayed that night in her head. And she had to ask.

"You said… you didn't act like it in the moment. What changed?"

He had the good grace to wince.

"I didn't react well and said things I shouldn't have. When I calmed down and thought about it, I realized something must have really set you off. But I didn't know what it was until last night with Robbie."

"You didn't know about the other women?" Brittany realized this was part of what was bothering her, the idea that Gus had known about Robbie's cheating this whole time and had never said anything. Somehow that betrayal would've hurt more than Robbie's.

Gus shook his head. "I'm not really on any of the social media, and Robbie never talked about her."

Brittany nodded, not trusting her voice but knowing she was going to be thinking about this conversation for a while, analyzing everything from his tone to how she asked the questions. For now, she focused on the fabrics in front of her to hopefully inspire the new designs she desperately needed.

After an hour of digging around, Brittany paid for the swatches she had settled on, grabbing a little black lace that had caught her attention at the last minute. She smiled wide in the face of Liam's complaining about having to open the register for the sale. With a big thank you, they left.

When they arrived back at the condo, Gus had work to do on his laptop, something about the constant report filing that a security officer has to do, and Brittany used the time to focus on her designs… only to come up blank. She had a block, and she didn't know why. She loved fashion and would often doodle outfits in her spare time. She shared with her followers how to alter thrift store clothes to fit better, or to fit a certain design aesthetic. But for some reason, now that her career was on the line, she was drawing a blank and didn't know what to do about it. Nothing was feeling right. Nothing was inspiring her. She was going out of her mind.

When she looked up at the clock, it was time to start getting ready for the evening. She put away her tablet where she had been sketching and got up to head toward the bathroom. Gus looked up from where he had been working in the kitchen.

"What's the plan for the night?"

Brittany hedged. She didn't want to lie to him, but she also desperately needed a night out, away from Gus and whatever this dumb crush was. But she also knew he wouldn't want her going anywhere without him, especially not now that her ankle was hurt.

"Depends on what you have planned."

He shrugged. "I need to meet Val, and I have more questions to ask the flower shop. If you're planning a night in, I can get that done while you're safe here."

She nodded. "Sounds good. I'm going to hop in the shower, so you do you."

Brittany took her time with the shower, knowing she was avoiding Gus but there was nothing to do about it. She focused on her makeup, her hair, and finally the dress she had brought just in case. It was one she had repurposed from one of her favorite thrift shops. There hadn't been a lot of the lace left to work with, so the dress was tight and shorter than she usually liked wearing. The lace did cover her body, but the nude underlayer made it seem like she was naked underneath, hints of her curves and skin peeking through the lace. This dress was sex, and it made Brittany feel powerful. Enough to pull on her lowest pair of heels and attempt her ankle, knowing she wouldn't be able to dance but not really caring. She slipped some fold-up flats in her clutch, along with her lip gloss, and fluffed the hair she had meticulously just curled so it looked beach-kissed. After layering on her Dirty Talk lipstick, Brittany was ready for a night out.

When she stepped out of the bathroom a while later, Gus had gone to meet Val, and Brittany had a brief moment of guilt. He only left because he thought she was staying in his condo, a building that had a secure door. Gus would hate knowing she was going out without him. But Brittany desperately needed to get him out of her head, and so with her teeth gritted, she left Gus a note explaining that she had to go out so he wouldn't worry, and then headed downstairs.

She had the elevator to herself and strode out onto the street, looking at the cars.

"Woooooo, sexy lady!"

Already smiling, she turned to find Dev and Randall hanging out the window of the rideshare, catcalling her.

"Watch out, Kimball, Brittany came to slay!"

"Shut up, you two." Brittany was smiling as she said it, carefully walking toward the car and sliding in next to her friends. The car took off the second her seat belt was buckled.

"Seriously, Britt, you're smoking. Gonna ruin some man's life tonight for sure." Randall winked at her. He was completely done up, his shirt one of his own designs fit him to a tee, the front buttons undone down his chest in obvious invitation. His locks were pulled back into a ponytail, and his eyeliner was on point.

"Me? How would they even notice me with you around looking that hot?"

Randall preened as Brittany took in Dev's outfit. Her style tended toward what Brittany liked to call "50s housewives chic" and tonight's bombshell wiggle dress was no disappointment, putting her lush curves on display. Dev had worn her hair down, her lips bright red, her glasses making her look cute rather than vamp. Her medical boot was still on, since she still had a lot of healing to do, but the whole outfit was so perfect for Devery that Brittany couldn't help but smile.

"Dev, you look amazing."

Dev flicked back her curly hair, her eyes twinkling. "Randall picked the dress. He insisted I follow some awesome advice I got at a panel today. 'Dress for the girl you want to be,' right?"

"Damn straight," Randall said, the two fist-bumping.

Brittany rolled her eyes, even though she was pleased to see her words had touched someone.

"How's it been at the booth?"

Randall got serious, as he always did when he discussed his business. "Busy. Next year I'm thinking I'll have enough product to stake out a larger section."

"He'll talk your ear off about profit margins if you let him," Dev warned with a smile.

"I'll listen to it all." Randall was one of Brittany's favorite people, and his success made her happy. He was a man with big dreams and big plans. Watching his mind work was always fascinating conversation.

"So…" Dev gave her a sly look, which was interesting to see on her otherwise guileless face. "Where's Gus?"

Brittany looked out the window. "I gave him the night off."

Randall and Dev exchanged a look. Randall answered.

"And he was fine with you going to this party by yourself?"

"I'm not by myself. I'm with you two."

Dev wasn't buying it. "You know what we mean."

"He's an employee, I don't answer to him. And I certainly don't have to ask him permission to go to a party."

Randall frowned, confused. "But I thought you had a stalker? Isn't that why your mom hired security in the first place?"

"My mom overreacted. And I'm sure she didn't realize she was hiring Robbie's brother, of all people."

"But you do have a stalker."

Brittany grunted, annoyed that they were right. But after the flowers at the meet and greet and then the text messages, Brittany couldn't deny that she felt safer having Gus with her.

Still.

"I need a night out. Having a babysitter is really starting to get to me, and if I don't let off some steam soon, I'm going to blow. The party we're going to has a lot of security and a strict guest list, so random people can't wander in and try anything with me. I'm not going to be alone anywhere. I just need some loud music, some fruity drink, and a hot guy to flirt with. I can't do that with Gus following me around."

Randall slid her another look. "Gus is pretty hot."

Brittany shook her head, even though it was true. "He's Robbie's brother."

"Robbie is an idiot. Gus is smart and kind and worth about a thousand Robbies. I don't see the problem."

Brittany turned to Dev, trying to prove her point. "You'd date Hayden if he and Min broke up?"

Devery snorted. "If Min and Hayden broke up, I'd have to drag him from the pit of despair he'd flung himself into and help him figure out what he did wrong. Min is it for Hayden. They're each other's person."

Brittany felt the implication that Dev wasn't saying—that she was never Robbie's person, nor was he hers. And Brittany knew Dev was right.

Randall leveled her a serious look. "If you think Gus could be the one, then it's worth trying. You deserve the best. Love is worth it. You only gotta look at Min and Hayden to see that."

Min and Hayden were over the moon for each other, fierce and protective, and loving. And Brittany did want that. Someone who supported her business as a streamer and fashion influencer. Someone to come home to at night, to watch terrible shows with. Someone who wasn't scared of her temper. Someone who cared what kind of footwear she wore.

Shit, she was in trouble. Which meant it was time to change the subject.

"What about you, Dev? Anyone on the horizon?"

Dev shrugged. "Not yet. But I can't imagine anyone's going to be panting after me."

Randall's head whipped around toward her. "Hey."

Brittany was also offended. She had never heard Dev so down on herself.

"That's my friend you're talking about. Why wouldn't someone pant after you?"

Dev shifted in her seat, uncomfortable with all the sudden aggressive friendship.

"I'm just not that outgoing, charismatic girl that people are drawn to."

Randall's eyes narrowed. "What people?"

"I don't know. People."

Brittany snorted. "Well, those people are trash, and if you

see any at this party, point them out so I can throw a drink in their stupid faces."

Dev smiled. "It's mostly just me being down on myself. I'm sick of the rehab and all the appointments and all the doctors. I just want to have some fun, you know."

"Fun with a cute guy?"

"Not… necessarily."

Brittany turned to Dev, eyes wide. "I'm sorry, are you coming out right now?"

"Don't pretend you didn't know. I told Min it was fine to tell you, since she tells you everything anyway."

Brittany and Randall's eyes met before they both laughed.

"Okay, fine, yes, she did tell me, but she also told me that you would come out to me personally and now I'm feeling a little cheated that I didn't get the whole experience. I would've given you this whole speech about women being superior to men, that you're going to lead such a happy life, and that I'm so glad you're able to live your truth—"

"Barf, no. I don't need a speech, I got enough of that from Mom and Min."

Randall clapped his hands to get their attention.

"Here's the plan. We're going to find Devery a cute girl to flirt with, we're going to find Brittany a cute boy to flirt with, and we're going to find the hottest guy there for me to dance with until my feet fall off. Let's see who can have the most fun tonight. Consider it a competition. Deal?"

"Deal."

Their car pulled up to the venue for the party. Waiting outside was a large man in a suit and a woman holding a clipboard, looking unamused as some cosplayers tried to convince her to let them into the party. Brittany, Randall, and

Dev made their way over slowly, gave their names, and were immediately ushered into the space.

The whole place was designed to be photographed. The number of stations set up, from backdrops to the dance floor to the bar, all with the intent for influencers to take selfies and post about the sponsor, some liquor company, made the club look chaotic and everything Brittany needed that night.

Her eyes zeroed in on the bar.

"First, we drink."

They made their way to the line, waiting patiently for it to shuffle forward while scanning the list of themed signature drinks. Dev went with a soda, while Brittany and Randall chose one of the signatures, something with an umbrella and a ridiculous amount of fruit garnish that would make a great picture their followers would love. Drinks in hand, they scanned the area.

"We need a home base. Something with seating. See anything?"

The night was just getting started, but the place was already packed, something about free booze and an exclusive guest list bringing everyone out on time for once.

Dev was eyeing the Photo Booth, currently being run by a woman with blue hair, several piercings, and black lipstick. "Maybe we do the pictures first while the outfits are fresh?"

Randall grinned. "Great idea."

At the booth, they again waited in the line, Brittany taking the downtime as an opportunity to snap a few photos of the space, as well as selfies with Randall. Dev was worrying her lip, her gaze drawn again and again to the woman with blue hair at the front of the line until Brittany slid closer.

"Dev. Just relax. It's a privilege to have your attention. Trust me."

They finally stepped to the front of the line. Brittany and Randall made a show of being entirely engrossed in taking pictures for their social media, giving Dev the space to small talk the attendant. Brittany attempted to commit everything she heard to memory to later relay to Min. It was the only way.

Finally, it was their turn to take over the booth. The space was small, cramped for two people, much less the three of them, but no one cared. They went all out for the photos, with more and more ridiculous poses until the three of them were laughing hard. Afterward, they took their printed pictures and wandered toward the dance floor in search of a space to sit. Brittany gave Dev the side eye.

"So?" Brittany asked. "Did you get the digits?"

Dev rolled her eyes. "Digits? Really?"

Randall crossed his arms, standing his ground. "Answer the question."

Devery glanced around as if to make sure no one was eavesdropping. "We exchanged handles, so we'll see where it goes."

"Handles, wow. You're practically married. Tell me where to send the bitcoin for the wedding."

Dev pinched Brittany hard as they stumbled toward a table just as a group of people snatched it up. Brittany glared at them, and Randall's eyes widened.

"Brittany, don't you dare."

"We were clearly on our way to that table. It's ours."

Dev shook her head. "They got there first. You can't get mad."

"Like hell I can't."

"Brittany?"

Brittany turned to find Kyle staring at her, grinning. He was in a button-up shirt, his hair perfectly sculpted, and his muscles were, of course, on display. His bright eyes danced with amusement as he focused them on Brittany.

"I don't mean this as a line," he said. "But you are absolutely stunning when you look ready to kill someone."

Brittany narrowed her eyes, trying not to smile.

"That is absolutely a line, and a terrible one at that."

He grinned even wider. "You're right. Can I apologize by offering seats at my table?"

He gestured toward a table in the corner with a couple other people, some of Brittany's former roommates, some she didn't know. Brittany hesitated. Kyle wasn't her first choice to hang out with at a party, but seating was limited and he was being decent so far. Brittany glanced at her friends, who nodded and then sniffed at Kyle regally.

"You may."

Kyle led them over to the table, pulling out chairs to help them both sit. Devery, who never met anyone she didn't find fascinating, immediately turned to the woman next to her and started a conversation. Randall managed to secure a spot next to Sam, and the two of them were already leaning into each other's space, vibing. Satisfied her friends were settled, Brittany rested her chin in one hand while she stirred her ridiculous cocktail with the other. Kyle, the big flirt, matched her position, leaning in.

"So, gorgeous. Tell me why you moved out of the hotel room. I thought you and I were going to get to know each other a little better."

"And you thought the perfect place for that was sharing a floor of a crowded hotel room with five other people?"

"Love springs in mysterious places."

Brittany snorted. Kyle was an idiot, but he could be fun, which was why he was so popular as a streamer. That, and he tended to stream shirtless.

Kyle adjusted his position, laying his arm across the back of her chair as he sat sideways in his, leaning even closer to her and Brittany willed herself to have some sort of spark. Anything to get her mind off the man she shouldn't be thinking about.

"So what happened to the guy?"

"What guy?"

"The one who almost ripped my head off. Did you finally ditch him for something better."

"He's just my bodyguard. Nothing more."

Brittany felt a warm hand slip to her thigh and squeeze.

"Then you and I could have some real fun, Brittany."

She stared at him, trying to feel anything but uncomfortable with his hands on her. All she could think was that she needed someone to replace Gus in her brain, and maybe that required a good old-fashioned hook up.

Plus she still had Operation: Get Laid to think about. Kyle was as deep as a sink, but Brittany couldn't help but think he'd probably be good in bed. So, for now, she ignored his hand on her thigh.

"How much fun?"

"Give me a chance, babe. I could make you scream."

He squeezed her again, his hand sliding farther up her thigh. He glanced behind her and furrowed his brow.

"I thought you said he wasn't your boyfriend."

"He's not, why?"

"Because he's over there glaring at me like he wants to take an arm off."

Brittany turned around to follow his gaze and froze, her heart stopping. Across the party, in the middle of a crowd that was getting progressively more inebriated, stood Gus. In an old T-shirt and jeans that he must have thrown on after the gym. His hair was a mess, as if he'd been running his hands through it in frustration. His whole body was tense, and his face... well, he was pissed. And staring straight at her.

Gus was moving toward her in a heartbeat, stomping his way through the crowd that easily parted for him, and Brittany felt her heart beat so loud and so fast she was certain the whole club could hear it over the music.

"Want me to take care of him?"

Brittany suddenly remembered Kyle was there, his gaze hard and dark as he glared at Gus. She had never seen him look like that, and it was... disturbing.

Brittany shook her head. "I'll handle him."

"You sure?"

"It's for the best."

Kyle didn't move as Gus reached her, a storm ready to touch ground.

"Get your fucking hand off of her."

Kyle gripped her tighter. "She's not here with you, bro."

"She is now. Get your hands off and get away from her before I make you."

Kyle stood, getting in Gus's face, the tension in both their bodies prompting Brittany to stand and get between them.

"Okay, both of you need to calm the fuck down. Kyle, go away and let me handle this."

Kyle backed away slowly, his eyes still locked on Gus's.

"She's not yours, bro," he taunted.

Gus narrowed his eyes. "No, but she sure as fuck isn't yours."

Kyle flipped him off, then headed to the bar, leaving the two of them standing and glaring at each other.

"What were you thinking?" His voice practically growled with anger, low enough that only a few people around them heard, but the tension was felt by the whole room.

"That we both needed a night off."

"A night off? Are you out of your fucking mind?" His voice rose a little at the end there. Randall, seeing Gus and realizing immediately what was happening, leaned toward them.

"Hey Gus, I get that you're pissed right now, but you need to chill before all these people think you're an abusive boyfriend they have to save Brittany from. This is an influencer event. You will go viral."

Gus didn't take his eyes off Brittany, breathing hard as he tried to control his temper. But he must have realized how right Randall was, because the next time he spoke, it was quieter, and through gritted teeth.

"I need to speak with you alone."

Brittany was already shaking her head, trying to ignore how breathless she felt in the face of his anger. "Gus, take the night off. We're both tired and need a break."

"You're in danger. I don't get a night off just because you're tired of being careful."

"This is an invite-only event. There's security everywhere. In fact, how did you even get in?"

"My company was hired for the event."

Brittany nodded, trying to speak as calmly as she could.

"Then I'm surrounded by qualified people. I arrived with Devery and Randall and haven't been alone once since I left your condo."

He came even closer at that, his eyes flaring at her mention of leaving his condo.

"Brittany," he ground out. "If you don't move your ass and come talk to me alone right now, I'm about to make a scene so big you will not recover from it."

They glared at each other, stubborn and angry and neither willing to give an inch. But Brittany didn't want a scene, couldn't stand the idea of them trending with Gus looking like the bad guy, so she nodded.

"Fine."

He immediately took her hand and pulled her with him, searching for a private area. But the place was packed to the brim, and private spots were all taken by drunk influencers. Finally, Gus headed to the Photo Booth, now unmanned by the attendant as most people had had their turn. He held the curtain open for her to enter, the set of his jaw daring her to argue with him, so she stepped inside the small booth. He followed her in, taking up so much space there was hardly room to breathe, and shut the curtain behind him before turning a death glare on her.

"Tell me you didn't sneak out wearing a fuck-me dress and inappropriate shoes for an ankle injury while a stalker is out there threatening you all so you could flirt with some asswipe."

Well, when he said it like that it did sound stupid. But that only made Brittany madder, and she was itching for a fight.

"You don't get a say in what I do with my free time, Gus. You're not my boss, and you're certainly not my boyfriend."

She wasn't sure why she put it like that, but she wasn't going to back down now. Her blood was boiling, both with rage and with his nearness. Gus must have sensed it, because his eyes narrowed at her words, and she could feel the moment the energy in the booth changed to something dangerous and exciting.

"Is that what you're doing here, killer? Looking for a boyfriend? Because I'll tell you right now, the only man you're going home with is me." His voice was smooth and dark and completely serious.

"Robbie—"

"Fuck Robbie." He leaned his hand against the wall of the booth behind her, blocking her in. The heat from his body was intense, overwhelming, and Brittany could hear how fast she was breathing.

"Brittany, I don't know what's going on between us, or where it's leading. But there is no way in hell I can leave here, knowing you're going out to flirt with other men, to let them touch you or caress you or kiss you."

Voices came from outside the booth, complaining at how long they were taking, so Gus tapped his phone on the payment device, never once taking his eyes off hers. He leaned even closer, and she could feel his breath on her lips.

"What do you need?" he asked. "Are you just looking to flirt? Or do you need something stronger?"

She felt his hand brush against her waist, stroking once, then twice, before gripping her there. The booth flashed with a picture being taken, but Brittany barely noticed, just stared at Gus, unable to answer his question. Not willing to dare it.

As if she had answered, he nodded.

"Okay, I'll tell you what. If you really think that asshole can get you there, then I'll let you go. I won't bother you. We'll go back to our professional relationship and never talk about this night ever again."

His hand moved lower just as the booth flashed again, and Brittany knew if he kept moving in the direction he was currently going, Gus would soon feel exactly how excited he made her.

"Or you can come home with me. Right now. And I'll take care of you. I'll take care of you so well."

For emphasis, his hand cupped her ass, the strength in his grip contrasting the soft tone of his voice. Brittany inhaled sharply, and she knew Gus must have felt it on his lips because he was so fucking close and if he didn't kiss her soon, she was going to burst. She desperately, desperately wanted to take him up on his offer.

But also knew if she did, it would ruin everything.

"Gus, we can't, and you know it. Robbie would hate you forever."

"I can handle Robbie."

But it was too late. The thought of the rift she would create between the brothers, all for what? A night of fun? Sex? She couldn't live with herself if that happened. Robbie was an ass, but Gus was special. And Gus loved his brother.

Which meant this couldn't happen.

Brittany took another breath, steadying herself, and then pushed him away. She felt the loss of his hand as it slipped from her ass, the loss of his heat as he stepped back, giving her the space she had silently asked for. They stared at each other as the booth flashed for its last picture.

"I'm staying."

He stared at her, and for a moment she wondered if he

heard her. But it was Gus. He always listened. With a nod, his energy changed, and he slipped back into his professional mode. He took another step back.

"I'll make myself scarce."

Gus turned without looking back, leaving her in the booth, and she wondered if she had just made the biggest mistake of her life. But she couldn't see how she could have Gus and he could still have Robbie.

Brittany took a moment to collect herself, trying to calm her racing heart and the overwhelming feeling that she had just made a horrible mistake.

"Brittany?"

Devery's voice came from outside of the booth, and Brittany let out a watery laugh at the absurd situation she had somehow found herself in.

"Dev?"

"Yeah, hey. So there are a lot of angry people out here who seem to want to use the Photo Booth. Are you, um, almost done?"

Instead of answering, Brittany stepped out, glaring at each and every person in line, ready to paint the floor with them if they actually caused her any trouble. She moved out of the way, and the next people in line pushed into the booth, not meeting her eyes. Something about their presence settled her. She was still herself. Reckless, angry Brittany. She hadn't been irrevocably changed just because she was spending time with Gus. Just because he had whispered some dirty things in her ears and put his hands on her in a way that made her want to beg for more.

Nope. Nothing had changed.

She turned to Devery, who was clearly concerned.

"You okay?"

Brittany knew she wouldn't like the answer, so she deflected.

"Could you hear us?"

"Only some of it. It sounded… rough."

Brittany just hummed, her eyes scanning the crowd against her will, searching for that tall build and that curl of hair.

"He said we wouldn't see him unless it was an emergency."

Brittany whipped around at that. "He what?"

"Said you had it under control, that the security here was the best of the best. He said you could have these."

Devery held out her hand, and Brittany automatically grabbed the picture strip, staring at the four pictures. Gus towered over her, and even in the Photo Booth, their body language was screaming sex. Their eyes were locked, both with desire. Anyone who looked at these pictures would immediately know they were drawn to each other, that they wanted each other.

Brittany shoved the strip in her clutch, not able to look at it a moment longer. Dev's eyes were full of sympathy, and Brittany found she couldn't stand that either.

"Let's go. There's an entire party of people to flirt with."

Dev hesitated. "We don't have to stay. If you don't want to. I'm fine to leave, and I'm sure Randall would understand."

"No way, Dev. The night is young, and this place is full of hot people looking for a make-out session."

Some costumed person walking by raised her glass. "Fuck yeah!"

Brittany waved, forcing a smile onto her face. "We're not

leaving. I just got into a public argument about how I need fun, and by god, we are going to have fun."

Dev gave her a look. "Brittany, I'm down for anything, but I heard some of that fight and that's not what it was about."

"Shut up and let's go."

Brittany grabbed her hand, pulling her toward the bar, convinced that this night was going to erase Gus from her brain for good.

CHAPTER 13

GUS

Gus stood on the sidelines of the club, keeping to the shadows, watching Brittany with an intensity that would probably make her stalker jealous. He was burning, pissed at her, but mostly pissed at himself. What did he expect? That she was just going to forget he was Robbie's brother? And even if that wasn't in the equation, she was a high-profile fashion influencer. What the hell would she want with some grunt like him? The truth was he was fucking kidding himself.

She was on the dance floor now, grooving in a way that he knew was killing her ankle, consuming a number of drinks. Gus was dying to check on her, to make her sit and drink a water and eat some of the shitty appetizers the place had laid out. But she had set her boundary, and he respected that. She wanted a professional relationship only. And Gus suddenly found that whatever Brittany wanted, he would make happen.

Including staying away.

He left a message for Val saying she needed to find Brittany a new guard, that he would switch out with whoever was on another assignment. While Gus hated trusting Brittany's safety to someone else, he also knew following her around while she flirted with other guys all weekend was going to slowly kill him.

Brittany stumbled a little, and Gus stood up from the wall he was leaning on, trying to get a better look at her through the crowd. He was relieved to see Dev was already there, talking to Britt, helping her stand, but when Dev looked around the room as if searching for help, he was already moving before she saw him and waved him over.

He pushed through the crowd until he reached Dev, who was currently propping up Brittany. And while Devery was probably a strong woman, and Brittany was quite small, Dev was in a medical boot, and Brittany was completely shit-faced.

Dev shouted to him over the music. "I need to get her out of here."

Brittany turned very, very drunk eyes on him, squinting at his face.

"Gus? That you, bro?"

Ignoring the 'bro,' Gus took her from Dev, easily scooping her into his arms, bouncing her a second until he had her balanced.

"I wouldn't do that too much," she breathed into his ear. "The last few shots aren't settling well, ya know."

She reeked of alcohol, she was pissed at him and had told him to leave her alone, and yet he still couldn't help but feel relieved she was finally in his arms and he was being allowed to take care of her.

"Gus, you smell sooooo good."

He grimaced. In another life, drunk Brittany would be adorable. But here, now, with too many people around him and their fight fresh on his mind, he wasn't loving it.

"Killer?"

"Yeah?"

"Shut up."

She gasped, but Gus ignored her, turning to Devery.

"Where's Randall?"

Dev grinned. "Found a hot guy an hour ago and texted me to 'not wait up.'"

"Are you ready to go?"

She nodded. "I've been ready."

They slowly made their way to the exit, Gus using his shoulders and glare to push people out of the way, Dev following slowly behind him. Brittany was mostly silent, her hand now in his hair, her nails lightly scratching his scalp, and he fought a shiver against the sensation.

The quiet of the night outside was a relief, one that Gus embraced.

"You need a ride," he asked Dev.

She shook her head. "No, I'm grabbing a rideshare. I'm going to call Min."

Gus nodded. "Sounds good."

"I'm going to have to tell her about you."

"I don't have a problem with that."

Dev bit her lip, glancing at Brittany, who was snuggled into Gus and not paying attention.

"She likes you, Gus. Like, really likes you."

He shook his head, not letting himself get his hopes up.

"She was the one who told me to leave."

"That's Brittany. A study in contradictions."

Gus wasn't going to let himself imagine it, this picture of his life with Brittany in it that was suddenly being presented to him.

"She wants more, Dev."

"Gus, she wants you. Up to you what you do about it."

With a wave, she went over to where the bouncer was standing, starting a conversation as she called a rideshare. Satisfied the bouncer was going to watch out for her, Gus strode toward where he had parked in the lot down the street.

"Gus," Brittany whispered in his ear.

"Not now, killer. I'm trying to get to the car."

"Gus, I didn't mean it."

"I'm not having a conversation with you when you're drunk."

"I didn't want you to leave. I never want you to leave."

Gus was pretty familiar with the ramblings of the inebriated. He had picked up his brother from enough bars and heard enough crazy stories to not take her rambling seriously.

He reached his car and managed to open the door, sliding her inside. When he leaned over her to buckle her seat belt, he felt her lean into him and inhale hard.

"You smell. So good."

"Cool. Warn me if you're going to barf."

He shut the door, trying his damnedest to shake her words from his head. By the time he slid into the driver's seat, he was relieved to see she had fallen asleep, her head back against the window at an awkward angle that would definitely hurt after a good amount of time. Her mouth was hanging open, and it was the most relaxed he had ever seen her.

They were at the condo ten minutes later. Gus easily carried her to the elevator and to his door, unlocking it. He immediately went to the bedroom, gently laying her down, and went about taking off her shoes, checking her ankle. It was a little swollen, but otherwise, not as bad as he had worried. At some point, Brittany had woken up, and now her eyes were locked on him, never looking away as he took off her earrings and necklace, setting them carefully on the nightstand next to a glass of water and a couple of painkillers she would need in the morning.

Done fussing over her, he headed to the door, ready for a shower and an uncomfortable night on the couch.

"Gus?"

He froze.

Brittany moaned. "Gus."

The way she said his name, that guttural calling out for him, was the sexiest thing he had ever heard in his life.

"Gus, touch me."

Okay, that was the sexiest thing he had ever heard. He turned around to see she was awake, watching him, her eyes bright and hot with way more focus than he was expecting.

"Brittany, you're drunk."

"Not as drunk as you think I am."

"No."

Frustrated, she kicked off the comforter he had laid over her, pushing it off her body in possibly the most awkward way he had ever seen, something that would've made him laugh if she didn't then completely focus on him.

"It would be sooooo much better than last time."

Gus's eyebrows shot up.

"Last time?"

"You weren't here, and I had to do it myself."

Gus should leave. He should leave immediately. Brittany

was drunk and likely wouldn't remember this. But first he had to know.

"Brittany, are you saying you touched yourself, here, in my bed?"

She bit her lip, and all the air left Gus's lungs.

"I pretended you were the one touching me. That it was your hand in my panties, making me wet. So wet, Gus."

She was looking at him with such anticipation, but there was no way he was going to cross that line when she was drunk. They could talk about this when she was sober. So he shook his head and walked to the door.

"You're drunk, Brittany. Sleep this off and then we can talk."

She flopped down onto the bed, defeated, staring up at the ceiling.

"You don't want me."

Christ, this woman was going to kill him.

"It's not that. You know it's not that."

"Then what is it?"

And suddenly Gus couldn't take it anymore. His control cracked, snapped under the pressure of this woman and how much he wanted her, and he abruptly had to tell her.

"Brittany, I've spent this weekend dying to feel you down there, wanting you spread open so I can look at you, study you, memorize every perfect part of you."

She didn't move on the bed, and Gus wondered for a moment if she had passed out, but then she whispered as loud as a scream.

"And then what would you do?"

"Once I had at least two fingers in you, could feel you

clench around me, could hear your moans, I'd need to taste you."

She squirmed at that, her body reacting viscerally to his words, and Gus needed to get the fuck out of there. He turned, ready to shut the door behind him.

"Gus?"

He froze, his hand on the knob, and turned back to see she had sat up, her skirt hiking up toward her hips and showing off those long, perfect legs, the lace of her dress doing nothing to hide her curves. Her eyes pierced him in his soul.

"Next time it better be your hand making me come."

"Next time, it will be."

And then he left her, knowing he was going to be awake the rest of the night with a hard-on he couldn't relieve. But fuck if he'd ever be able to forget tonight.

CHAPTER 14

Brittany woke up the next morning certain she had not died, since death had to feel better than she currently did. If it were up to her, she would fall back to sleep and try to be unconscious for the worst of her hangover, but alas. Her mouth was a desert of sand, and her bladder was full enough to be threatening an accident she'd never forgive herself for.

She forced herself to roll over in bed, discovering that she hadn't actually woken up on her own. Her phone was on the nightstand, plugged in next to a large glass of water, and the alarm was currently going off like it was begging to be thrown out the window.

Brittany sat up the least amount that she could manage and drank from the cup, guzzling the whole thing down in a way that had her stomach rioting almost as much as her head. Memories from the night before flooded in—the horrible fight with Gus, dancing with Dev, and the many, many shots of something called "The Health Potion" that was proving to actually be quite the opposite. She remembered Gus appearing out of nowhere, scooping her up in a way that made her breathless and taking her home. Putting her in his bed, that still smelled like him and drove her wild.

And then, with horror, she remembered exactly how much she had told him while she was drunk. Last night, Brittany would've given anything for him to join her in that bed, and with a wince, she remembered pleading with him to touch her.

Of course he hadn't. But she remembered his words, weaving together what he would do to her if the situation were different, if she wasn't drunk and they were allowed to touch each other, and oh lord, she now had to spend all day with him at a convention pretending she didn't know what he would do to her body if they both just gave in.

She steeled herself, standing with only a slight swaying of the entire room, and carefully made her way to the door, noting with chagrin that her ankle had a lot to say about how she had danced the night before. Brittany pushed into the bathroom, doing her business and then staring at her reflection in the mirror. She was practically green. Her makeup was a shallow approximation of what it had been the night before, the circles under her eyes showing exactly how little sleep she had gotten. She washed up, leaving her skin bare, and carefully stepped out of the bathroom toward the main area, ready to face whatever lecture Gus had prepared for her recklessness last night. She knew she deserved it.

Brittany stepped into the living room, her eyes finding Gus in the open kitchen, working on breakfast. He looked up, immediately putting down what he was doing and coming to her, nothing but concern in his eyes.

"Hey, let's get you to the couch."

He helped her sit, only touching her as was necessary to steer her there, propping her foot up on a pillow. Satisfied, he left and came back with more water, a sports drink that promised electrolytes, and a bottle of painkillers.

"I'm doing some plain toast and eggs right now. Coffee will be ready in a minute. Stay here."

He went back to the kitchen to do whatever he was doing. So far, Gus was patient and kind and understanding and Brittany suddenly found she was very, very annoyed.

"Just say it."

"Say what?"

"Whatever lecture you've had brewing in you since we got back. Lay it on me already. The suspense is killing me."

"I haven't been working on a lecture."

She snorted. "Please. You probably have a list of grievances in the notes app on your phone."

"I've never used my notes app in my life."

"That's weird and you know it."

He just shook his head, focusing on his sizzling pan.

"You have nothing to say?"

"Not a thing."

"Not even about Kyle?"

He paused at that, and Brittany felt a moment of victory as well as a moment of disgust with herself. Who was this person itching for a fight?

"If I had anything to say about last night," he finally said carefully. "I would keep it to myself. It's not my place to question your actions, or to lecture you on your behavior. I'm an employee, and you're my client."

Brittany hadn't really been prepared for how much that

hurt, even though she recognized the words. She felt the bitterness, the unfairness of it all rising inside her, and needed to unleash it somehow.

"So you don't care if I spend the rest of the weekend fucking Kyle."

Gus walked toward her, his eyes stormy, and she wondered if she had finally gotten to him, but all he did was hand her a plate of scrambled eggs and toast, and then placed her coffee on the table where she could reach it.

"Who you fuck isn't my business, Brittany. You made that very clear last night."

She stared down at the breakfast he had made her, after taking care of her the night before, after watching her act like an idiot on the dance floor, after the horrible fight they had had where he laid out what he wanted and she had been too scared to try.

"What if I want it to be your business?" She almost whispered it, so quiet it was possible he didn't hear her. But the tension that filled the room, the electricity that felt like a current zapping through everything around her was palpable. She glanced at him, saw his eyes were dark with thought as he stared at her so intensely her hair stood on the back of her neck.

"What changed? Last night you didn't want me near you. What's suddenly different?"

Brittany didn't know how to answer that. Because the truth was, she felt the loss of him when he left her in that photo booth, felt the deep regret and pain when he walked away that she didn't think she could stand it. That emptiness was why she had thrown herself into the party, and why she had started on the drinks.

She looked away from him, not able to meet his eyes. But she told him the truth.

"I can't watch you walk away again."

It was so quiet she wouldn't have been surprised if he had left the room.

"If we do this…" his voice trailed off just as Brittany's eyes snapped up. He was still in the kitchen, his hands on the counter, leaning forward as if bracing himself. His tone was calm, but his eyes were burning. He swallowed hard, and she watched his throat, wondering what it would be like to taste him there. To taste him everywhere.

"If we do this, we do this together. I can't be thinking that you're waiting to sneak out to go meet up with douches at parties."

She nodded, excitement building. "Same for you. If we do this, it's just us."

"And once one of us is done, we're both done. No hard feelings. No temper tantrums. No water damage to my condo."

He gave her a stern look at that, and fuck her life, it was sexy.

"Don't give me a reason to torch your place, and I won't."

He smirked at that before growing serious.

"I'll handle Robbie."

Brittany winced. "He doesn't have to know. If you want. We can keep this secret."

"I want him to know."

"Oh."

They stared at each other, the tension building, and Brittany could feel herself grow warm. Fuck, if he could do this just by looking at her…

"When?" Even she could hear how husky her voice had become.

Immediately, he stood up from where he had been leaning against the counter and started toward her, his steps purposeful and his eyes so full of heat Brittany was sure she was going to come before he even touched her.

And then, because the universe hated her, there was a knock at the door.

"Fuck," Gus bit out, and Brittany agreed with the sentiment wholeheartedly. He stormed to the door and pulled it open to reveal a tall, slender Asian woman with a short-cropped hairstyle that Brittany liked to call "I'm hot, go fuck yourself." Another man was with her, muscular, a little shorter than Gus, older and bald. The Asian woman didn't flinch at the stormy look on Gus's face.

"Good morning to you, too," she said. She strode in like she had been to Gus's condo before, and Brittany sat up straighter, not sure what was going on, but knowing somehow that she wasn't going to like it. The woman scanned the area, and then approached Brittany on the couch, putting on a professional expression.

"Ms. Jenssen, my name is Valerie Shang. I own Shang Security. It's nice to meet you in person, even under these unfortunate circumstances."

Brittany eyed her warily. "You're Gus's boss?"

"Mr. Lozano is an employee, yes."

"Okay."

Brittany didn't know what was happening, and the whole situation was weird. She didn't know how to talk to this woman and the man she had brought with her when only moments ago, she had been ready to strip and beg Gus to touch her. The whiplash was discomforting.

"I've been notified that you would prefer a different security agent, so I've come personally to introduce you to Curtis. He's been with me for almost ten years, is ex-military, and is one of my most requested security personnel."

Curtis stepped forward at that, holding out his hand for her to shake, which she did on reflex, still trying to figure out what was going on.

"Um, it's nice to meet you, but I think there's been a mix-up. I didn't ask for a new guard."

Val glanced at Gus, so Brittany followed her gaze to find Gus was glaring at Val as if he could shatter her with his eyes. Unfazed, Val turned her back on him and focused on Brittany.

"Mr. Lozano mentioned he was going to be unavailable for the remainder of your trip here in Kimball, and he wanted to transition you as smoothly as possible."

Brittany's blood froze. He had asked for someone to replace him. He was going to leave her. The fight last night had been too much for him, so he had pulled the parachute with his boss. Brittany didn't even know what to say to that. She was shocked and hurt, and even though she understood it, she was sliced down the middle.

"Oh, okay. Sorry, this is a surprise to me. I guess just let me get my things together and—"

"Fuck that, no. Brittany, stay where you are. Val, my schedule's opened up, you don't need to replace me."

If Gus was a live-wire, Val was nothing but cool, calm water. She gave him a neutral look, then turned back to Brittany.

"Let me speak with my employee for a moment. Curtis will be here if you need anything."

And with that, Val stepped out of the condo and into the hall, Gus hot on her heels. The room was silent once they left, either speaking incredibly quietly or the door was super thick, because Brittany couldn't hear anything.

Trying to gather herself, Brittany turned to Curtis. "Can I get you anything?"

He nodded. "I'll get myself a glass of water. I saw in your file you've injured your ankle, so it would be best if you rest it as much as possible. I've been briefed on your schedule."

He went to the kitchen and helped himself, and Brittany didn't know what to do. He seemed like a nice guy. Capable. Ready and willing to keep her safe.

He just… wasn't Gus.

But Gus had apparently told his boss to get him off her case. Which meant she needed to move on.

"Curtis, I actually have to set up a stream for today. Could you help me?"

CHAPTER 15

GUS

Gus was so livid he could punch a wall. Several walls, in fact, especially the ones with the stupid wallpaper in front of his nosey neighbor's door. The second he was in the hall, he spun to Val, ready to tell her to fuck off hard and fast, but she cut him off first.

"Not here."

Without pausing, she strode to the elevator, leaving Gus no choice but to follow. He hesitated only a moment, not wanting to leave Brittany alone, but she had Curtis, and as much as Gus hated him in this moment, Curtis was damn good at what he did.

In the elevator, Gus opened his mouth to let Val have it, but again she cut him off.

"Before you start yelling at me, I want to remind you that I'm here with a replacement for you, just as you asked me to do last night. If you're mad at anyone, be mad at yourself."

"What makes you think I'm not?"

The doors opened, and Val headed straight for the exit.

"Val, where the fuck are you going?"

"We're going to get coffee, Gus. You're going to explain to me why you're being such a shithead, and then you're going to try to convince me that you're able to act as security to our client. And your argument better be damn good, because right now, I'm not feeling it."

It was unfair. But it was unfair because Gus had made it this way, calling Val last night and demanding a replacement after that horrendous fight with Brittany. So he followed her, ready to do whatever he needed to undo the damage.

They went to the usual coffee shop, with Val once again ordering a muffin that tasted like wood chips. Gus ended up with a cup of something that he had no memory of ordering, and they sat themselves in the corner of the café, far enough away from people to have a quiet, private conversation, but close enough to people that if Gus started yelling, he'd cause a scene. Gus dropped into the too-small chair across from her and ran his hand through his hair, knowing he looked like baked shit but not able to do anything about it.

"So," Val began. "You've changed your mind, I take it."

"Yes. I don't need a replacement. It was a misunderstanding."

Val took a long sip of her blended sugar whatever and Gus knew she did it on purpose to drive him nuts.

"What kind of misunderstanding?"

"The private kind." Like fuck he was going to tell her about last night. About Brittany in his bed, begging for him.

"We have a problem here, Gus."

"No problem that I see."

"I have a client that hired us to keep her out of danger. And the security personnel I assigned to protect her seems to be prone to misunderstandings."

"That's not what happened here."

"Then tell me."

"Brittany and I have a history. You knew that when you gave me the assignment."

"Your history was that you were friends until your brother dumped her. You said you could handle this and keep it professional. What changed?"

"The client and I had an argument last night that got a little… heated. We've since made amends and are ready to continue our relationship."

"Relationship?"

"Working relationship."

Gus steeled his jaw, not willing to give more, and Val could probably sense it because she sat back in her chair.

"Gus, you're damn good at your job, but you've been emotionally compromised and we both know it."

"Emotionally compromised? What does that even mean?"

"It means you've fucked the client, and that's not what you get paid to do."

A rock sunk into Gus's stomach at Val's words.

"I haven't. We haven't."

"But with the way you're going, I'm guessing you will. And that's a problem for me and my company. If you're thinking with your dick, you're not thinking with your head."

"It's not like that."

"Then what is it like? Explain it to me, so I can understand. Because right now this looks like a clusterfuck."

Gus's mind whirred with explanations he could offer, excuses or diplomatic reasons, but settled on the truth. Val was one of his best friends, and if he couldn't be honest with her, he was truly fucked.

"I don't know how to explain it. We were working together, we were fine, everything was fine."

"And then you moved her into your condo."

"She got hurt. She wasn't going to be safe in that revolving door hotel room."

"Don't bullshit me. You've never let a client stay in your home, even when their residence was compromised."

She was right. "Brittany's a friend. She had already been to my home several times. It was easier this way."

"Fine. Let's pretend that's a totally normal thing to do. What happened last night?"

Gus hesitated. He was not going to come out of this story looking good, and he knew it.

"She snuck out without telling me. Went to a party unprotected."

"It's my understanding she went with friends of hers and that the party had my security agents everywhere, as well as a tight guest list."

"You and I both know that doesn't matter if someone's aiming to hurt a client."

"Fine. She snuck out to a party. I assume you showed up and talked your way inside."

Gus nodded. He knew all of Val's employees, had worked with most of them at some point or another. It had been easy to convince them to let him in.

"I'll be sure to chat with the party staff later, but let's move on. What happened when you got to the party."

"I found her snuggled up with some guy in a corner."

Val leveled him with a look. "She's allowed to do that."

"I fucking know she's allowed to do that, Val." The fact made him burn, that he had no claim to Brittany, that she could touch and kiss and more with anyone she wanted because she wasn't his.

"Gus, tell me this wasn't some alpha male jealousy thing that I'm getting pulled into. I thought you were better than this shit."

He had thought he was, too, but Brittany changed everything.

"I pulled her aside and we had words about her sneaking out." Among other things, Gus sure as fuck wasn't going to tell his boss. "It got heated, and she made it clear at the time that she would prefer someone else on her case."

Val nodded. "So you called me. Makes sense. Now tell me what changed."

"We… worked it out."

The look on Val's face said she wasn't buying it, which made sense since Gus was working overtime to not talk about the truth.

"What about Robbie?"

Gus snorted. "Why does everyone care so much about what Robbie thinks?"

"The better question is, why don't you care more about what Robbie thinks? Everything up until this conversation led me to believe that he was the most important relationship in your life, and you didn't want to do anything to ruin that."

Gus paused to think about it. How he took care of Robbie, went out of his way to make sure he was happy and thriving, fixing whatever problems may come up, telling himself that's what good brothers do. And Robbie definitely hated Gus hanging out with Brittany. But Gus was finding that while he cared about Robbie, he didn't give a shit what Robbie thought about Brittany. Not even a little bit.

"My relationship with Brittany has absolutely nothing to do with Robbie. And if he has a problem with that, he can work that out on his own."

Val's eyebrows shot up. "You're really not making me feel better about keeping you on this assignment."

"But you'll keep me."

He stated it, rather than questioned, even though his heart was pounding with the possibility of her refusing. Val glared at him, more serious than he had ever seen her. Which was saying something, since he and the other guys had a running bet on if she ever smiled.

"I'll need you to check in with me twice a day rather than once. No more public displays with this woman. No more drama. No more late-night calls. You hear me? You want out, you remember this moment and why you wanted to stay, and you do your fucking job. Understand."

"Copy that."

Gus smiled at her, even as she glared at him, and relief flooded him. He stood, anxious to get back.

Val beat him to it. "I'll tell Curtis to expect you. Don't fuck this up."

Gus was out the door, his coffee forgotten in his mission to get back to Brittany.

At the condo, Gus let himself in, staying quiet when he heard Brittany's voice describing her outfit for the day, realizing she was streaming. He nodded at Curtis, who nodded back before heading out the door. One thing Gus loved about Curtis, he knew when to fuck off.

Gus turned his attention to the corner of his living room,

where Brittany had set herself up. She was standing, which he didn't like, thinking of her ankle, but she seemed well enough as she showed off the small shorts she was apparently planning to parade around in the convention center that day. And she was currently in some sort of bra, something that covered more than a swimsuit but was still clearly underwear. Gus knew she did this often, that part of her stream was showing people the undergarments that could work for various outfits, but still the sight of her in it, posing for her stream, was enough to stop him in his tracks. Fuck, he was going to be hard for hours.

At the thought, the memory of their conversation right before Val interrupted came back to him. He slowly made his way to the living room, knowing the moment when Brittany noticed him by the tension that shot through her body. She was clearly determined to ignore him, which suited him fine, because he was in the mood to work for her attention.

He sat on the couch, facing her but far away from her camera set up, watching as she held up two different shirts to her body.

"What do you all think? I was leaning toward a vamp look, but I've also been enjoying the nerdy T-shirt vibe at the con, so I'm torn."

She continued reading her chat, responding to questions, debating the shirts, and she was so fucking cute Gus couldn't stand it anymore and let his hand fall right at the pressure on his zipper, rubbing himself through his jeans.

"Y-you're right, the nerdy aesthetic is what I'm here for, I can vamp anytime."

Brittany pulled the T-shirt over her head, fast, and Gus felt satisfaction deep inside him at her stutter. She was doing her best to ignore him, but she wasn't succeeding. He was getting to her. Gus rubbed himself once, hard and slow, through his jeans. Color rose up her neck as she kept her attention on her stream, but her eyes flickered toward him, and he knew he had her.

So he reached for his zipper.

"Now let's talk about sunglasses because it's extra sunny today and you all know how sensitive my eyes are."

Gus's eyes traveled down from Brittany's face, enjoying how she swallowed as he folded back the sides of his jeans, making room, and reached his hand into his boxer briefs. Her eyes flicked to him right when he touched himself, and he felt the look as if it caressed him.

She showed off the two sunglass choices, probably trying to hide her eyes and where she was looking, but from him or her stream, he wasn't sure. And then Gus pulled himself out, letting his length free and Brittany dropped both pairs of sunglasses.

"Sorry, everyone, one second, just a little clumsy today. Should we talk earrings? I found a cute thrift store down the street with some stellar choices."

She turned to grab the earrings, her back to the camera, but her eyes immediately went to him, and the hunger he saw there had him giving himself one stroke, slow and strong, loving that she was watching him. Fuck, this woman was perfect.

Brittany spun back to the camera. "Hmm, I can't seem to find the earrings now, so maybe it's a casual day? In any case, I should run, my next panel is soon, and I got a lot of ground to cover in the convention center to get there. Thanks so much everyone for tuning in! I'll see you tomorrow!"

After a few more goodbyes, Brittany hit the button on her camera, double checking that everything was off. Gus watched her, stroking himself, dying with anticipation of what she was going to do now that they were finally, finally alone.

Brittany stepped toward him, the look in her eyes unidentifiable.

"I can't believe you just did that," she said.

"Tell me you're wet."

She just shook her head, moving closer to where he was still seated on the couch. He reached out a hand for her.

"No." Her voice was sharp, and he obeyed immediately, letting his hand drop, freezing the movement of his other hand on his dick. Her eyes scanned over him, and he couldn't breathe waiting for whatever was going to happen next.

"Show me," she said, and Gus felt a break in his mind as it hit him how much he wanted to please this woman.

He stroked himself slowly, from base to tip, giving himself a twist at the end, covering his hand in the precum that was coming just for her, because she was watching him.

"Is that what you like? Slow and hard?" she asked, her voice mild and neutral as if she was asking how he liked his coffee.

"Sometimes."

"Show me what else you like."

Brittany stepped closer as his hand on his cock sped up, unconsciously mirroring the speed of her steps until she was right in front of her. She placed a finger under his chin, drawing his gaze up to meet hers.

"All that for me?"

He nodded, unable to speak as she slowly straddled him,

her knees going to either side of his thighs. She sat her cute ass on his legs, his cock hard and long between them. She stared down, watching him stroke himself.

"I'm close," he admitted.

"Already?"

"It's you. You have me on edge just by looking at me. It doesn't take much as long as you're here and watching."

"I turn you on that much?"

"You know you do."

She rocked in his lap, nowhere near where he wanted her, where he wanted to touch her, but he kept his hands to himself, sensing she wanted to be in charge of this moment. She leaned over him, her hair tickling his face as she lightly, so lightly, bit his earlobe.

"Then show me how you come, Gus."

With a half-grunt, half-moan, he did just that, his hand flying up and down his cock, harsh and fast. His eyes were locked on hers, staring deep into those baby blues, and the excitement and desire he saw there was his undoing. With a shout, he came, erupting between their bodies. Brittany leaned back to see better, and something about her watching him defile himself, all for her, was the biggest turn-on he had ever experienced.

Gus leaned back when he was done, a complete mess. He was going to have to shower and change clothes, but he had managed to miss Brittany, which was a shame. He'd love to see her covered in him, to rub it into her skin. Next time, he promised himself.

Brittany was still in his lap, had watched every moment of his orgasm as if committing it to memory. She took his hand, the one that had been stroking his dick, and licked it from wrist to fingertip, cleaning the come off, and then gently kissed his palm.

"Thank you for showing me. You did a very good job."

He was warm inside, even as she stood up, brushing down her shorts and adjusting her top.

"Wait, where are you going?"

"Busy schedule today, Gus. We need to leave soon, and you need a shower."

"Brittany, get your ass back here." He was practically growling, and he could hear it in his own voice. Frustrated as fuck that she was walking away instead of letting him put his hands on her, letting him have the privilege of giving her an orgasm.

Instead of listening, she turned to him, the look on her face saying that she was still apparently very, very pissed at him.

"Gus, you tried to fire yourself off my case. I'm still angry with you. So if you want to touch me, ever, you're really going to need to work for it."

She strutted to the bedroom and shut the door behind her, and Gus let out a frustrated groan. He hated knowing she was turned on, how turned on he had made her. She wouldn't let him take care of her, and that was torture for him.

Which was obviously what she had in mind. Gus was fucked. He went to clean himself up and change clothes to prepare for his day of being frustrated.

CHAPTER 16

BRITTANY

Her hands were shaking when Brittany shut the bedroom door behind her. She'd had time to think while Gus had been out telling Val whatever it was that meant Curtis would leave with only a nod, so she assumed he took back quitting. And while she had set up for her stream, she went over the events of the night before. Brittany cringed when she thought of what she had said to him at the party in that Photo Booth. She had meant it at the time, but she realized now it was a defense mechanism. She didn't want to be the one to get between brothers.

But she also couldn't help herself around Gus, as showcased by how she shamelessly begged him to touch her last night. And the memory of him stroking himself off in front of her was going to be in her spank bank forever. They had a chemistry that she no longer thought she was strong enough to deny.

In thinking about it, she assumed he must have called his

boss after their argument at the party, and that made sense. She had asked him to back off, after all. Brittany couldn't be mad about that. She shouldn't be.

But she was.

Brittany adjusted her outfit, pulling on some knee-length socks to wear with her sneakers. Brittany still wasn't certain she could rock heels with her ankle, but she could definitely play into her online name.

As she checked her hair, Brittany's phone dinged with a message from Kyle. She opened it to find a picture of the door to the hotel room she had been staying at with him—the floor now covered in shredded flowers. There were tears in the wallpaper that looked like they were done with a razor blade, scratching deeply into the walls. And taped to the door was a card with her name on it in very, very familiar writing. Kyle's message was a simple "what the fuk?" Brittany didn't know what to tell him. Her stalker was still in town, and he was apparently super, super pissed.

With a quick application of her "Dirty Talk" red lipstick, and a deep breath to steady herself, Brittany stepped out of the bedroom to find Gus there, his hair still damp from the shower, leaning against the kitchen counter. His eyes found her almost immediately, raking her from head to toe in a way she felt in her blood.

"So I'm not allowed to touch you, but you're going to dress like that?"

Brittany stuck up her nose. "Like what?"

"Like every wet dream I've ever had come to life."

She ignored his comment, handing him her phone.

"There's been a development."

He studied the picture as Brittany grabbed her small backpack and strapped it on. When she looked back at him, Gus had a frown on his face and was texting on his phone.

"Curtis is going to meet your roommate to check this out and deal with hotel security."

Brittany nodded, feeling numb, and Gus stopped to grab her shoulders, pulling her closer.

"Hey," he said, his voice soft and kind. "You're safe. Curtis will handle this. The asshole's mad because he hasn't gotten to you yet, and we're going to make sure he doesn't. Don't let him ruin your day."

She nodded, feeling emotional but agreeing. Brittany bumped her hand into his hard chest, aiming for humor.

"Keep it in your pants, Lozano. We got a full day ahead of us."

He held open the door for her, smirking a little, probably recognizing how full of shit she was.

"Yes, ma'am."

They headed out onto the crowded streets of Kimball. It was Saturday, the busiest day, and even though they were blocks from the convention center, the excitement and sheer amount of people hit Brittany like a blast of hot air.

It was still a little early, though, and Brittany had plans with Min, so they walked toward the restaurant. She and Gus weren't speaking, weren't touching, but Brittany couldn't think of anything else. That's how aware she was of his presence. Lord, she was going out of her mind.

They somehow made it to Insatiable, and Brittany stepped inside, glancing around for Min, who she found tucked away in the corner.

She turned to Gus, who was casing the place as if masked gunmen were going to come for her at any angle.

"This is supposed to be a private girlfriend brunch. No boys allowed."

Gus's eyebrows went up. "I'll find a place at the bar if that makes you more comfortable."

She nodded. "Good."

"But you should probably know I'm already hard for you again."

He was doing this on purpose, annoyed that she hadn't let him touch her earlier, and also distracting her from the latest from her stalker. She knew it, but it still made her heart beat like crazy. She glanced down at his crotch, then immediately glanced away.

"Fucking Christ, Gus."

"Can't help it. You drive me crazy, killer."

"Go douse yourself in cold water or something."

Without looking back, she strode toward Min, doing her best to keep her shoulders straight and look unaffected. But when she finally made it to Min, she practically collapsed in her chair, putting her head on the table. Min was surprised.

"Rough morning?"

"You could say that."

"Anything to do with that gorgeous mountain of a man you walked in with who is currently fucking you with his eyes from the bar."

Brittany sat up, looking only at Min, who was definitely amused by the situation.

"Min, I don't know what to do."

"Looks like he has a few ideas."

"It wasn't supposed to be like this. He's Robbie's brother. What am I doing?"

"I'm hoping you're realizing that you're worthy of love and

affection and great sex, just like everyone else. And if that's the man who gets your motor running, maybe the drama is worth the ride."

Before Brittany could answer, the third chair at their table is slid out, and a large man in a chef's jacket and a ponytail collapsed into it.

"I hate my life," he announced.

Min smiled at him. "You're just saying that because you hate working mornings."

"Brunch is an overrated invention of the wealthy looking to waste their money on something they could just eat at home but instead will lord over others in social media posts filled with pretension."

"At least you get to charge them a lot?" Brittany offered. Theo turned his dark eyes to her, and Brittany smiled. They had become friendly over the year since Min and Hayden had started dating, the two of them thrown together often in social situations. Brittany knew that Min secretly harbored fantasies of her and Theo getting together, but Brittany had never felt anything more than brotherly affection for the volatile chef.

Unlike a certain broody security guard who she could feel glaring at her from the bar.

"Brittany," Theo said. "Have you fixed your palate yet?"

She snorted. "Theo, I can't fix a genetic predisposition to hate cilantro."

"Have you even tried?"

"Not once."

"It's a shame the flavor combinations you're missing out on."

"The second you make soap taste good, I swear I'll eat it."

Shaking his head, he turned back to Min.

"Min, you have to convince my brother she isn't working out."

Min didn't even blink. "Rosa? I heard she's amazing. I heard the dinner service she covered for you ran the smoothest the restaurant has ever run."

"First of all, restaurants are supposed to be chaos. Second, do you know what she did?"

"Ground up your wagyu?" Brittany guessed.

"Baked pasta without cooking it first?" Min grinned.

"Cut your onions unevenly?"

"Used canola instead of grapeseed?"

"I know you're making fun of me," Theo said. "But all of those are horrifying, and I need you to stop before I get nightmares."

Min took pity on him. "What did she do that was so horrible?"

"She put ricotta in the ravioli."

Brittany blinked, meeting Min's confused eyes.

"And that's... bad?"

"It's a simple recipe. Ricotta changes the entire concept of the dish."

"Could you... serve both ravioli?"

But Gus wasn't listening, already on to the next grievance. "She moved all the utensils in the kitchen. Said it was better for the workflow, whatever that means."

Min was bewildered. "Umm..."

"And she changed the spice racks around. Grouped them by flavor profile. Who does that?"

"I'm not seeing the problems here, Theo."

"It's just not working out. You'll have to trust me. She

needs to go."

Min gently placed her hand over his.

"Theo, she is the fourth chef you've tried in this position. She's damn good, she has amazing ideas, and she puts up with your shit. You can't fire her."

"I'm not that difficult to work with."

There was really nothing to say to that, so both women stayed silent. Theo slapped the table.

"Fine. But when my kitchen is a disorganized mess because of her, you're the one that has to help me fix it."

"Deal."

With that, he was gone, off to torture the new chef in fun and exciting ways, and Brittany silently congratulated herself on not going into the culinary industry.

Picking up her menu, she glanced over to the door just as it opened. And that's when her whole body froze.

"Holy shit," Min said. "Is that Robbie?"

It was. Robbie had just walked into the restaurant, his arm around a young, beautiful,

Asian woman that Brittany recognized as a makeup influencer she had met briefly at a networking event a few months ago, known as Diamond. Her eyes flew to where Gus was sitting to see he had spotted his brother as well, his whole body stiff.

As Brittany stared, Robbie spotted Gus, and they walked toward him. Brittany wondered if Gus had this planned for the day before dismissing the idea. This must just be the universe fucking with both of them.

"Brittany?"

Brittany snapped her attention back to Min, who nodded at the server who must have approached at some point.

"Ready to order?"

Brittany pointed to the omelet on the menu and then took a deep sip of her coffee, trying to balance her nerves.

"Are you okay?"

Brittany heard the sympathy in Min's voice and nodded, keeping her own voice down.

"Yeah, I'm just worried about Gus."

Min's eyes went behind her, back to the trio at the bar.

"He seems to be handling it well."

Brittany glanced over to see now that Diamond was laughing at something Gus said, placing her hand on his arm, and while it was a perfectly innocent touch, Brittany couldn't help but feel something clawing inside her at the sight. Something ugly.

As she watched, the three of them were led to a table. Apparently her bodyguard was going to use this opportunity to have brunch with his brother. Which was fine, but the way the influencer was sizing up Gus made Brittany's blood heat.

Brittany hadn't felt jealous the entire time she dated Robbie. Women would flirt with him on stream, at parties, and everywhere he went, attention seemed to follow him. And that never bothered her. It was simply part of who he was.

But now this beautiful woman was laughing at something Gus said, was watching him with a look that said that she wasn't stupid, she knew quality when she saw it, and Gus was the absolute best man at that table.

And all Brittany could do was sit there and stew about it.

"Brittany, you can't cause a scene here just because some woman touched your man."

"She's not just some woman," Brittany shot back. "Diamond's one of the most popular cosmetic influencers in the country. She does work for charities, works with brands on their sustainability practices, hosts functions to benefit the homeless."

"Oh. She's perfect."

"Yes."

"I hate her."

Brittany snorted, happy to have a loyal friend like Min, even during these more irrational moments.

"You wouldn't if you met her. She's one of the kindest people I've ever met in my life."

"Ugh, the worst."

"She's perfect for Gus."

"Hey." Brittany looked up at Min's sharp tone of voice. "If Gus likes her more than you, then he can go fuck himself. I don't care how nice she is, or how much good she's doing in the world."

"You have to say that because you're my friend."

"No, I get to say it because you're my friend."

Their food arrived then, saving Brittany from the overwhelming feeling engulfing her. Once the server left, Min got right back into it.

"I also find it interesting that of the three people there, you're more worried she's flirting with Gus than you are that she's clearly dating your ex."

That made Brittany pause. When she had first heard Robbie had cheated on her, the thought of him dating other women the entire time they were together had made her feral. But now, confronted in person with a woman he was clearly getting naked with or wanted to get naked with, she didn't care. All that was running through her head was that woman's hand on Gus's arm, touching him like she was allowed, an arm that only hours earlier Brittany had fantasized about wrapping around her while she ground herself in Gus's lap.

Brittany dropped her head in her hands with despair.

"What the fuck am I doing?"

Min gave her a sympathetic look. "Eating breakfast."

"And then?"

"And then you're going to go make sure that man knows he's claimed."

"Am I even allowed to claim him?"

"Brittany, I don't know how you keep missing these cues, but from where I'm sitting, I think he desperately wants you to."

Brittany finally took a bite of her food, thinking. Her options were to pretend that everything was fine, to play it all casual and not get mad when he looked at other completely perfect and gorgeous women. Or she had to tell him she wanted to try being together, and that meant other women can't touch him.

She stood up suddenly, not sure what she was doing but knowing she needed a second alone.

"I need the bathroom."

"Are you okay?"

"Yeah, I just need a minute."

She beat a hasty escape to one of the single-stall restrooms in the joint, breathing deeply as she paced the floor. It was only a moment before there was a knock at the door. She yelled, tired of all people everywhere.

"Occupied."

"Brittany."

She'd recognize that voice anywhere. She unlocked the

door, opening it a few inches to stare up into Gus's hard, unsmiling face.

"Let me in, killer."

She stared at him a moment, and he let her, giving her that time to think, not rushing her until she finally pulled the door open the rest of the way and he stepped inside.

"What are you doing, Britt?"

"I'm in the bathroom. What do you think I'm doing?"

"Are you okay?"

Brittany looked away from him, leaning against the sink and crossing her arms.

"I'm fine. Having a great time. The best."

"Anyone ever tell you that you suck at lying?"

"Everyone I've ever met."

He nodded, moving closer and leaning over her, caging her near the sink as he propped his hands lean on either side of her.

"Why are we in here?" he asked.

"You let her touch you."

Brittany knew it was going to sound ridiculous, and it definitely did, but she couldn't help it. The moment kept replaying in her mind, making her angrier with each repetition.

Gus lifted a hand and touched her cheek gently, stroking back toward her ear.

"Diamond is a toucher. She doesn't mean anything by it."

"She shouldn't be touching you."

"Oh yeah?" His hand cupped the back of her head, burying itself in her hair, and he leaned so close she could feel his breath on her lips. "Why's that?"

Brittany thought about it, realizing something stupid and

wonderful. He was hers, and she didn't want someone else touching him, and she no longer cared if that was weird or over the top. She stared at Gus, her eyes wide with shock, her mouth a little open, and he must have realized her thought process because he was smiling a little.

"We haven't even kissed yet," is what she ended up saying.

"Brittany, when I kiss you, I'm not going to stop. So you better be absolutely certain this is what you want, because there is no going back for me."

She stared at him, still trying to figure out how this happened, still trying to figure out how she missed all the signs, but one thing became very, suddenly clear.

"Gus, if you don't kiss me right now, I'm going to punch you in the nuts."

He breathed a sigh of relief. "I thought you'd never say that."

And then his mouth met hers, and she was fucking done. Fireworks exploded in her head as the hand at the back of her head held her firmly in place, tilting her so he could get a better angle. His tongue invaded, claiming her mouth, stealing her breath, marking her as his in a way that made her want to melt into a puddle. Her hands went to his chest, then slid up, wrapping around his neck and pulling to get him closer, closer, wanting to feel his heat and electricity, wanting him practically inside her, engulfing her, never wanting him to stop.

He reached down with his free hand, grabbing behind one leg and pulling her up, landing her butt on the narrow ledge of the sink and then stepping between her legs.

"You drive me fucking crazy," he growled in her ear. "With your red fucking lips and these tiny shorts and those fuck-me knee-highs. I've been dying to feel your skin since you left me this morning. Can I please touch you?"

"God, yes," she moaned into his mouth, pulling up his T-shirt so he could feel her nylon socks against his skin as she wrapped her legs around him, and he groaned.

His hand dipped low on her back to keep her balanced against him and then dipped lower, sliding under her waist-band, slipping into her panties and grabbing a handful of her ass and squeezing. Brittany's nails dug into his back where she was gripping him, gasping for breath as his mouth left hers to find her cheek, her ear, her neck, giving each place its own little bite.

"You taste so fucking good. Tell me you're wet for me, Brittany. I need to feel you."

She couldn't answer, so lost in the sensation of his teeth nipping her just above her breast, the buttons of her blouse somehow open and exposing her bra. His hand on her ass slipped out of her shorts, and she felt its loss for only a moment before he zipped open her shorts and slid his hand down exactly where she needed him. He caught her moan with a kiss, swallowing it.

"Keep it down, killer. I'm guessing this would ruin Theo's yelp rating."

But Brittany couldn't think about anything but Gus. "Touch me before I die."

"Yes, ma'am."

His whole hand cupped her, grabbing her, his grip pulsing on her in a way that she would've said she hated in concept but in practice had her back arching, her breasts thrusting in his face. He gladly took the hint, sucking one nipple into his mouth.

"That's it. Take what you need."

His fingers began moving in circles, slow to start and then speeding up until she was panting, her nails gripping his shoulder, the wave of sensation rising within her as she thought of how this was Gus's hand touching her, Gus's mouth on her breast, Gus's hard cock pressed into her thigh.

And then he slid a finger inside her and she saw stars.

Her breath stuttered as he rubbed against that magic spot, the one that very few men had found at this point in Brittany's life, and he must have sensed her spiral because he slowed his finger.

"Not yet, killer," he breathed into her breast. "I'm not done. You can't come yet. You have to wait a little longer."

"I can't."

"You can and you will. I promise I'll make it worth your while."

Her fingers clenched in his hair, not letting him move from where he was teasing her nipple with his teeth, but she nodded.

With a grunt of approval, Gus moved his hand again, this time slower, stroking inside of her, teasing that spot just as his thumb found the perfect angle to drive her clit crazy. Faintly, Brittany heard herself panting, whimpering, but all she could do was hold on to him and focus on the sensations he was causing inside her. Just as he slid a second finger in, he moved to her other nipple in his mouth and sucked hard, creating a tug that ran through her entire body straight from his mouth to her pussy.

"Please," she heard herself beg. At that moment, she couldn't even find it in herself to be embarrassed. She just desperately needed him to make her come.

He lifted his head, looking into her eyes, and she saw everything at once: his desire, his heat, his care, and something else, something deep that she wasn't quite ready for.

"Come for me, Brittany. I want to watch you break apart."

He punctuated his words by thrusting a third finger inside her, hard and deep and at the exact angle she needed to explode.

She was lost to her shivers, her muscles contracting around his fingers, her wetness sliding between them as he kept working that spot, not letting her move away, watching her every reaction as he held Brittany tight against him. And when she finally fell limp in his arms, he cradled her to his chest, matching his breath with hers, the smell of him filling her every sense, and she realized with a panic that she was not going to be able to let this man walk away. There was no getting over him if he decided to leave.

Dazed from both the orgasm and the revelation, Brittany looked up to meet his eyes, realizing vaguely that his fingers were still inside her, that his other arm was keeping her balanced against the sink. Her red lipstick was smudged on his face, and he was looking at her with such a tender expression she was certain her heart would break.

"You did so well," he whispered, pulling his fingers out of her, out of her panties, and she whimpered with the loss even as all of her bones felt like liquid. As she watched, he raised his hand to his mouth, sucking a finger inside, tasting her juices while never taking his eyes on her and she felt desire flicker inside her again.

He removed his finger from his mouth with a pop and then held his hand toward her, waiting. Not saying anything, but he didn't need to. She instinctively opened her mouth, and he dipped his middle finger inside, letting her taste herself. She let her tongue wrap around his finger, moaning at how dirty the act itself made her feel. The twitch she felt between her legs, where his cock was pressing against his jeans, let her know that he felt the same way.

Brittany reached down to touch him, but he stepped back before she could make contact, his other finger still in her mouth, now holding her there.

"People are probably looking for us." His voice was raspy, torn, clearly wanted to stay in that bathroom forever, and boy, was she eager to agree. "We should go before they get more suspicious."

And then he stepped back, his finger slipping from her mouth down to her waist to help steady her as she lost the anchor of his body, helping her back down to her feet. With shaky hands, she buttoned up her shorts, turning to check her makeup, her hair, and grimacing as she realized Min was definitely going to know what had happened. Brittany had that 'just got my back blown out' look to her, and there was no way she was going to be able to hide it.

In the mirror, she watched Gus adjust himself, running his hands through his hair to try to repair the damage she had done with her hands buried in it, wiping his face where her lipstick had lived up to the hype and stained his skin. Their eyes met in the mirror.

"Don't let her touch you again." Brittany's voice sounded suddenly loud in the bathroom, but she couldn't help it.

He met her glare with a calm look. "Stop flirting with Theo."

"Theo flirts with parked cars."

"He can flirt with anyone else. Just not you. Not anymore."

There was a challenge in his eyes as if he expected her to lose her temper of this control he was trying to establish. But she wasn't angry. She almost craved it, craved him claiming her as his so thoroughly that no one would question it.

"Deal."

Gus nodded once, and with a final glance raking over her body, he unbolted the bathroom and opened the door.

Only to find Robbie standing there, looking pissed as hell.

"Nothing going on, huh?" Robbie sneered, betrayal and anger and a lot of other petty emotions crossing his face, his jaw locked, his eyes on Gus.

Gus's jaw clenched, but otherwise his expression stayed the same.

"Things have changed."

"No fucking shit." Robbie took a step forward into Gus's space, a move that was threatening and male and everything Brittany hated about men. Gus stood his ground, letting his brother get closer.

"If you need to hit me, go ahead and hit me."

"I need you to stop fucking my ex, Gus."

"That's not up to you anymore, Robbie."

Robbie really didn't like that, and Brittany wasn't interested in having some stupid fight ruin her post-orgasm euphoria, so she slid closer, standing near Gus.

"Don't be a dick, Robbie."

"You're one to talk. Hopping from brother to brother. Guess I should've known when I first took you home. Couldn't take your eyes off of him, from what I recall."

Brittany's memory of meeting Gus for the first time was Robbie introducing them and then ditching her to stream for hours. Gus chatted with her at the time, served her some lemonade, and seemed more like he pitied her than anything else.

Brittany really should've seen the red flags then.

Gus maneuvered himself between her and Robbie.

"You don't talk to her like that," he said.

"Or what? You're going to hit me?"

"Or I'm going to teach you the lesson in manners you should've learned a really long time ago, Robbie."

Brittany grabbed Gus's arm just as movement behind Robbie caught her eye. There was a small, Latinx woman in a chef's jacket, her hair pulled up into a dark bun, holding a kitchen knife and looking pissed as hell.

"Look, dickwads," she said. "I don't know what's going on here, but if you don't get your asses the fuck out of this restaurant and deal with whatever male machismo bullshit this is far away from here, I'm going to call the cops and then show you why I got high marks in knife skills in culinary school."

Brittany gaped at her, instantly falling in love with her energy. And then Theo appeared, looming behind her from the hall.

"You heard her," he said, his voice devoid of his usual exasperating playfulness. "Your food is in boxes. Take it elsewhere, and don't come back until you sort this shit out."

For a moment, it looked like Robbie and Gus weren't listening, hadn't heard anything for the last minute or so. But then Gus very deliberately turned his head to where Brittany was standing behind him and held out his hand to her. She took it on instinct, and he pulled her out of the bathroom, down the hall toward the exit. As they were passing Robbie, he couldn't take his eyes off Gus.

"This really how you want to do this?"

"It's the only way you've left me, Robbie."

Keeping a firm grip on her hand, Gus pulled Brittany with him out of the bathroom hall, stopping to say something to Theo that Brittany didn't hear. When they reached the dining room, Gus headed for the door, but Brittany tugged his hand until he glanced back.

"Min."

Gus nodded to the front of the restaurant, where Min was standing holding a couple to-go boxes and Brittany's bag. Brittany allowed him to pull her closer to the door, where Min smirked at her, her eyes sliding down to where Gus still had a grip on Brittany's hand.

"You were gone for a while. Everything okay?"

"There may have been a bit of a scene."

"In a good way or a bad way."

"Both." She and Gus said the word at the same time and then stared at each other. Min snorted.

"Well, let's go before Theo starts throwing bread around. He doesn't like people ruining the vibe of his restaurant."

They stepped outside, and Brittany let the sun hit her, feeling warm and luscious after such a weird, tense encounter.

"Didn't he once have a shouting match with a food blogger who gave him a bad review while sitting in the dining room?"

"He only likes it when he's the one causing drama."

Outside, Gus stepped away to give her a moment with Min, who handed Brittany her bag and box of food.

"So," Min said in a suspiciously innocent tone. "Anything you want to talk about? Or are we going to pretend everything's the same as always?"

Brittany loved Min, but really, this was ridiculous.

"As I recall, you didn't even tell me someone broke into your hotel room and trashed the place, much less that you were hooking up with your sworn nemesis until you both had broken up."

"Fine. Throw my own actions in my face. Be that way."

They smiled at each other, and then both went in for a hug.

"I love you, you know."

"I know."

Min laughed and pulled back. She glanced at Gus and then got serious.

"But for real, if you need anything, if it gets too much, or he starts being an ass or something, call me."

"You'll be my first text. Ride or die. Accomplice to arson."

"That's all I ask."

One more quick hug, and then Min headed off with a wave, leaving Brittany and Gus alone for the first time since she came on his fingers in the bathroom. Suddenly not sure what to do with her hands, she clasped them together in front of her.

"So," she ventured. "How's your morning going?"

The corner of his mouth twitched. "A bit of a mixed bag, to be honest. How about you?"

Before she could answer, the door to Insatiable opened, and Diamond stepped out. She blinked at them, clearly surprised to find that they were still there, but then steeled herself and approached.

"Hey. You have time to talk for a minute?"

Brittany felt her stomach drop. Did she want to talk with the woman Robbie was dating? The answer was obviously no, but here she was.

"Honestly, I don't have a lot of time. I have to get to the convention center."

"It'll only take a minute."

Brittany peered around her.

"Where's Robbie?"

"He left out the back."

"Did he send you out here for this?"

"No."

Finally, Brittany nodded, stepping away from Gus to be away from the door, somewhere not necessarily private, but about as private as Brittany was willing to get.

Diamond started talking once they settled.

"I didn't know."

Brittany blinked at her. "You didn't know what?"

"That he had cheated on you. I wouldn't have given him the time of day if I had known. I don't fuck with cheaters."

Brittany nodded, trying to process. She had never really blamed the women Robbie had hooked up with for his cheating, so it wasn't like she felt that Diamond owed her an apology. But Diamond clearly felt that way, so Brittany was willing to listen.

Diamond continued. "We were dating when the… incident happened with his equipment. He told me you were crazy, unhinged. And I believed him at first. But I started asking around and doing some digging and finally connected with someone who told me the real timeline of your breakup."

Brittany felt awkward, not knowing what to say. "Okay."

"I just wanted to say I'm sorry. For believing him. Sorry that he treated you like that."

Brittany sighed a little. There was no relief here, probably because Diamond wasn't the one she wanted an apology from.

"He's the one that cheated, he's the one that should apologize."

Diamond nodded, relieved.

"I dumped him when I found out. A man with a history of cheating lies like that to your face, there's no way to trust him afterward."

"But you're here with him?"

Diamond looked a little embarrassed. "He said he wanted a chance to get me back, and in a weak moment, I said yes. And then he threw that scene in there. I told him to lose my number."

"For what it's worth, you deserve better."

"So do you, but I suspect you've known that for a while." Diamond glanced at where Gus was on the sidewalk, keeping his distance so they could talk privately, but staying close enough in case Brittany suddenly needed saving or something. Diamond leaned closer.

"He's a good one."

Brittany glanced at Gus. "He is."

"But he loves Robbie."

"I know."

Diamond nodded, and Brittany pulled her into a hug.

After that, Diamond said her goodbyes, stopping to say something to Gus, and left with a wave. Brittany gave him a curious look.

"What was that about?"

"Nothing important. We should go."

Brittany glanced at her phone.

"Shit, I'm running late."

CHAPTER 17

They get to the convention center just in time for Brittany to eat the rest of her breakfast before starting her panel, one of the last ones for her weekend at Kickoff. As Gus watched her answer questions on stage, he couldn't help the affection that lodged in his chest as she effortlessly charmed hundreds of people. Brittany was amazing, and Gus was done pretending he wasn't crazy about her.

His phone buzzed in his pocket for the fiftieth time, and Gus ignored it once more. Robbie had been blowing up his phone. After the fourth time he had accused Gus of betraying him, Gus began to hit ignore, not wanting to engage with Robbie when he was in his ranting mode. Gus was used to Robbie's moods, used to calming him down and de-escalating whatever situation they were in. But he found when it came to Brittany, he just couldn't. The only way to de-escalate would be to stop seeing her. Stop touching her. And that just… wasn't something Gus was going to be able to do.

And yes, that should worry him. Watching her, seeing the fans around her who loved her and loved her content, made him think back to Robbie's original warning: that she wanted more than some regular guy like Gus.

Shaking the thought out of his head, he found himself suddenly caught as Brittany looked at him, a small smile on her face. Someone else on the panel was answering a question, and her eyes had found him in the back of the crowd. Gus refused to look away. While her eyes were on him, he brought his hand up, the one that had recently been inside her, and rubbed it on his mouth. The shiver that ran down her body was worth it, as was how she shifted in her chair, uncrossing and recrossing her legs with a restlessness he felt in his cock. Gus decided then and there that however long she wanted this to last, he was along for the ride. And when she broke his heart, he could at least say that he'd had her, if only for a little bit.

She was worth it.

After Brittany wrapped her panel, they went to another conference room, this time to watch Hayden's panel as he talked about his new game. Hayden was known online as DeathsHead, a popular video game streamer who, up until last year, had never shown his face to the public. But after a lot of drama and a big tournament, where Min had trounced him, Hayden had revealed his face to everyone in order to clear Min of the accusations of cheating... and to be with her.

Now, Hayden was releasing his own video game, something he and Theo had been developing in secret for years. The release party was that evening, and Brittany was attending, which meant so was Gus.

Inside the room for the panel, they found seats toward the

back. Gus tried to step away to stand against the wall where he could keep a better eyeline on everything, but Brittany pulled him down next to her.

"Just sit with me," she said.

Helpless to argue with that, he sat in the hard, too-small chair, having a small elbow war with her. When he caught a couple guys down the aisle giving Brittany an interested look, he draped his arm over the back of her chair casually, not enough to be obvious, but definitely enough to make it clear she was with him.

"Smooth." She smirked at him.

Okay, maybe a little obvious.

He let the hand behind her slide up to grip her neck, firm but not hard, and he heard her catch her breath.

"You love it."

"I do."

Caught off guard by the admission, by the look in her eyes that made him want to drag her out of here and find somewhere they wouldn't be interrupted, Gus just gave her neck another squeeze and then left his hand there, loving the feel of the soft hair in her ponytail against his fingers.

Finally, Hayden was announced, and the crowd lost their minds. Even after exposing his face, Hayden was incredibly popular, and the people here were excited about his game. As Hayden started the showcase for the game, someone pushed down the aisle toward them.

"Sorry, sorry, sorry."

They plopped down next to him, and Gus tensed until he recognized Devery, Min's little sister. She leaned over him to talk to Brittany.

"What did I miss?"

"Just the intros," Brittany told her.

Devery nodded and then really looked at them, at the arm Gus had around Brittany.

"Wait, are you two… two?"

Gus had no idea what that meant, but apparently Brittany did.

"We're figuring it out. Don't make a big deal."

"Me? I would never."

She pulled out her phone to start texting, and Brittany was immediately suspicious.

"What are you doing?"

"Texting Min to see if she knows, and then yelling at her if she says she did but didn't tell me."

"Dev, that's literally the definition of making a big deal."

"It's a small deal. Minuscule. Besides, Min's seen Hayden's presentation many times. She's probably bored back there in the green room."

Gus didn't think Min would be bored by anything to do with Hayden, but he certainly wasn't going to speak up, even when Brittany shot him an exasperated look.

The panel went well, enthusiasm high for the game, and then the three of them waited for Hayden and Min to join them to walk to Brittany's next meet-and-greet since Min was doing one at the same time.

At the meet and greet, Gus let the women have the green-room to themselves as he scouted out the rest of the area for the event, making sure there were no more surprises from Brittany's stalker. Though their relationship, or whatever you wanted to call it, had changed, he had absolutely no intention of slacking on his duties. She was still in need of his services, and he was going to deliver.

Even if he couldn't wait to get her back to his place to pick up where they left off at the restaurant.

The meet and greet began with much excitement from the lines in front of both Min and Brittany, and Gus found himself standing next to Hayden, both watching the proceedings with a cautious eye. Hayden spoke first.

"If you're with Brittany as some sort of revenge thing against your brother, then I gotta warn you it won't end well for you."

Gus gave him his whole attention at that. Hayden was a little taller, but Gus had a good fifty pounds of muscle on him and was trained to fight.

"I appreciate the protectiveness, but that's not what's happening here."

Hayden nodded. "Good."

They were silent for another moment, and then Hayden spoke up again.

"No offense, but your brother's a dick."

"I know."

"I've had to stop Min several times from going over there to punch him in the nuts."

Gus grunted. These women.

"If it makes her feel better, Brittany poured soda all over his rig and then fried it."

"Ouch."

"After deleting all his save files."

Hayden winced at that one, understanding as a gamer how devastating it was to lose those files.

"You gotta appreciate her attention to detail," was all Hayden said.

Gus let his eyes trail back to Brittany, where she was

smiling full and wide for the camera, enjoying her time with her fans. Looking beautiful and irresistible as fuck.

"There's a lot to appreciate about her."

He felt Hayden look at him, but ignored him, focusing instead on the guy that had just smiled for the camera with Brittany at his side… just in time to see his hand slide down to grab her ass.

Gus saw red.

Before he knew it, he was ripping the guy's arm off her, shoving him to the side of the room, the guy's back against a wall as Gus points a finger in his face.

"You don't touch her like that."

Even he heard the cold in his voice. The creep looked acceptably scared just as security approached to take him away. Gus turned his attention to the crowd gaping at him, still waiting for their turn, and turned his glare up to full power. But before he could say anything, Hayden was there, his hand clamped on his shoulder, blocking his eye contact with the crowd.

"They get it, man. Come take a walk."

He tried to pull Gus away, and at first Gus resisted, but Hayden hissed at him, his back to the crowd.

"She's now surrounded by security, and you're scaring people. Besides, she can handle that shit on her own. Take a fucking walk with me."

Gus's eyes flew to Brittany, where she was glaring at the guy that security was hauling away. Immediately he felt himself soften, realizing what a tool he had just acted like, and let Hayden drag him out into the nearest empty hall.

Once there, Hayden let him go and Gus leaned against the wall, trying to regain whatever sanity he had had before this.

"He had his hands on her."

"I saw."

"Fucking grabbing her, groping her."

"I know, man."

"What the fuck would you have done?"

Hayden took a minute to answer.

"I would've lost my mind and done the exact same thing. Although knowing Min, she would've decked the guy twice before I got there."

"Then why are you looking at me like I fucked up?"

Hayden threw him an incredulous look. "Min is my girlfriend. More than that, she's the love of my life."

"Okay?"

"So what does it tell you that you're reacting the same way I would?"

Gus was silent, thinking about that, realizing exactly what Hayden was implying and also exactly how right he was. He leaned against the wall, smacking his head back against it.

"I'm fucked."

"That's one way to put it."

Gus let out a deep breath, trying to calm himself down, trying to block the image of the guy touching Brittany.

"Look, man, work yourself out. But Brittany is family to Min, which means she's family to me. And that means I can't let you go all toxic alpha male out there without her permission. Whether you like it or not, she's a public figure, and you know she can handle herself without you losing it on some asshole in front of a hundred camera phones. Understand?"

Gus nodded. "Yeah, I get it."

"Good. Now, I know you're coming to the release party as her security. Tonight is important. You're not allowed to pull something like that. You're not allowed to ruin it. Do you understand me? If you think you can't handle it, you need to find her another guard for the night."

"I can handle it."

Hayden studied him a long time, and Gus felt his respect for the man grow even more. Finally, he nodded.

"Good. Now get your shit together before you go in there. And stop scaring the fans."

And with that, Hayden was gone, leaving Gus alone in the hall to figure himself out. He had never reacted like that before, never been the jealous or overprotective type. But it was different with Brittany. He didn't like to think she was in danger. Didn't like some other guy touching her, especially without her consent. Sure, she was obviously good at handling those problems herself since they've now happened twice during the convention. But Gus found he could no longer stand by when it happened, and he didn't like how crazy he felt watching things like that go down.

But this was Brittany's life. If he wanted to be involved in it beyond the convention, and lord knew he did, then he had to trust her to take care of herself. He couldn't stomp around like an idiot yelling at people.

With a deep breath, he resigned himself to standing on the sidelines for a little bit longer and then went back into the room, ready to take care of her however she needed. Inside, the meet-and-greet was wrapping up, Brittany smiling for the camera with one last group of people, and then she thanked them for coming and their support. Once done, she ducked into the green room. With a glance around, Gus followed her.

"I'm sorry," Gus said the second he walked in. "I was an ass.

You are fully capable of handling situations like that without me going all alpha and making it worse. I'm an idiot."

Her body sagged, the tension suddenly leaving, and Gus was reminded of how rarely Robbie would apologize for the stupid shit he would do.

"Why did you do that?" she asked. "There was security there to deal with things like that, they were already on their way."

Gus held his hands out, feeling exposed.

"I don't like seeing someone else touch you like that."

"Don't tell me you were jealous of that guy."

"Fuck no." He struggled to find the words, but he knew this was important, even if he sounded crazy in the explanation.

"Brittany, the stalker, your public profile, how I know Robbie treated you… you deserve better than all of that. You deserve your boundaries and your space and your ability to feel safe, and I get really, really angry when I think about the people in your life who haven't respected that. I'm sorry that came out today. But you deserve the best, and you haven't been getting it for a while now, and that pisses me off."

Brittany stared at him, and Gus found himself holding his breath, knowing this moment was somehow going to decide something and not exactly knowing which way he wanted this to land.

And then her arms were wrapping around his torso, her face buried into his chest like she never wanted to let go. Gus's arms immediately wrapped around her, holding her tight and firm, letting his head tip down to smell her hair, and the world felt so right that he knew he was fucked. He wasn't going to be able to let her go. If she wanted to leave, it would gut him.

He held her tighter, enjoying this moment for as long as possible if only because she was in his arms and that's where she wanted to be.

"You have to let me handle those situations," she said into his chest.

"I know."

"I mean it."

"I know."

She was quiet then, just letting him hold her, holding him in return, and then he heard a throat clearing.

"Sorry to interrupt," Min said with a wry tone. "But we're leaving. Britt, you coming?"

Brittany gave Gus one last squeeze and then looked up at Min, nodding.

"Yeah, we'll be right there."

Min stepped out, and Gus met Brittany's eyes, letting himself drown in them.

"Where are we going?"

"I told Min we'd get ready together for Hayden's party. He has to be there early to set up, and she wanted to look nice."

Gus nodded. "So that's where we're going."

"If you don't mind. We can stop at your condo first if you need your things."

Gus shook his head, not willing to let her go.

"I had packed a bag, just in case you were on the go."

"Oh."

They stood there for another moment, feeling each other, enjoying each other, until Brittany pulled back.

"We should probably go."

She wasn't meeting his eyes, but Gus guessed she was feeling as out of sorts as he was. Whenever he imagined his Kickoff experience, it certainly didn't involve feelings for his brother's ex.

Robbie. Fuck. He was going to have to deal with that at some point.

But not now. Robbie's angry text messages had mostly stopped, which either meant he was finally getting over himself or he was stewing something up for a big explosion. Only time would tell, but Gus couldn't find it in him to really care. Robbie was going to need to get over himself. And if he didn't, Gus was prepared to make him.

CHAPTER 18

BRITTANY

Brittany's mind raced while she walked with Gus to where Min and Hayden were staying. Once at their room, he did a quick sweep of the place and nodded, then stepped out, warning her not to leave without him. Where he went was a mystery, but Brittany couldn't help but be grateful because she was in desperate need of time alone with her friend.

Once the door closed behind him, though, Brittany felt his loss. Was she really this far gone? That she now missed him when he wasn't in the room with her? The answer was an obvious yes, and she knew exactly how pathetic that was. When she turned to find Min staring at her, her arms crossed, tapping her foot like she was waiting for a story, Brittany gave in to her patheticness, throwing herself back onto the bed and covering her eyes.

"Okay," she said. "Just let me have it."

"Since when are you fucking Gus?"

"Define fucking."

"Brittany, I swear to god, if you don't answer me, I'm going to shave an eyebrow while you're sleeping."

"I could rock that look." Brittany peeked out from under her arm to see Min wasn't going to give this up, so she sighed.

"We're not fucking."

"Bullshit."

"We're not. But to be honest, it's probably only a matter of time."

Min paused. "If you're not fucking, then what happened in the bathroom this morning."

Brittany grimaced. "Some light… heavy petting."

"That doesn't even make sense."

Brittany let her mind wander to the bathroom and exactly what happened there, and she felt herself getting warm.

"Do you really want to know?"

"Fuck, not now, with that look on your face."

She felt Min flop down on the bed next to her.

"What are you doing? Should I be angry at someone? Who do we hate? You need to give me details because otherwise, as your best friend, I could get lost and deck the wrong person."

"I like him."

"Yeah, I figured that part out."

"It's a mess."

Min grimaced in sympathy. "Because of Robbie."

"Yes. And other things."

"What other things?"

Brittany waved her hand vaguely in front of her.

"You know."

"I don't."

"He's, like, a really good guy."

Min's eyebrows raised. "He is."

"He has a real job where he protects people."

"Where's this going?"

Brittany didn't know how to say the next part without feeling like an ass. But this was Min and they told each other everything, so she just ripped the Band-Aid off.

"I'm some fluffy influencer who posts on social media for a living. He literally saves lives."

"Britt, if you're about to talk shit about my best friend, we're going to have a problem."

Brittany huffed. "You know I'm right."

"No, I fucking don't. You have a real job that's a lot of hard work and hustle. You're successful because people like you, and you've created content they want to engage with. And no, you're not throwing yourself in front of bullets for your fans, but you're making an impact on people's lives."

Brittany kicked her leg, uncomfortable with the praise.

"I wasn't really looking for a pep talk."

"Too fucking bad. Is he the one making you feel like this? Has he said something?"

"No, he would never. He helped me set up a spot in his condo to stream while I'm staying there."

"So where is this coming from?"

Brittany thought about it, really thought about why she was feeling so negative about herself, about what she and Gus could be. And she realized.

"Robbie."

Min's eyes narrowed in a bloodthirsty look Brittany had only seen on her stream when she was about to blow some zombie's head off.

"What about him?"

"He… he never got the fashion influencer thing or what I was doing."

"He's a gaming streamer, and a mediocre one at that. Could he not see the similarities?"

"Yeah, but he said people watched him because he had skill and put on a show, whereas all I did…"

Brittany paused. Min was breathing deeper, which was a sign she was about to get really loud.

"Just spit it out, Britt."

"All I did was wear clothes and look pretty."

Min shot up in the bed, glaring down at her in disbelief.

"Brittany, what the fuck? I've watched you slash tires for less than that."

"I know."

Brittany was known for her temper, and she would get pissed when Robbie would bring it up. But his statements always hit close enough to home, to her own insecurities about what she did for a living, that she couldn't find it in herself to get that mad. To her, it was always more like he was telling her some hard truths.

And yes, she knew how fucked up that was.

Min must have seen her mental struggle, because she rolled over onto her stomach, looking down at Brittany with a fierce look she usually reserved for schooling other gamers on her stream.

"Brittany, you are the whole package. You're kind, you're a hard worker, and you make damn good money because you hustle hard. You're the best friend I could have ever been blessed with. There is not going to be a man that's worthy of you, but if you like Gus, then I think you should go for it. And whatever garbage Robbie put in your head, you need to release it immediately. I'm going to put rusty nails in his shoes for ever making you feel this way."

Brittany took a deep breath.

"I like Gus."

Min nodded, not surprised.

"So what are you going to do about it?"

"Fuck him."

"Great. Feel free to spare me details."

"I'm going to send you minute-by-minute updates."

"Please don't."

"PowerPoint presentation afterward?"

"I hate you."

Min rolled off the bed, heading toward the closet where her dress for the night was hanging.

"I'm done with girl talk. We both need to look hot tonight, so we need to get started. Put on a playlist already."

Min's little sister, Devery, arrived a short time later with Min's mom, Iris, in tow, both having traveled down for Hayden's release party to celebrate. Brittany cranked up the music, Min ordered some snacks from room service, and it was basically a party for the women as they did their makeup and hair.

"What time do we have to be there?" Brittany asked as she finished a glass of champagne.

Min glanced at the clock on her phone and winced.

"Thirty minutes ago."

"I can't believe Hayden hasn't been blowing up your phone asking where you were."

Just then, Min's phone rang. Everyone burst out laughing, even as she shushed them to answer the phone.

"I swear, we're on our way."

"No, we're not!" Brittany sang, pouring another glass of champagne for herself. Min flipped her off just as there was a knock at the door. She was the closest, so Brittany went to answer... and stopped dead in her tracks, her mouth dropping.

Filling the other side of the door was Gus as she had never seen him. Crisp button-up white shirt, blue suit jacket. His hair was combed and mostly under control except for that one stubborn curl on his forehead. He looked more delicious than she had ever seen him in her life.

His eyes took in the loose, sequined minidress she was wearing. She had curled her hair, letting it fall down her back in waves. Her legs were smooth and showcased well by the short skirt and the flat sandals she had strapped on moments ago. When she finally looked back at his face, he looked like someone had punched him in the gut.

"Are you fucking kidding me?" he said, a growl in his voice.

She looked down at herself, confused. "What?"

"Brittany, if that's how you're going to walk around this party, I'm going to be spending the entire night hiding my erection."

She let her hand touch his chest, sliding up toward his neck, lightly tugging him down toward her.

"What if I don't want you to hide it?"

He moved into her space, intent on something that Brittany was excited to discover, when he stopped at the sight of three other women staring at him. Gus straightened, looking more responsible than he had moments ago.

"You ladies let me know when you're ready to go."

Dev's mouth quirked up. "You're our ride?"

"Yes."

Iris gave him the once over, probably trying to decipher his driving record from his face, but Min just grabbed her clutch.

"Let's go. I'm ready to dance with my man."

After a few more last-minute checks of outfits, lipsticks, lashes, and hair, they trooped out to the elevator together, pushing into a crowd of other people clearly heading to their own parties. Gus pulled Brittany to him, his arm wrapping around her waist as more people filled the elevator.

"You look absolutely beautiful," he said in her ear, loud enough for a few people near them to turn and look. Min and Dev grinned from the other side of the elevator.

"You're making a scene," Brittany whispered to him, not able to stop herself from smiling.

"Good," was all he said before the door opened at the lobby, and everyone spilled out.

Gus led them to where his SUV was parked, helping everyone into the car. Brittany was stuck in the back seat, crammed with Min and her sister, while Min's mom got the coveted passenger seat. Iris smiled at Gus as he helped her up.

"You have excellent manners."

He winked at her. "I'll tell my mother you said so. She'll be proud."

"She should be."

He hustled around to the driver's side, and then they were off. At Brittany's eyelash flutter, he cranked up the music, and the back seat was hopping in anticipation of the party. When he pulled up to Insatiable, the valet was practically blasted to the side by the volume of the music.

Before the valets could get to the doors, Gus was already

there, opening them and helping the women out. Brittany scooted toward the door, and Gus basically scooped her up, pulling her against his body and letting her slowly slide down until her feet hit the ground.

"That was dramatic," she teased.

"But enjoyable."

He held her hand, handing over the keys to the valet, and pulled her inside the restaurant.

Brittany stopped in the doorway. The place had been completely transformed, with realistic scenes created around the space all pulled from Hayden's video game. The music was pumping, and though the crowd hadn't really started arriving yet, Brittany could already feel in her bones how good of a party this was going to be. The air practically crackled with it.

"Where to first?" Gus asked.

She grinned. "The bar."

CHAPTER 19

GUS

When Brittany grabbed his hand and pulled him into the crowd, Gus realized suddenly that this was exactly where he wanted to be twenty years from now, following Brittany on whatever adventure she had decided the day was going to be. It was humbling realizing so much of your happiness relied on a woman who had the ability to drive you out of your mind.

When they got to the bar, she somehow managed to shift people away, snagging a spot up front. She flagged down the bartender, who immediately changed directions to come help her, another of Brittany's superpowers. She glanced at Gus.

"You still a beer drinker?"

"Just water. I'm technically working."

Brittany frowned, but placed the order, then turned to him. He found himself leaning over her, almost shielding her with his body in his attempt to carve out privacy for them at the bar that was becoming more crowded by the second.

"What's that face for?"

"I didn't realize you considered this working," she said.

"You're at a public event, one that you had posted you would be attending."

"You think the stalker would come here? There's a guest list."

"There are ways around that. I'm just making sure you're safe."

Still, she frowned, looking more bothered than Gus felt the situation warranted.

"What's really the matter?"

After a short debate in her head, Brittany shrugged.

"I guess I just thought we could be here just as us, you know. Not working, not a client. Just… two people who like each other who get to hang out while they're dressed really hot."

Brittany looked uncomfortable as she said it, as if she hated how vulnerable she sounded, but all Gus could hear was the blood rushing in his ears.

"Hey."

He let his hand slide to her waist, pulling her closer, closing his eyes at the feel of her body pressed up against his.

"I really, really like you," he said into her ear.

"I'm not just a client?"

"You never were."

She searched his eyes as if trying to find the lie, and Gus let her search. He was telling the truth, and he didn't care if she knew.

Finally, she nodded, slipping her arm into his jacket and around his chest.

"I really, really like you, too."

Their drinks arrived then, which they grabbed and made their way to a corner booth where Min, Hayden, Dev, Min's mother, and Randall were all crammed in. Brittany slid in next to Randall, and Gus took his place next to her, her leg pressed up against his. Without thinking, Gus slipped his hand onto her thigh, letting it rest there with a possessive squeeze.

The next hour or so went by in a rush of catching up on everyone's Kickoff experience, Randall's sales, Dev's latest role-playing game, and different panels. It was fun, more fun than Gus could remember having in recent experience, and he realized part of that was because he had missed these people. These were Brittany's friends, after all, which meant that when she and Robbie broke it off, they no longer hung out with Gus. And Gus, a solitary introvert used to keeping to himself, didn't realize how much he had missed being part of this family, even when he had just been the third wheel. These people, though, had never made him feel like that, and he marveled again at what an idiot Robbie was for ruining everything by cheating on Brittany.

A chair moved next to him, and Gus was ready for it before he even saw Theo plop himself down. He was out of his chef's whites, in a button-up shirt and nice slacks, and was drawing more than a few interested glances from the people around them.

"Okay, I'm ready. Let's get this over with."

Min burst out laughing just as Hayden shook his head.

"Only you would consider listening to Hayden's speech about the launch something to get over," she said.

"It's been a long day, I wasn't able to work on recipes, Rosa threatened to set the kitchen on fire if I tried to help with the service tonight, and I'm tired of hearing about what an awesome brother I am."

Theo was disgruntled, crossing his arms in front of him. He threw Gus a look while he was ranting, clearly not done.

"And you're banned from ever using the bathroom in my restaurant ever again."

"What if it's an emergency?"

"Then you better be kind to the bookshop next door, because you're out of luck here, you heathen."

Brittany clamped her hand over her mouth, trying not to laugh while still looking pretty embarrassed by the whole situation. Gus squeezed her thigh, letting his hand slide a little higher.

"Worth it."

The table burst out laughing, and then Hayden was standing, pulling Min from the booth.

"Excuse me, I'm going to go 'get this over with.'"

Min waved, and they pushed their way over to where the party planner was waiting with a microphone.

Brittany breathed into Gus's ear. "Worth it?"

"I would literally do everything exactly the same right now if I didn't think Theo would kick us both out."

Brittany laughed, leaning into him just as the music cut out. A spotlight moved to Hayden, where he was standing with Min, holding her hand.

"Hey, everyone," his deep voice reverberated over the speakers. Cheers went up, and he waved them down to be quiet.

"I was told I had to give a speech, which I hate, so we're going to be quick. This game was a work of love and wouldn't be here without my brother, Theo."

Theo waved at the applause, the lines of his face softening, his pride in Hayden showing through.

"Theo is a huge asshole, but he's always been there for me, and I don't know what I would do without him."

Theo raised his glass, rolling his eyes at his brother before taking a drink, and Gus was suddenly struck with how different their relationship was from his and Robbie's. They worked together on this game for years before Hayden was able to finish, and Theo was always supportive of Hayden's dream. More importantly, before that, Hayden's streaming helped to fund the restaurant, which turned into a smashing success. The brothers were there for each other, always, closer than they like others to see, and Gus suddenly realized that he and Robbie were not like that. He wouldn't trust Robbie with money for a new career. When Robbie had first announced he was going to stream, Gus had assumed it was yet another weird 'get rich quick' scheme. And while Robbie had stuck with it longer than his last few jobs, Gus still wasn't really convinced it was something that would keep him going. And Gus knew, without a doubt, if he needed anything... Gus knew Robbie wouldn't be his first call for help. And that made him really, really sad.

Gus shifted his attention back to Hayden, who had been thanking various developers on the game, but had just gripped Min's hand tighter, pulling her closer to his side.

"And most of all," Hayden continued. "I want to thank this beautiful woman next to me."

Catcalls from the crowd resounded, and Gus joined in as Brittany screamed loudly for her friends. Min blushed as Hayden turned to her.

"Min, you are everything I didn't know I needed in my life.

The game wouldn't be here without you. My life would be a sad shadow of what it could be. You brought me out into the world and showed me love and beauty and exactly the best ways to kill zombies."

The crowd laughed, then gasped as Hayden pulled a small box out of his pocket. From the way Min's mouth was hanging open, she hadn't known this was coming. Brittany was up, trying to kneel on the seat of the booth to get a better look, and Gus steadied her with a hand to her back.

"Min, I can't imagine my life without you. You are essential to absolutely every aspect. So, once again, I'm going to do this big, public grand gesture, and hope like hell you're willing to take a leap with me."

He went down on one knee, and flashes went off around the crowd as everyone took pictures and video. Hayden slowly opened the box, and even from this distance, Gus could see the glint of a substantial diamond.

"Minerva Hayes, will you marry me?"

Tears were pouring out of Min's eyes, but she was nodding "yes" as emphatically as she could. A cheer went up over the crowd as Hayden slipped the ring on her finger and then pulled her tight into an embrace. Brittany was doing her best to jump up and down on the seat as their entire table vied to be the loudest.

Brittany turned accusatory eyes to Theo.

"You knew he was going to do this."

Theo shrugged.

"Of course, I did."

"I can't believe you didn't tell me."

"Well, I can't believe you had sex in my bathroom, so I guess we're even."

Brittany laughed and rushed out of the booth with Devery and Iris, making their way over to where the newly engaged couple were taking pictures and accepting well wishes.

This left Gus alone at the table with Theo.

"Congrats, man," Gus said, meaning it.

"Thanks."

There was a wistfulness about Theo then, something Gus had never seen in the chef's expression.

"You okay?"

Theo nodded.

"Yeah. It's just… it's been just me and him for so long, you know? It's hard to think of another person being there with us. With him."

Gus nodded, understanding. He felt the same way about Robbie.

"It's hard watching your little brother grow up, I guess is what I'm saying. Especially when…" Theo's voice trailed off, his eyes glancing back to the kitchen.

"Especially when you feel stuck?"

Theo met his eyes at that. Gus shrugged.

"I'm an older brother, too. And Robbie sure doesn't have his shit together, but there are times when he's out, or he's streaming, or we're just hanging, and he seems so happy I just sit there and wonder what I'm doing wrong. I spent our childhood taking care of him, and now he's this adult doing adult things, and what am I doing with my life?"

Theo nodded to where Brittany was admiring Min's new engagement ring.

"You doing something there?"

Gus let his eyes trail over to her, her cheeks flushed with

excitement, her eyes watery with tears, so happy for her friend. A surge of affection flooded him. Gus nodded.

"I am."

"Then I'm going to tell you. After you two left, your brother stuck around, throwing a tantrum, saying some dumb shit about how betrayed he felt. Said you two must have been going on behind his back this whole time, that he knew from the jump you had feelings for her but that he thought you would respect him and keep it in your pants."

Gus's anger rose. He knew Robbie wasn't taking it well, but to have a public meltdown like that was too much.

"We didn't do anything while they were together. I never saw her as anything but Robbie's girl until this weekend. And he's the dumb shit that cheated on her for months before she broke it off with him."

"The point is, he's playing the victim and writing a story. And he's a guy with a pretty healthy platform to get that story out into the world."

Gus snorted. "I'm not on social media. I don't care what his followers say."

"You're not. Brittany is."

Gus's heart dropped. Brittany had more followers than Robbie, had been building her channel for a lot longer and acquired very loyal fans. But the internet was vicious and sexist. If Robbie painted her as the villain, trolls would be all too eager to agree and jump on that bandwagon. Gus realized vaguely that he was gripping his glass of water too tightly.

"I'll talk to him."

"You need to. If you want this thing with Brittany to go any further than this weekend."

Just then, a shorter woman in a chef's coat stormed up to

their table and leaned down to Theo, getting in his face. Gus recognized her as one of the audience who caught him and Brittany in the bathroom before, but now with an extremely murderous expression. Theo, however, merely gave her a bored look.

"It is counterproductive of you to move everything in the kitchen after I have reorganized it." She was practically biting her words through her teeth, radiating anger.

Theo didn't even flinch. "Your reorganization was impractical. The staff couldn't find anything and were stumbling to complete the complicated recipes you left for them to prep because nothing was where it should be."

If anything, the woman seemed to get angrier, and Gus started to wonder if he should step in.

"Why even hire me if you don't let me do my job? You think I don't notice you undermining me at every opportunity?"

"If you were doing your job correctly, I wouldn't have to undermine you."

Even Gus knew that wasn't the thing to say. The woman straightened immediately, glaring at Theo for a moment before starting on the buttons of her jacket.

"Chef, consider this my notice. I think we can both agree I'm not a good fit for your restaurant."

Theo finally blinked. "You're really going to do this in the middle of a party we're catering?"

"You've left me no choice."

Her jacket was off, revealing the tank top and her sleeve tattoos she had hidden underneath, her full curves suddenly on display, which was probably part of the reason Theo was sitting up.

"This is unprofessional."

"*You* are unprofessional. I don't care what an opportunity this is, you have made the situation horrendous and I won't subject myself to it anymore. Your staff is lovely. You should give them a raise. But you and your Michelin star can fuck off."

She stormed out, Theo's eyes tracking her through the crowded restaurant until she was out the door, before relaxing back into his chair, looking both troubled and relieved.

Gus took a sip of his water, feeling awkward.

"It's for the best," Theo said. "Her bechamel was sub-par."

Gus nodded as if he knew what that meant.

"And now she's left in the middle of her shift. Who does that?"

"People who are fed up with their bosses?" Gus ventured. Gus wasn't close with Theo, but the chef had a reputation for being loud and emotional. He demanded a lot from those who worked under him and didn't take criticism well.

"If you can't take me at my worst, you don't deserve me at my best. You know?"

Gus shot him a look.

"Are you at your worst?"

Theo looked away.

"If so, you might need to look into that. Because it might be why you feel stuck."

"Strong words coming from a guy dating his brother's ex."

Gus felt the deflection for what it was and refused to rise to the bait. He stood up.

"Sorry, I only have room for one unreasonable person in

my life and that position is currently taken by my brother. You might actually have to do some soul-searching here."

Gus turned and walked toward Brittany, leaving Theo to think about the mess he had made for himself, grateful that he had moved beyond the need to self-sabotage and was ready to admit exactly what he wanted.

Brittany.

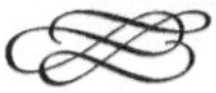

CHAPTER 20

BRITTANY

Brittany brushed the tears from her eyes for the hundredth time as she pulled Min in for yet another hug.

"I can't believe it! I'm so happy for you!"

Min was beaming, having already gotten hugs and congratulations from her sister and her mom, and the other friends around them. The diamond on her finger glittered in the low lighting, and Brittany found herself once again hopping up and down in excitement.

"When do we start planning?"

Min laughed. "Let me enjoy the night first, and then we'll talk, okay?"

Her eyes slid over to where Hayden was talking with Randall. At the same moment, his eyes met hers.

Brittany squealed. "This is so cute. You both have the same stupid smile on your faces."

"Our smiles are not stupid," Min said, the stupid smile on her face growing.

"I'll take a picture and send it to you."

"Don't you dare."

Brittany and Min grinned at each other.

"You happy?" Brittany asked.

"I am. I really, really am."

Brittany pulled her in for one more hug. She was so happy for Min, overjoyed that her friend had found her person and that they were going to make a commitment to each other.

But there was also a twinge of... something. Not necessarily jealousy, because Brittany wasn't the type to be jealous of her friend's success. But the sense of missing something that should be there, of feeling a hole that a person should be filling, was making itself known. And while Brittany enjoyed the hell out of her single life, she still felt that twinge.

But she pushed the feeling down, pulling back from Min to plant a big kiss on her cheek, leaving a bright Dirty Talk lipstick mark.

"I'm happy for you. I love you. Go get your man and celebrate."

Min squeezed her one more time and then went to Hayden, who watched her approach like a thirsty man would watch a glass of water. When she was close enough, he pulled her to him, wrapping his arms around her and pulling her up against him. When he kissed her, the crowd cheered.

"Seems like that went well."

Brittany turned to see Gus smiling down at her, his eyes glittering with interest and heat and something that looked a lot like affection. She beamed at him.

"I'd say it went really, really well."

"They sure know how to throw a party. Although if you want any food, I suggest snagging it now. Theo's chef quit."

Brittany winced.

"Yikes, another one."

"Yeah."

All while they were talking, he was leaning closer and closer, and Brittany realized she was also leaning toward him, wanting him close.

"Have I told you how gorgeous you look tonight?"

"It doesn't hurt to hear it more than once."

His hand reached up for her cheek, caressing her there, and Brittany felt like she could melt into a puddle right in front of him.

"Just fucking great."

They whirl around to find Robbie there, staring at them, leaning a little to one side and more pissed than Brittany had ever seen him.

Gus was already walking toward him, trying to head off the classic Robbie meltdown that was clearly about to happen.

"Dude, don't cause a scene, they're trying to have a nice party here."

Robbie scoffed. "How am I the one causing a scene? Me? I'm the victim here."

Brittany snorted, which she knew wasn't helpful but also knew was inevitable. Robbie was a baby when things didn't go his way, and he had apparently decided that this situation was exactly that.

And he was also drunk as a skunk.

Still, Gus tried to calm him down.

"You're not a victim. You are no longer dating her. You moved on a while ago."

"You moved on when we were still together, Robbie, remember?" Brittany added, not really feeling like being the bigger person when he was being such an ass. Brittany was a strong believer that if they went low, you dug a trench underneath to let the sinkhole swallow them.

Robbie turned glazed eyes to her.

"I can't believe you'd do this to me."

"Weird that I have to break this to you, but me and Gus actually have nothing to do with you."

"You're replacing me with him. The boring brother. No one even likes him."

And that's when Brittany saw red. She stormed up to Robbie, leaning up on her toes to get in his face.

"You listen to me, you waste of space. Gus is the best man I've ever fucking met, and if you think I'm going to let you talk shit about him just because he's your brother, you better adjust your fucking mindset. He has done nothing but care for you and clean up every stupid shit thing you've done, and he deserves a lot more respect than anything you've ever shown him in your useless life. If I ever hear you speaking of him like that again, this stiletto is going to be making a sharp entry straight into your eye, you understand me?"

The entire restaurant was quiet, and Brittany vaguely heard her voice echoing in the crowd. At some point, Gus had wrapped his arm around her waist, probably to hold her back just in case she started swinging. She couldn't blame him for quick thinking. But she never removed her eyes from Robbie, waiting for him to say the wrong fucking thing so she could clock him.

But instead of getting mad, Robbie suddenly looked sad. Distraught.

"I was never good enough for you," he said. The crowd around them had widened, giving them space, watching what was proving to be an even greater show than a proposal.

"You could've been," Brittany told him, not willing to give him an inch. "You could've shown up. You could've tried. Instead, you cheated."

Robbie nodded.

"I'm a fuck-up. Always have been. Just ask Gus."

At that, Gus tried to speak low just for Robbie, but Robbie pushed him away.

"No, I don't want to hear it. You've always been better. And now it's going to get thrown into my face every single day for the rest of my life. What a loser I am."

Hayden approached at that, Theo behind him. "Gus."

They didn't need to say anything else. Gus gripped Robbie, not letting him slip away.

"I'll get him to his hotel room."

He stopped in front of Brittany, keeping Robbie away from her.

"I'm hoping this won't be long. Stay with your friends. Don't go anywhere alone."

"I'm safe, Gus. I promise."

"Stay that way."

He didn't kiss her then, even though his eyes said he wanted to, and Brittany felt the loss of it as he dragged Robbie across the dining room and out the door. There was something about the moment that made it feel more real than it probably was. Like Gus was walking away. Like he had made a choice, and he hadn't picked her.

After Gus left, Brittany threw herself into the party and celebrating her friend. She and Dev managed to get Iris out on the dance floor, where they cut a rug, made friends with the DJ, and basically had one of the best nights Brittany had in recent memory. It was glorious.

She just wished Gus could've been there.

He sent her a text about an hour after he left, saying that he wasn't going to be able to make it back to the party and that Brittany should catch a ride home with Devery and her mom. He had already been in contact with the security at the party to ask them to assign someone specifically to watch out for her. Brittany was disappointed, even though she understood. But it still begged the question, was Robbie ever going to be okay with her and Gus being together? And if he wasn't, could she handle walking away? A few days ago, that answer would've been an easy 'yes.' After all, she and Gus had just started being intimate, and while they had crazy chemistry, Brittany had no plans to get between brothers.

But now... now she had come to know Gus. Rely on him. He was warm and caring and kind, but also vulnerable. He wasn't used to being the center of attention, always assuming that people would ignore him in favor of Robbie. He had put himself in the background for so long he had made a career out of it, the protector who faded into the shadows. But Brittany wanted to put him first and center him and make him feel how he made her feel: cared for. Special. Loved.

Shaking her head, definitely not ready to deal with those feelings, Brittany called a ride share for her and Devery, with Min and Hayden saying they would take the trolley 'for the memories,' whatever that meant. When she let herself into Gus's place, the lights were dim, meaning he was still out dealing with whatever drama Robbie felt like unleashing at the moment, and she was disappointed.

Determined not to dwell on a guy when she had things to do, Brittany changed into her comfy clothes, a tank top with a hoodie and her silk pajama shorts and went to her computer. Kickoff and the convention were overwhelming, as was her schedule, so while she checked her email often, she didn't always have time to respond.

Clicking through, she winced at the emails from her mother, the ones asking for updates on her designs, or for her to approve scheduled appearances for after Kickoff. Brittany didn't know how many times she had to tell her mom that Kickoff was busy and she wouldn't always have time to respond, but still. Kathleen would continue to do what she had been doing for years—running Brittany's life.

Brittany just wasn't so sure she wanted to let her anymore.

She loved the channel, loved helping people find their outfits and their confidence in turn. But there was a lot she couldn't do on the channel. She wanted a lot of things, and she just wasn't certain how she could get it.

She sat down with her tablet, the swatches she had picked up, and a soda, determined to get some new designs ready for the meeting on Monday. She tried to clear her head, to think of nothing but lines and shapes, of fabrics, of feelings. But every time she let her mind wander, it went to Gus. What he was wearing. His smile when he was trying not to. The anger on his face when someone grabbed her.

She shook her head after a minute or two, gazing at the drawing. Without realizing it, she had designed lingerie—something strappy and lacy and sexy that had her fantasizing about how Gus would react if he saw her in it. She realized she had laid out the black lace she had grabbed at the last minute, on a whim, and was running her hands over it while she was drawing. And Brittany had to admit that the sketch would look amazing in that lace.

And once it was in her head, she started a new drawing, and then another, and another. Ideas flying out of her stylus faster than she could get the lines down. Something had unlocked in her, a floodgate of creativity as she tried sketching lingerie for every type of woman she could think of. She imagined Min in a loose, silky negligee, something with tasteful slits cut out in just the right places that would drive Hayden wild. After a blink, she stared down at the simple drawing she had done, and even though it was rough, she knew... Min would love it.

Brittany wasn't sure how long she worked, but after a while her eyes were burning so she sat back, looking at her tablet in a daze. She had been struggling with designing for a few months now, and she realized why. She hadn't been feeling it, not with the high-end clothes her mother was insisting she design all while knowing that's not Brittany's style. But now she had new inspiration, and she knew in her soul that this was the right direction for her. A huge chunk of Brittany's channel was always spent on the first layer of clothing, the undergarments, and something about designing those intimate pieces was bringing out Brittany's creativity from its long hiatus.

An hour later, Brittany was tired, her eyes bleary, but she was somehow so amped up she knew she wouldn't be able to fall asleep. She was on the precipice of something. Her mother would hate it, but Brittany was finding that to be less and less of a motivator. She felt good for the first time in a long while, and she was going to revel in it.

CHAPTER 21

GUS

Robbie was a mess in a way that Gus hadn't seen since college, when Robbie had first discovered the Long Island Iced Tea had zero tea in it.

Gus managed to wrangle him into a cab, and then back to his hotel room. After a brief wrestle for the door key, Gus got him inside, noting that the hotel room looked a mess.

"Jesus, Robbie, what happened here?"

Robbie cast a bleary look around the place.

"I don't know, it just looks like this."

Gus managed to get Robbie on the bed. There was something so familiar about this, cleaning up after Robbie had fucked everything up. Dropping his plans for the night just because Robbie needed help. And Gus resolved that this was going to be the last time. He couldn't keep putting Robbie first. He was a grown man and could take care of himself, and Gus had to let him.

But since he was here, he'd try one last time.

"Robbie. What the hell are you doing?"

Robbie groaned. "Just leave if you're going to be an ass."

"I'm not being an ass, I'm genuinely asking. You were cheating on Brittany, so it's not like you were invested in your relationship. You lost Diamond, a woman who seems incredibly nice and intelligent, and you lied to her face for months. And now you keep digging your own holes, tripping into them and falling. What's the plan here, man?"

Robbie didn't answer at first, and Gus briefly wondered if he had passed out. And then Robbie started talking.

"I knew you liked Brittany. When I first brought her home."

Gus startled. "I never—"

"You didn't have to. I saw it on your face. You practically lit up from the inside. And when I took her hand, I saw your face fall, like you had lost something important. It haunts me."

Gus thought back to that moment, how struck he felt when he first looked at Brittany. Once he had learned she was with Robbie, he had immediately shut off that part of himself and never really thought about it again. But apparently Robbie had known the whole time.

"We didn't do anything while you were together. You have to know that."

"I do."

"Then why are you being such a tool?"

Robbie mumbled something into his arm.

"You're going to have to speak up, I can't hear drunken ramblings."

"It's another failure," Robbie said, a little too loud. "It's yet another moment of proof that I have no substance. That I'm not worth sticking around for. That I can't follow through on anything."

Gus gaped at him. "What the fuck are you talking about?"

Robbie rolled his eyes.

"I've heard it my whole life. From Mom. From teachers. And now, apparently, from women. 'Why can't you be more like Gus?' 'Your brother is such a solid man, why can't you follow his example?' Everyone that ever meets the two of us always, always prefers you."

Gus didn't know what to say. Since Robbie was born, Gus had stepped into the background, joining his mother in making sure that Robbie's needs were met, that he was happy, that he was taken care of. Gus could recall times through school, through college, in adulthood that people had flat-out ignored him when Robbie was in the room. Gus had no idea Robbie felt this way.

"Robbie…"

"You're always everyone's first choice."

"That has not been my experience. You are pretty universally beloved by everyone you meet. I'm always the afterthought."

Robbie snorted, a move that somehow caused him to throw himself off balance, even though he was lying prone in the bed.

"I'm loud, Gus. People like loud people for a short amount of time. My problem is I can't convince them to stick around for the long haul."

"Have you tried giving them a reason to?"

Robbie threw him a glare. "What the fuck is that supposed to mean?"

"It means you're self-sabotaging. You had a good thing with Brittany and you fucked it up."

"Hey, I broke up with her before she found out."

"How is that better?"

Gus was getting angry again. Robbie was a smart guy, which meant he was being purposefully obtuse when it came to how he treated women. And Gus couldn't stand it. He had a hand in raising this man, and there was no way Robbie was going to turn out to be one of those assholes who treated women like garbage. Not anymore.

"You did this, Robbie. If you were serious about Brittany, she would've been able to tell. But you weren't. She was an afterthought to you, and it was so obvious to everyone around you two that it was hard to watch. You fucked around, and you're mad that you fucked around and you're trying to blame it on other people. And now you're here bitching because she's moving on."

"With my brother."

"She was going to move on regardless. I'm just the lucky asshole she chose."

Gus took a deep breath, trying to calm down the rant that he hadn't realized had been building for years.

"You need to apologize. To her."

Robbie groaned. "Apologies are always so lame. The internet rails you for them."

"I'm not saying post an apology, numbnuts. I'm saying call her up, and apologize, preferably in person. You fucked up. It doesn't have to be a public spectacle, it just has to be sincere."

Robbie didn't say anything, just laid in the bed with his arm over his eyes, and for all Gus knew he had finally passed out. In the past, he would set Robbie up with painkillers, water, and have breakfast the next morning. But suddenly, the absolute last thing Gus wanted to do was take care of his brother.

He wanted Brittany. Wanted to make sure she was okay after the scene Robbie had caused, make sure she wasn't having second thoughts about them. He knew she was sensitive to causing tension between him and Robbie, and he loved her for that, but Robbie wasn't going to change anytime soon, and Gus was done waiting for him to get on board.

It was time to get Brittany and make sure she knew she was important.

Gus let himself out of Robbie's hotel room, a million thoughts flying through his head. He got in his SUV and drove the short distance to his condo. When he arrived, Gus was jittery with nerves and anticipation. The party had been a big deal, an even bigger deal than either he or Brittany originally thought. And Robbie had ruined it, in a huge scene involving Brittany and Gus. Gus wasn't sure where that put him and Brittany.

With a deep breath, he let himself into his condo… and froze. Snacks were out in full force, potato chips mixing with popcorn and soda in a rivalry for the decades. There was a lump of blankets in the middle of the floor in his living room that was surrounded by a laptop, a tablet, and printed-out paper scattered a little haphazardly.

"Brittany?" he called out, cautious. At the sound of his voice, the lump stirred, revealing that it had been Brittany cocooning herself underneath what appeared to be every single blanket he owned. Her head popped out from the mound, the look on her face excited.

"Gus! Guess what?"

He glanced at the kitchen.

"You made a pot of coffee late at night and are now too caffeinated to go to sleep?"

"Yes, but only technically."

She struggled through the blankets to stand as Gus made his way toward her, talking the whole time.

"I got home from the party and was going to work on my designs for Champagne, but instead I started drawing underwear, and look."

She got to him with her tablet, two blankets draped over her like shawls. When she approached him, she lifted her arms, and on instinct Gus grabbed her, scooping her up so her legs wrapped around his middle, his hands holding her under her ass. Her arms wound around his neck, and he felt her soft hair against his cheek as she buried her face in his neck.

"Hi," she said into his skin, and for the first time in hours, Gus felt himself relax.

"Hi."

"You okay?"

"Robbie's rough, but he'll sleep it off in his hotel room and hopefully wake up a better man who knows how to apologize."

Brittany lifted her head to look him in the eye, her hand at his neck sliding into his hair.

"Gus, I asked if you were okay."

He shook his head at himself, old habits dying hard.

"Yeah. I'm okay. Getting better every second, actually."

She grinned at that and then pulled her tablet around to show him. On screen was a drawing of something filmy but daring.

"You've been sketching lingerie?"

"I've been drawing a dozen of them."

She used her finger to scroll through on the tablet, showing him sketch after sketch, all loose but with enough details mapped out to show exactly how special each one was.

"Holy shit, killer, how long was I gone?"

"Too long, but I'm too excited to be mad. My followers are always talking about trying to find underwear and lingerie that works for their outfits, but still makes them feel sexy. I think they would seriously love these. What do you think?"

She was breathless when she asked, speaking in one long sentence, and Gus's chest tightened with how alive she was, how passionate and open in a way that he hadn't really experienced with her yet. She was sharing something she loved with him, and the privilege of the moment threatened to overwhelm Gus.

"I think Champagne is gonna flip."

She bounced up and down on him in excitement, and he felt an answering pull in his cock from the movement. He angled his hands to have a better grip on her, letting go of some of the blankets to better hold her, only to have his hands slide against smooth, warm skin.

Gus froze.

"Brittany," he said carefully. "Are you not wearing any pants?"

Her grin grew wider.

"I'm wearing what I sleep in. I was getting ready for bed when I thought I'd do some work."

"And just to be clear, what do you sleep in?"

Instead of answering, she let the last blanket drop, revealing that she was in the tiniest silk shorts known to man and a tank top so sheer, he could see the valley between her breasts and the hint of her rosy nipples.

Gus forgot how to breathe.

"Should I change?" Her voice was throaty, innocent in a teasing way. Gus gripped her tighter.

"You need to give me a minute, all the blood just rushed out of my head."

With a wicked grin, she leveraged her hand on his shoulder and rocked herself into him, dragging her core against his rapidly growing erection. It was a lot, too much, and Gus gripped her to make her freeze. She tugged his hair in warning.

"Gus, I swear to god, if you're about to tell me that Robbie is in too fragile of a state—"

Gus turned and set her on the kitchen counter, placing his hands on the counter on either side of her lush thighs.

"Let's go ahead and not mention my brother for several hours."

She leaned back, resting on her hands behind her.

"Hours, huh?"

"Days. Weeks." His eyes raked down her body, and he noted how she arched her back a bit, enjoying his eyes on her, pushing her breasts up for him to admire.

"This is what you've been wearing when you sleep in my bed? In my sheets? On my pillow?"

"Maybe less."

She bit her lip, a move so sexy that Gus both wanted to watch and also got jealous of her teeth.

His eyes landed on the small silk shorts currently covering her pussy.

"Tell me you're wet for me."

CHAPTER 22

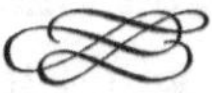

She didn't hesitate, so turned on by the command in his voice.

"Gus, I'm so wet for you."

"Show me."

He didn't move his hands from the counter as she sat up, sliding her shorts down as far as she could get, shimmying until they fell to the floor.

"You weren't wearing underwear."

His strained voice rang out in the condo, almost echoing in the otherwise quiet space. His eyes were zeroed in on her pussy, where it gleamed with her arousal. Teasing, Brittany lifted one leg, hooking it around one of Gus's arms that were still caging her in, leaving her spread open before him.

"It's a little warm for underwear, don't you think?"

His eyes finally traveled up to hers, seeing the tease, the heat, the desire, and his jaw visibly tightened.

"You owe me, Brittany."

"Owe you?"

"I showed you what I liked. Now you need to show me what you like. It's only fair."

The memory flashed through her of him working his cock while she was streaming, watching her as he got excited, his hand moving faster and faster. She had been in the mood for revenge, and she knew it would torture him not to help her finish that day. And now, apparently, he was going to pay her back.

"I'd rather you touch me," she tried. "I've been waiting for you all night."

"You started this game, killer. I'm only insisting on you finishing it. Show me how you touch your pussy, and I'll make sure you scream when you come."

Fucking hell.

Her eyes on him, she let her hand slide down her body, where her sex was exposed. She rubbed slowly at first, spreading her wetness, loving the feel of her own softness as she watched Gus watch her. His gaze was intent, like he was memorizing her movements, which knowing him, he probably was.

"It nearly killed me when you walked away yesterday," he bit out.

"I knew it would."

His eyes met hers, piercing her in place.

"Don't do it again."

"Don't deserve it again."

They glared at each other, both stubborn. Then he smiled. "Deal."

He glanced down where her hand had paused on herself.

"I didn't tell you to stop."

"You think you're in charge?"

"Brittany, I have wanted you for so long that the very cells of my soul burst with it. I have to be in charge or else I'm not going to last. The dream of you, your body, your warmth, everything I've ever wanted… it's too much for me to hold back. So let me be in charge this time and I promise to be at your mercy next time."

She lost her breath at his intensity, only nodding in response.

"Then get back to it."

She started working herself over again, letting the feeling of him so near affect her, letting herself inhale his scent and his heat and revel in the fact that they could finally touch.

Something must have shown on her face because he leaned forward, taking her mouth, hard and possessive, his tongue sliding in through her open lips to move in a rhythm that Brittany imagined perfectly matched what he wanted to do when he was inside her.

"Gus."

Her voice was broken, everything was broken, and only he could fix it.

"Baby, I can't wait. I need you to lie back."

He helped her, the cool quartz top of the kitchen island contrasting how hot she felt. He stared down at her, displayed for him. His hand went to the bottom of her tank top, playing with the edge.

"What are you thinking?"

"You're so fucking beautiful," he said. "Just when I think I've wrapped my brain around how gorgeous you are, I look at you again and it's all blown to pieces."

He leaned over her then, his mouth to her neck, letting his

teeth rake over the soft skin there before kissing his way down to the vee of her tank top.

"I can't believe you've been sleeping in this wet dream of a shirt. In my bed."

"Not just sleeping."

He licked her collarbone.

"That's right. You've been in there touching yourself, all while I was stuck out here on the couch."

His eyes glittered as one of his hands slid down the length of her body, right down the middle, from Brittany's neck, down the middle of her breasts, caressing her stomach, and then pausing right under her belly button. Brittany felt herself writhe, trying to inch his hand lower.

"Gus, please."

"Tell me what else you've been doing in my bed, Brittany."

"You know what."

"Running your fingers all over this beautiful pussy and making yourself come all while I was on the other side of the door trying to talk myself out of a hard-on?"

His hand slid millimeters lower, driving Brittany out of her mind with want. He leaned closer, teasing her, not letting his body touch hers, just hovering, letting her sense his warmth.

"What did you think about, Brittany? When you got wet, when you put your fingers inside your gorgeous body. Who were you thinking about when you came?"

"You."

"That's fucking right."

A wicked grin spread across his face, making him so handsome Brittany couldn't help but continue.

"I thought about you, and how you were always nearby,

always ready to have my back. Your broad shoulders and your insane body and those fucking eyes that always found me in a crowd no matter what. I imagined what you would feel like if you were there, how hard you'd be, where your hands would go. Your expression when you were inside me. Would you be soft and sweet? Hard and fast?"

"Whatever you want, baby. Just say the word."

"Then fucking touch me already. You promised you would."

Something flared in his eyes and finally his hand slipped down, touching her just as his mouth lowered to her breast, sucking her nipple into his mouth through the flimsy shirt. Brittany felt that tug everywhere, shooting down her body to where his big hands were circling slowly, spreading her wetness, teasing near her clit with each stroke.

"I'm going to make you pay for that," Gus said into her breast.

"We were trying not to do anything, remember?"

"Doesn't matter. I want to be near you when you come from now on. If you're shaking or clenching, I want to watch."

"If you'd just get a move on, you could do it right now, asshole."

He smiled, then worked her nipple again, letting his teeth bite into her just enough to have her moaning.

Gus was done talking. His hand on her pussy finally, finally stroked her clit, making Brittany's back arch with the sensation, just as Gus's other hand slid under her shirt, massaging her other breast. He lifted his head long enough to wrench the skimpy shirt over her head, throwing it some-where in the condo, where Brittany didn't care, because his mouth was now on her bare skin and she was drowning.

His hand slipped lower, stroking her entrance, pushing deeper and deeper with each stroke until she felt his finger slip inside her. Her hands, which she vaguely realized had worked their way under his shirt, raked her nails into his back.

"Gus—"

"You're doing so well," he said. "I can tell how good you're going to feel when I'm finally inside you."

"Hurry."

"No, baby. We're not hurrying anything."

And then a second finger joined his first, curling up into her, hitting a spot that had her spiraling just as he gave her nipple a hard suck... and she exploded. His fingers were relentless, working her as she clenched and moaned and shook, holding her tight and not letting her go. Never letting her go.

When the last of her convulsions subsided, his touch gentled until he was almost petting her. When she could breathe again, she opened her eyes to find Gus staring at her with worship in his eyes.

"You're incredible."

Her skin was flushed, she was naked and spread out on his kitchen island, and she was certain her hair was a mess. And then she got a good look at him.

"Gus, why the fuck are you still dressed?"

"I got distracted by watching the hot piece of ass in the kitchen come on my fingers."

His words made their way inside her, and Brittany guessed he could probably feel exactly how much they affected her.

"I'm feeling really fucking empty right now, and I need you to do something about it."

In response, he pushed a third finger into her, stretching her in a way that had Brittany grabbing his wrist.

"One more time, baby. I promise I'll fill you up, just one more time."

Brittany didn't release her hold, glaring at him. "Get your clothes off, asshole."

She was holding his wrist prone, but that didn't stop his fingers from curling inside her, and though she was doing her best to remain unaffected, she wasn't sure how much longer she would be able to hold out.

"Just one more. I want to taste you while you come apart for me. I want to sear it into my brain forever."

She was shaking with the effort it took to not get distracted, gritting her teeth, but he was relentless, using micro-movements to stimulate her.

"I'm going to make you pay," Brittany threatened.

"Looking forward to it."

She let go of his wrist, giving up for now, and he grunted in satisfaction.

"Thank god, because I was about to cave."

Before she could answer, he was moving down her body, pulling her thighs so that her bottom slid closer to the edge of the counter, and hooked a stool around his ankle, pulling it toward him so he could sit, giving him an angle on her body that she had never experienced before.

He lifted her legs, pulling them over his shoulders, and lowered his head, and Brittany forgot everything except his mouth, softly kissing around her, and his tongue, licking up and down, teasing her clit before finally drawing it into his mouth and sucking gently.

"Fuck, Gus."

"I'm working on it."

He buried his face in her, and Brittany felt like she was running a marathon as sensation hit, his tongue on her, his hands gripping her thighs, the cold of the quartz beneath her. But most of all, it was looking down and seeing it was Gus, with his face between her thighs. Gus, lapping at her like she was a treat, and Gus, whose tongue teased her clit. Her hands went to his head, buried in his hair, clenching and pulling until she finally managed to yank him off of her. His eyes were glazed, his face wet with her, his hands still clutching her thighs.

"If you don't get your fucking clothes off in the next ten seconds, I'm going in the bedroom alone to finish myself off."

Gus darkened at the challenge, not liking the idea of her walking away from him even though all evidence pointed to her not being able to walk anytime soon, thanks to him.

"Fine. But you're sitting on my face later, and you're not moving until I'm drenched with you."

He stood suddenly, pulling her legs off his shoulders and spreading her knees apart.

"Don't move."

His shirt was off in a blink, his pants and shoes gone shortly after. And then his arms were around Brittany, scooping her up, pulling her against him. She could feel him at her core, long and hot and thick, and she couldn't stop herself from rocking against him.

"How far is the bedroom?" she breathed into his ear.

"Too far."

He made it to the couch, sitting down with her straddling him on top. His mouth found hers, devouring, consuming, his hands kneading her ass in a grip that was on the edge of pain but only made Brittany's desire skyrocket.

Gus easily pulled her up to her knees so his tongue could reach her nipple, loving it so well Brittany forgot there was anything but his mouth.

His hands left her, and she heard a small rip as he angled her away for a second, not knowing where he got the condom but so grateful he had one that she leaned down and bit his collarbone. Once the condom was in place, Brittany felt him nudging at her entrance, and all she could think was that she was finally going to know what he felt like.

"You're going to ride me now, killer. Show me how bad you've been craving my cock. Show me how dirty you're willing to get to feel me inside you."

Brittany leveraged her hands on his shoulders, keeping her balance, and pushed herself down onto him. She was wet enough, but he was so large, stretching her in a way that his fingers had only hinted at. She sank slowly, wanting to savor this first moment when he would finally be inside her.

And then she was flush with his body, full of him, panting with need and so much more. He kissed her, one hand pulling her head toward him, one on her waist holding her down, tight on top of him. She wound her arms around his neck, falling into him, letting him set the pace, knowing this was exactly where she wanted to be. He pulled away, his lips hitting hers as he spoke just two words.

"Use me."

She sat up a little, adjusting her angle, sitting up a little just to slide right back down. He hissed at the sensation.

"Yes, baby. Just like that."

Brittany couldn't stop the moan that echoed through her. "Gus, please."

"You're doing so good. So fucking good."

His eyes were down, focused on where they were joined, so Brittany started rocking, bouncing, chasing the perfect angle, the perfect slide that would drive him crazy. She grabbed one of his hands that was clenching her waist and dragged it to her breast, pushing it into his hand. He immediately wrapped his fingers around her nipple, plucking and twisting and driving her insane. Her movements were wild as she moved to filling herself, chasing her pleasure.

"Yes, fuck, baby."

She was losing herself to him, to sensation, to the feeling that this was exactly where she wanted to be in her life, with this man, with his hands on her.

Brittany leaned back, overwhelmed with both the direction of her thoughts and with how good he felt. His hands caught her, holding her at the perfect angle as he lifted his hips, driving into her from below again and again in a steady rhythm that was pushing her to the brink.

"Gus..."

"I got you. Just let go."

But she didn't want it to end, didn't want to lose this feeling of him and how complete they made each other. So she fought back her orgasm, wanting this moment to last and last.

Gus, somehow sensing what she was doing, yanked her up, holding her tight to his chest, that glorious cock still driving into her in this new angle, hitting a new spot that had her whimpering.

"Brittany, you need to fucking come for me."

Those words sent her over the edge, a broken scream that he swallowed with his mouth as he kept up his pace. She bit his lip, holding it between her teeth, and she could feel him spasm inside of her, his moans and everything filling the space as he spent himself inside her.

They stayed like that, wrapped tight into each other, her face in his neck, his in her hair, his cock lodged inside her, neither of them wanting to let go. And it felt so right Brittany wanted to cry at the perfection.

Instead she pulled herself up, her body heavy and sated.

"Gus."

"I know." He kissed her shoulder, her neck, her ear. She flexed a muscle deep inside her, just an experiment, and he froze.

"You're going to have to give me a minute, killer. You just ripped my fucking soul out."

She slid her hand down to where they were joined, caressing his lower stomach.

"I could say the same for you."

"Your hand is saying otherwise."

"My body may have a mind of its own."

"Your body is fucking perfect."

He kissed her to make his point, long and slow, seeming to luxuriate in her, and Brittany melted, letting him set the pace, letting him kiss and play and tease her.

Finally, he pulled back, resting his forehead on hers.

"Snacks or bed?"

She grinned. "Snacks in bed."

He smacked her ass in agreement, making her laugh, and then stood up, still holding her to him, kissing her as he walked them to the bedroom before lifting her up and then dropping her on the bed.

"Stay here."

He was gone, and Brittany got the sight of his glorious naked ass in action as he walked back to the kitchen. She laid back, unbothered by her nudity, propping herself up on Gus's pillows in the middle of the bed, letting her mind clear and relax for the first time in a really, really long time.

When he came back holding two cups of water and two sandwiches, he stopped in his tracks when he saw her spread out on the bed.

"I don't think I've ever seen anything better than you in my bed."

"I wasn't sure what side was yours."

"Whatever side you're on."

"It doesn't work that way."

He set down the water and the plate, then kneeled on the bed, leaning over her, wrapping his entire body around hers.

"It does now."

He started kissing his way down her body, and Brittany could feel her breath quickening.

"I thought we were snacking."

"Right, sorry, you're distracting."

He kept her with him, rolling until he was seated next to her, then handed her one of the plates from the nightstand.

"Eating in bed?"

He shrugged. "I'm fine if you're fine."

They sat in companionable silence, eating their sandwiches and drinking their water. Brittany draped the leg closest to him over his leg, and he kept one of his large hands on her thigh. When she was done, he took her plate, placing it with his back on the nightstand. She stayed where she was, leaning her head against his shoulder, staring at where he had taken her hand and laced his fingers through hers.

"What are we doing, Gus?" Her voice was quiet. She hated to bring reality into this perfect moment, but she couldn't help herself.

"What do you want to do?"

"I don't know what I'm allowed to ask for."

He blew out a breath at that.

"Brittany, I'll be honest. You could ask for anything right now, and I'd give it to you if it meant you were here with me for even a few minutes longer."

He squeezed her hand for emphasis.

"I think I want to try, Gus. You and me. If you're down for it."

"I am very, very down for it."

"But I can't come between you and Robbie. We gotta fix that somehow. I don't want you to resent me."

He nodded. "We talked a little tonight when I took him home, but I think we need a full conversation when he's sober and ready to listen. And I do think he's ready to listen."

Brittany wrapped her arms around him at that, holding him tight, and he pulled her into his body.

"So we're really doing this?"

"Brittany, all I know is that if this weekend ends and I'm suddenly not seeing you every day, touching you every day, hearing your voice, I'm going to go out of my mind. You have become essential to me in all the best ways."

She was overwhelmed by his words and how right they felt. Not knowing what to say, Brittany kissed him, letting herself express with the kiss what she couldn't find words for.

Gus kissed her back, the feeling somehow familiar yet completely different from every kiss before, like they were coming together in a way that was unbreakable. And although she was absolutely terrified about what that meant, Brittany knew there was no going back from this. As much as she was it for him, she knew he was it for her.

CHAPTER 23

GUS

The sound of his alarm woke Gus up to find he was warm, sated, and completely draped by Brittany, who he vaguely remembered pulling onto him right before he fell asleep. She was there now, her head on his chest, her leg thrown over his thighs, and her arm wrapped around his stomach, holding him as tight as she could even while she was unconscious. Gus felt a warmth invade his chest, the feeling of how right this was, an affection of knowing that she was safe and satisfied and his. And he felt like an idiot for denying himself for so long.

"Shut that monster off," she mumbled into his chest. Gus grabbed his phone, which was blaring his alarm, and silenced it. He then pulled Brittany even tighter against his body, running his hands down her length. He couldn't get enough of the feel of her.

"Absolutely not," she mumbled. "It is too early and I need sleep."

Gus laughed. "As I recall, you were the one begging for more."

"That was last-night-Brittany. Morning-Brittany is more practical."

"Hmm."

He let his hands wander, stroking her slowly up and down her body, pulling her legs around him, letting his hands tease the sides of her breasts. He could feel her getting warmer and more pliant with each stroke.

"Gus."

"Mmhmm?"

"I know what you're doing and it's not going to work."

"So that's someone else's pussy wetting my stomach?"

At that, she struggled to sit, and Gus let her, grinning at how sleepily disgruntled she looked. Brittany was a lot of things, but she was never boring. She straddled his stomach, hands on his chest to hold herself up, that long blonde hair flying everywhere as she glared at him.

"Just because you have some weird chemical power over me doesn't mean I can go without sleep. It's the crack of dawn—"

"Six a.m. is not the crack of dawn."

"It is if I say it is, and I'm not going to be explaining to my live audience why I look puffy and sleep deprived."

"You can. You can tell them everything about what we did last night."

She shot him a look of disbelief. "You want me to tell them about our sex life?"

"I want you to tell them you're mine."

Brittany paused at that, staring at him, and he could tell the wheels in her head were grinding, processing something.

He sat quietly and waited for her to come to whatever conclusion she needed to. He wasn't going anywhere, and if she was going to be skittish about it, he'd rather know now.

But instead of bolting, she melted a little further into him. "Fuck, that was hot. Okay. Fine. Fuck."

She started moving, scooting down his body, and Gus was confused.

"What just happened?"

"You said something that really turned me on and now I'm blowing you, okay?"

His brain short-circuited.

"That's, ah, not why I—"

"I know, just shut up."

Her head was there before he could blink, her hand working his already half-hard erection with a familiarity that he savored. Brittany started slow, just gripping him tight and watching him get harder and harder as she worked him with her hand.

"Fucking hell, Gus. I'm going to have a sore jaw."

"You don't have to. Come up here, I'll show you how well my jaw works."

"Absolutely not. You wanted me awake, so here I am. Shut up and enjoy."

And with that, she lowered her head, her tongue giving him a small lick before she put the whole head in her mouth, twirling her tongue, and Gus saw stars.

"Goddamn."

She looked up at him, still holding his dick, her lips wet, her naked body nestled between his legs, and she was so beautiful he ached.

"Say my name."

She reached over, taking one of his hands and putting it on her head, before sucking his cock in again, taking him even deeper down her throat. When she started to bob up and down, he couldn't help himself, clutching her hair, pulling her back and forth on his cock.

"Brittany, you are so goddamn good, so fucking hot, with your perfect mouth and that fucking body screaming for me to fuck you."

She hummed, the vibration hitting him with a new sensation. In reflex, he pulled her harder onto his cock, driving into her and holding her for a second before releasing.

"Sorry, baby, you're driving me crazy."

She let his cock out with a pop and looked up at him, her eyes glazed.

"I love it. Use me, Gus."

And then she sucked him back into her hot little mouth and he lost his mind. He gripped her hair, fucking her mouth, his mind alive with her scent and the sight of her and everything. And when she slipped a hand around to his ass, squeezing, Gus lost it. He erupted, hoarsely groaning her name over and over again as she swallowed every bit of him.

When he was done, Gus collapsed, his grip now loose on her head. She took the opportunity to lick him clean before crawling back up to him.

"You've destroyed me," he told her.

"Don't wake me up next time."

"That's not the threat you think it is."

He pulled her in for a kiss, smelling himself on her and loving it. And then he yanked her up higher on his body until her knees were on either side of his head. She blinked down at him, dazed.

"Hold the headboard, baby."

And then he yanked her down onto his mouth, going to work doing what he loved.

Later, after Brittany had come on his mouth twice, Gus finally let her rest. While he was making coffee, he got a text from Val asking him to meet her at their coffee shop. After making Brittany swear she would stay in the condo with the doors locked until he came home, he headed out to meet Val. She was already sitting at the usual table, yet another terrible scone untouched. She glanced up as he walked in.

"Oh good, you're here. Got an update on the case," she said as greeting.

"Hit me."

"Florist called. The guy called in another order for our client. Wanted the driest, deadest roses they had to be sent to her."

Gus froze. "That's new. He's usually about wooing her."

"Something must have changed, because they said he wanted the card to read, 'you're going to regret betraying our love.' The florist was concerned to say the least."

"So, our guy thinks she's no longer his."

"Gee, you think that has anything to do with her tall, hot bodyguard?"

Gus leveled a glare at her but thought about it.

"If he knows about me and Brittany, it means he was at that party last night. And since the guest list was locked up—"

"He was a guest at your friend's party. Get the guest list so we can go over it. And start thinking of anyone you saw last night that looked suspicious."

"There wasn't anyone I could recall, but…"

She rolled her eyes.

"Just tell me, I hate the dramatics."

"Robbie showed up part way through. Drunk as fuck. Made a huge scene."

Val's eyes narrowed. "And then what happened?"

Gus shifted, uncomfortable with his past actions now that he knew Brittany's stalker was there.

"I took him back to his hotel. Brittany caught a ride with a friend."

To Val's credit, she didn't even blink at his confession. "You left the client unattended for a personal matter?"

"It was unavoidable. I contacted the security at the event and asked them to keep an eye on her."

Val pinched the bridge of her nose between two fingers, something Gus had only seen her do when faced with incredible stupidity.

"Where is our client now?"

"At my condo."

"You sure about that?"

"That's where I left her after she swore she would stay behind the locked door. I've installed a number of safety and security features. She's safe."

"That's good to know, because the address our guy gave the florist for delivery was yours. I would appreciate it if you wouldn't leave her unattended from now on. I'm adding Curtis to your detail, he should be there any minute. I already texted the client to know to expect him."

"Understood. I just wish you had called with this update instead of asking me to come meet you."

She threw him a confused look. "I didn't ask you to come here. You just... came here. I assumed you came looking for me."

Blood rushed to Gus's head, roaring.

"I got a text from you asking to meet."

"I never sent a text."

He didn't even realize he had started moving until he felt Val grab his arm and yank.

"Stay calm. We'll call 9-1-1 and head over. Curtis is probably already there."

"He's going for her, I have to get to her."

"I'm right behind you."

Gus was gone before she finished the sentence.

CHAPTER 24

"Coming!" Brittany yelled, hearing the door knock from the bedroom. She was already running behind from her day because of Gus and his bedroom antics. She'd had to cut her live stream short, which was annoying, so she already felt off when Gus's boss texted saying she was sending Curtis over to her while she was meeting with Gus. Now Curtis was knocking on her door. She was nowhere near ready for her busy day, and Gus wasn't back yet. Hoping Curtis being there meant she could head to the convention center so she wasn't late for her panel, Brittany rushed to the door. She stopped to look out the peephole, but the guy she saw was leaner and taller than Curtis, with a ball cap pulled down his head, a large bulky jacket covering his body. With that said, she couldn't deny there was something familiar about him.

"Can I help you?" she yelled through the door. The guy had heard her moving around already, so she couldn't really pretend the condo was empty.

"I was sent by your security team." His voice was deep but a little garbled, like he was trying to make it sound deeper than it was. Still…

"What's your name?"

"Curtis Davis."

Brittany froze at the blatant lie. The guy she could see through the peephole was definitely not Curtis, and if he was here saying otherwise, then she was in deep, deep trouble.

"You're not Curtis," she told him. "I've met him, and you are not him."

As Brittany watched through the peephole, the guy seemed to hesitate, the hat still pulled down over his eyes, angling himself from the peephole. But she still caught a glimpse of the side of his face finally, and realized…

"Kyle?"

As if he was dropping a mask, the man outside stood up straight, no longer bothering to hide his face. As she watched, Kyle raised his hand, one that Brittany hadn't been able to see through the hole, revealing he was carrying a hammer—which he slammed into the doorknob.

"What the fuck are you doing?!" she screamed through the door. He didn't answer, but Brittany sure wasn't sticking around. She sprinted for the bedroom where she had left her phone, grabbing it to call 9-1-1—only to find she wasn't getting a signal. Weird, since Gus's place usually had five bars, but she there was no time to troubleshoot it. Instead, she put her phone in the pocket of her shorts and locked the bedroom door. The banging on the front door continued as Brittany fought with the heavy dresser to push it against the door as a barricade. She got it in place just as she heard the front door bang open.

And then silence.

She took the time to look around the room, searching for anything that could be used as a weapon, but didn't find anything. The room had windows, but no balcony, no fire escape.

Trapped.

Kyle's voice came through the door, sounding familiar now that he wasn't trying to disguise it.

"I didn't want it to happen like this. You have to know that."

If Brittany wasn't so terrified, she would've laughed.

"Get the fuck out of my house."

"This isn't your house. This is <u>his</u> house." There was bitterness in his voice at that, deep and righteous anger, and Brittany knew if he got that door open, she was in real trouble.

"I'm on the phone with the cops right now, asshole," she lied. "Get the fuck out while you can before they arrest you."

"You're not calling anyone. I jammed the signal."

Fuck, okay. So there was no calling the cops, and no escape unless Brittany felt like jumping out of a four-story window. And, doing the rough math in her head of her chances of survival, she decided that would fall into the 'stupid' category.

Brittany went to the closet, searching… and then gasped in relief. A baseball bat. Gus kept a baseball bat in his closet, and she was going to go to so many of his games to thank the universe for this gift.

She just had to survive first.

Brittany peeked out of the closet toward the door. Kyle hadn't made a peep since he announced he had a jammer. Which was suspicious considering how much her stalker liked to ramble in his notes. Whenever she had thought about a future confrontation, she had always assumed he would be giving some lame villain speech about being misunderstood, but now he was silent as a cemetery.

As Brittany strained to listen at the door, she glanced down in time to see the doorknob jiggle. He was testing it.

"It doesn't have to be this way," Kyle yelled through the door. "Just apologize and open the door. I'll forgive you. We can move on from here."

"You're out of your mind. I'm not apologizing for shit. Get the fuck out of here."

"You won't apologize? After all the gifts I sent you. The love notes. The poems. They really mean so little to you? Hell, I even offered you my hotel room to stay for the weekend. And here you are, completely ungrateful."

Brittany felt her blood run cold. She had always known Kyle was handsy, and he constantly hit on her, but she had assumed he did that with every woman. She should've known, really. She blamed the adrenaline that had been coursing through her since she realized he was lying, that she hadn't had time to put two and two together. But this was her stalker, the guy who had been sending her all the fucked-up things for over a year. The one the police had said they couldn't do anything about unless he actually tried to hurt her. The one that her mother had hired security to protect her from.

And here she was. Unprotected. Alone. Fucked.

Brittany tried to remember how long ago Gus had left, but she couldn't. She had been in a post-orgasmic haze and hadn't looked at the clock. But he would be back eventually. She just had to survive until then. So Brittany gripped Gus's bat and planted her feet.

She called through the door. "My boyfriend's on his way back. He's going to fucking murder you."

"You're not understanding, sweetheart. I'm your boyfriend. And if that fucking meathead you've been screwing behind my back shows up, I'm going to put an entire round of bullets into his fucking head."

Well, that wasn't going to happen as far as Brittany was concerned. She'd leave with Kyle if it meant Gus was unharmed.

As she watched, the doorknob jiggled again… and then the lock turned. The fucker had found the stupid flimsy key, which meant the only thing standing between Brittany and him was the dresser and her backswing.

The door started thumping as Kyle threw himself against it, slamming the dresser away from the door inch by inch. Brittany gripped the bat, trying to remember all the things her eighth-grade softball coach told her, never realizing how it would actually transfer into the real world.

Brittany ducked into the closet. There was nothing to keep Kyle from getting in there, not if he had the interior door key, and there wasn't more furniture to use to block. The bed was too large for her to move, and the dresser was already on duty. If she survived this, she was going to talk to Gus about living a more maximalist lifestyle.

A shattering noise had Brittany ducking into the closet, gripping her bat tighter as the asshole managed to destroy the lock on the door, leaving only the dresser standing in between him and Brittany.

"You're making this very difficult on yourself, Brittany."

"Kyle, you're a fucking psychopath. You need to have your head examined."

"That's not a very nice thing to say."

"Well, it wasn't nice to send me a bunch of weird paintings you whacked off on, so consider this karma coming back to you."

There was more banging, and Brittany knew he was making progress on moving the dresser.

"I wish you could understand that we're meant to be together."

"You're meant to be in prison, Kyle."

"We'll see about that."

After a few more shoves, it was suddenly silent in the bedroom, which was somehow even worse.

"It's better for you if you just come out," he said. "I won't have to punish you. We could just move on from this and finally start our lives together."

Brittany closed her eyes, fighting the nausea that the dread brought. She didn't dare speak to reveal her location, but Kyle wouldn't have to search for her long.

"But if this is really how you want to play it, then fine. I can teach you a lesson in what real love is."

His footsteps were soft on the rug, but she could still make them out if she held her breath. She forced herself to wait, knowing Kyle was probably planning some move, something to catch her off guard, and Brittany couldn't let that happen. Another step, another…

And then she stepped out, already swinging the bat and catching Kyle as hard as she could in his shoulder. Fuck, she had been aiming for his head. But still, it pushed him to the side, and she took the moment of distraction to attempt to sprint past him, still holding the bat as she raced to the door.

But just as she got back into the living room, her hair was yanked back, pulling her along with it.

"Fuck fuck fuck—"

He pulled her to him, and she felt the heat of him and his breath near her ear and had to swallow back the bile that rose in her throat. His arm clamped around her waist, holding her still, but she struggled as much as she could, doing her best to ignore the stinging pain in her scalp.

"You feel so good in my arms. We can finally be together, Brittany. I've waited for you for so long."

Brittany thought about playing along but knew she couldn't do it. She wasn't strong enough to pretend like that. Instead, she struggled, trying to get an angle to kick him, but Kyle anticipated her move.

"Let go of me, you sick fuck."

He pulled harder on her hair, her eyes watering with the pain.

"You'll change your tune shortly. Just have to teach you a lesson first."

"Fuck your lesson."

Kyle's hand rose, cupping her chin, digging into her face and cheeks in a way that Brittany knew would leave a bruise.

"Lesson one: bitches don't get to talk to their master that way."

Kyle shoved her then, knocking her off her feet and onto the ground, and she instinctively dropped the bat to catch herself on the ground. Which was a big mistake since he immediately kicked it away. She scrambled to stand, but before she could he kicked her, hard, right in her side in a way that she figured her ribs were gonna have words about later. He flipped her over, kneeling while straddling her body, and her whole body fought and fought, scratching and swinging and kicking and bucking to get Kyle off of her.

"Stop fighting me."

"Fuck you."

His hands came around her throat, cutting off her air supply, and she grabbed his wrists, trying to ease the iron grip he had on her, struggling for breath. He leaned over her, in her face, his eyes alight with manic energy, and she knew this was the last thing she was going to see before she died.

"We could've been something. You finally ditched that loser and we were going to be together. I had been so patient, so kind, everything a woman wanted."

He leaned closer, his grip even tighter, and Brittany's vision started to go dark.

"And then you fucked his brother like the whore you are. How could you do that? Have you no self-respect?"

It took everything in her to drive her knee up into his groin, but Kyle shifted at the last minute and she hit his thigh. His chuckle was wet in her ear.

"I'm an idiot for loving you. You know that, right? I could've had any girl, but I thought you were special. But you're not. You're just like every other woman. You use men and spit them out. Well, that ends here. Hopefully you'll serve as a lesson to women as what happens when they—"

Whatever garbage he had been about to spout was cut off as he was grabbed and thrown off of Brittany. She gasped for air, turning over on her side as she took in gulp after gulp, not sure what happened but grateful for the second chance she had been given. Spying the bat in the corner of her eye, she lunged for it, grabbing it before staggering to her feet... only to stop dead in her tracks.

Gus was there, broad and strong and angry as fuck, judging by the flush of his skin and the way his powerful fist drove into the stalker's face over and over again. Brittany watched, her body still tense as she gripped the bat, just in case the guy made a move against Gus.

Finally, Gus dropped the guy to the ground, a crumple of clothes and blood where a man used to be. He turned, finding Brittany immediately and going to her. Gus pulled her tight against him, and that's when she heard him muttering to himself, his words barely above a whisper.

"You're okay, you're okay, tell me you're okay."

"I'm okay," she croaked, wincing at the sound, her throat already hurting. "Are you okay?"

She felt him nod against her.

"What do you need?" he asked.

"Don't let me go."

"Baby, I'm never letting you go again."

CHAPTER 25

GUS

Gus stepped into the hospital room where Brittany was waiting to be released, two cups of tea in his hands. She dressed in the clothes she had been wearing when they got there, staring at the floor. When she heard him, she looked up, the ghost of a smile on her face.

"I was wondering where you got off to."

"Heard the café had a secret stash of tea. Thought we'd indulge."

She smiled, wincing slightly, and Gus felt rage all over again for what that asshole had done. He gave her a searching glance.

"What did the doctor say?"

Brittany grimaced. "Cracked ribs. Some bruises and scrapes. Nothing that won't heal with some patience and TLC."

Relief rushed through Gus, even as his eyes landed on the bruising on her neck, his thoughts dwelling on what could've happened if he didn't get to Brittany in time. His blood running cold.

Brittany's hand landed on his, gently squeezing. "Doc says I'm good to go."

"Then let's get out of here."

Brittany had refused the ambulance ride but agreed to let Gus take her to the emergency department. Kyle, the stalker, had been taken into custody, and was already confessing to everything, from spoofing his number to trick Gus, to breaking into his condo and attacking Brittany. Apparently, Brittany wasn't the first woman he had done this to, but she was the first he had become physically violent with. And now he was going to prison for as long as the prosecutor could manage.

Gus couldn't remember the last time he had felt such terror than coming home to find his door busted open, and a man on top of Brittany, his hands choking her. When Brittany told him Kyle had pretended to be Curtis, the flames of anger had entered Gus's brain and still hadn't let him go. If she hadn't already met Curtis, Gus couldn't imagine how this night would be ending. After the police had taken away Kyle in handcuffs, a quick search of the building had found Curtis in the parking garage, knocked out with a head wound and stuffed into his car. Kyle had apparently been very thorough in his plan to kidnap Brittany.

The thought made Gus shudder as they walked out of the hospital.

"How's your door looking?" she asked, breaking him out of his thoughts.

"I've got a replacement coming tomorrow, along with some new fancy locks."

She nodded, and his mind raced.

"Are you okay with going back to the condo? If not, I can get us a hotel room somewhere without the memories."

Gus didn't want to think what it would mean to him if she didn't want to go back to his place. He'd have to sell it, find somewhere new, maybe somewhere closer to Los Angeles.

"I'd prefer the condo. All my stuff is there. That asshole doesn't get to ruin your home."

Relief flooded him, and they fell into silence as they stepped outside, Gus leading her to where he had parked. He helped her in, buckling her seat belt for her in a way that had her smirking at him.

"I'm not an invalid."

"No, you're not. You're a strong, resourceful, powerful woman that I consider a privilege to take care of. And since you scared twenty years off my life tonight, you're going to indulge me in my helicoptering for a few days."

Brittany nodded, still smiling, and he climbed in the driver's seat, taking her hand as he drove them out of the parking lot.

"I called Min to tell her what happened," he told her. "Fair warning, I convinced her not to come over tonight, but you will absolutely be bombarded tomorrow."

"Fuck. She's an early riser, too."

"I told her to bring breakfast."

They rode in silence until he parked in his building's garage. He shut off the engine, not making a move to leave, and Brittany must have sensed his mood.

"What is it?"

"I almost lost you. Because I was an idiot. I can't stand that I let you down."

Her brow furrowed. "You didn't let me down. You left me in the safest place you knew and were gone less than an hour. You did everything. I'm grateful to you, Gus. Don't you dare beat yourself up."

"A little late for that, killer."

He stepped out of the car before she could answer, walking around it to the passenger side to open her door and help her out. They made it all the way to the door, where the locksmith had rigged up a solution until Gus could get a new door installed.

Gus paused, wanting to take this slow.

"Hey, look at me." He cupped Brittany's chin and waited for her eyes to meet his. "I'm here with you. I'm not going anywhere. We're going to do this together. And if at any point you change your mind and want to go somewhere else, you say the word. Got me?"

She took a deep breath and nodded.

"I'm good. Let's do this."

He took her hand again, and pulled out his key, unlocking the makeshift lock.

Inside was still a mess from both the attack and from the police presence afterward. The interior door to the bedroom was still broken, but the locksmith had clearly done what he could to clean it up.

Gus watched Brittany closely for any sign of distress. But so far, she was taking in the scene, studying the wreckage from the attack with a clinical air. She moved toward the bedroom and looked in, surveying the damage.

"It's crazy," she said. "At the time it felt like the entire world was falling apart. But aside from the doors and some of your things, it's like nothing happened."

"You good?"

She took a deep breath before nodding. "I'm good. I'll help you clean."

"No. You'll sit on the couch under a blanket with a fresh cup of tea, watching whatever dumb dating show you want while I clean."

Her lips twitched. "Yes, boss."

And that's exactly what she did. Gus tucked the blanket around her, made her tea with honey to help her throat, and went to work righting the condo. Soon, the only evidence that something had happened were the doors. When he was finally done, he sat on the couch, pulling Brittany into his lap, draping her legs over his and tucking her into his side.

"This is nice," she said. And it was there, with her in his lap, her warmth slowly sinking into him, her body loose with relaxation, that it hit Gus exactly how close he had come to losing her.

He attempted levity. "Not to be dramatic, but I'm going to be attached to your hip from now on. To an annoying degree. Better get used to it."

"Okay, but Theo's never going to let us use the restroom again."

He couldn't bring himself to laugh, just held Brittany tighter, and she seemed to realize something was going on.

"Hey," she said softly. "I'm okay. You made it in time."

"I almost lost you." His voice broke, but Gus couldn't find it in himself to care. This woman had become so important, had become everything good in his life, and he almost lost her. He couldn't stand the thought, couldn't think of what this day would've looked like if he had shown up five minutes later than he did.

"But you didn't." She sat up, curling her hand around his neck. "You showed up when I needed you."

"Brittany, I don't know where this leaves us. I don't know what's going to happen after today, or after the convention, or anything. But I need you in my life. You're essential."

She gave him a skeptical look. "Is this the adrenaline talking?"

"No, this is me. Terrified at how bleak my life almost became because the woman I love was attacked and almost killed. Adrenaline is just a nice bonus."

She kept staring at him, her eyes darting from one eye to the other.

"Say it again."

"What?"

"That you love me."

Gus didn't hesitate.

"Brittany, I love you. And it may seem fast, but I'm suspecting that I've loved you since I met you. And I know you love me too, but you don't have to say it yet if you don't want to. It's enough that you're here, in my arms, letting me hold you after this terrible fucking day."

She smiled then, big and wide in a way that made Gus's heart turn over.

"I might love you, too," she whispered.

He kissed her, keeping it soft, sweet. Letting her know through the kiss how much he cherished her, adored her, worshipped her, and could feel the tension leave his body the longer it went on. He was home, right where he was supposed to be, with the woman he loved, and he was going to enjoy it for as long as he could.

CHAPTER 26

BRITTANY

The first feeling Brittany had upon waking up was how warm she was. There was a delicious weight on her, and when she lifted her hand, Gus's hair slid through her fingers. A glance down showed that he was holding her in his sleep, his body half on top of hers, chest to chest, his head tucked into her neck like she was his lifeline. She let her hands drift down his broad back, loving the feel of his smooth skin under her palms.

Last night Gus had helped her to bed, tucking her in before stripping down to his boxer briefs and sliding in next to her. She'd been worried she wouldn't be able to sleep, but with Gus there, she had knocked out in record time.

And now here he was, clutching her like a teddy bear, one of his legs thrown over hers, shielding her with his body even in his sleep. The wave of love and affection that hit her was strong, and she breathed in his scent, grateful to be there in that moment with him.

"Tell me you're awake."

His voice was rough with sleep, and he didn't raise his head from her neck. But his hand slid from her torso along to her side and down to her hip in one long stroke. Brittany couldn't stop what she knew was a goofy smile on her face.

"Define 'awake.'"

"Alert and ready to beg for my mouth on that gorgeous pussy of yours."

Holy fuck, okay. He woke up much faster than her, which meant Brittany was going to have to get her brain going. Hard to do when his hands kept slipping closer and closer to exactly where she wanted him to be.

She hummed. "Not quite that awake. But maybe awake enough for something else." She slid her own hand between them, grabbing him beneath his boxer briefs, loving the hitch of his breath as she held him, firm and possessive.

"Fuck."

"You've taken such good care of me," she said into his ear. "Let me take care of you."

She ran her hand up his length as she spoke, wanting him mindless, wanting him under her spell and command. And he must have sensed that in her, because he gave a soundless laugh.

"You're seducing me."

"Damn straight I am."

She gave him a small shove, and he turned onto his side, resting his head in his palm as he stared at her. She continued teasing him through his underwear, loving how his eyes darkened with each stroke. When she reached down to cup his balls, still feeling him through his underwear, his hips shifted, tensing for a moment before he fell onto his back.

"Okay, killer, take what you need. Just remember who gave it to you."

He sounded resigned, but the breathless growl he spoke in gave him away, his excitement, his desire, his needs. Brittany carefully sat up in the bed, being cautious about how she moved her ribs, and then slowly drew his underwear down to his ankles, throwing them to the side once they were off.

At first she just admired him. The muscles he earned both through the gym and through his job flexed under her gaze. Those long lines led straight down his abdomen to his navel to where his cock lay on his stomach, hard and ready. Brittany licked her lips at the sight, and Gus groaned.

"Fuck, the look on your face. Like you're going to devour me."

"I am."

And then she lowered her mouth to his cock, licking him up in one long lap from base to tip, and he shifted his legs. She leaned over him, laying her forearm across his thighs in an attempt to hold him still, and took him in her other hand, letting her tongue swirl over the head, tasting the precum there. She teased him with her mouth, her tongue, losing herself in the moment. His legs once again attempted to shift under her arm.

"Hold still," she warned.

Brittany went back, taking him into her mouth, down her throat, as much as she could, and Gus groaned, his hand landing on her ass with a light slap as if he was overcome and needed to get the energy out. His hand stayed there as she began to suck, rubbing her in circles, and she found herself pushing back against his hand. When he slipped into the loose leg of her sleep shorts, he stroked her there.

"Killer, you are fucking soaked."

Brittany hummed in response, too full of him for actual words. She felt him slip her shorts down along with her underwear, hearing his exhale when she was revealed from the waist down.

And then he lifted her and shifted her until she was straddling his face.

She stopped looking down at him as best she could from this angle.

"Gus?"

"I need to taste you, I can't wait."

Gus pulled down on her thighs with both hands until his mouth was right against her. His lips moved, and Brittany moaned, feeling his tongue twist and tease her. Needing to give as good as she was getting, she sunk her mouth back onto his cock, diving up and down, determined to beat him at this game where they both came out winners.

Their pace elevated, with Gus lifting her up enough to dive two fingers inside her, plunging in deep and hard enough to make her gasp, choking a little on his length. His mouth found her clit, sucking her in, and she felt that pull everywhere inside her, driving her higher and higher and higher as she frantically worked him over. When they broke, they broke together.

Brittany did her best to swallow as much of him as she could while her body shook and spasmed with pleasure, and then she lay on him like a blanket, no bones left in her body, no will existing to get her up and moving. She could feel Gus's rapid heartbeat against her stomach, heard his deep breaths as he floated back down to earth with her, and she knew she wanted this forever.

And then someone banged on the door.

Brittany didn't move.

"They'll go away," Gus told her.

They waited, but if anything, the banging got louder, added in with the ringing of Brittany's phone. She groaned, not wanting to move from where she had decreed was the most comfortable spot in America. Gus fumbled for the nightstand and answered her phone with a grunt. Long moments passed before he hung up.

"Who was that?"

"Min. She's at the door. She says she can hear your phone, and if we don't open up and give her proof of life, she's going to murder you herself."

Brittany pulled herself up with a groan, still straddling Gus's chest as she brushed her hair back. She felt his hands on each of her butt cheeks, kneading them.

"Not now. I have to get dressed before my best friend loses her mind."

Gus sighed but he let her go, and she stepped with shaky legs out of the bed. Brittany grabbed a pair of joggers and pulled them on, then pulled Gus's T-shirt on. If Min wanted to show up at some godawful time in the morning, then she'd deal with seeing Brittany less than dressed.

The banging on the door continued, and as Brittany approached, she could hear Min yelling from the other side of the door.

"I know you're in there, and I'm not leaving, so you might as well just open the door."

Brittany yanked the door open with a glare, only to be met with Min who had nothing but a relieved look.

"Oh, thank god." And then Min grabbed her, pulling her into a hug so tight Brittany lost her breath.

"Fuck, Min, I need to breathe," Brittany managed to croak out. Min immediately loosened her grip, pulling back to look Brittany in the face.

"Sorry, sorry, but I was scared shitless and even though Gus said you were okay, I couldn't help but worry and I had to see you and please tell me you're okay."

"I'm okay."

Min hugged her again, and Brittany noticed Hayden was behind her, holding a carrier of coffees and a few bags that smelled like food.

"You brought breakfast."

Hayden shrugged. "Just following orders."

They came in, setting up the food, and at a certain point Gus wandered out in a T-shirt so old it was almost see-through and sweatpants, and Brittany could do nothing but enjoy the show. He smiled at her, noticing her noticing him, and pressed a kiss against her temple before heading for the coffee, grabbing himself a breakfast sandwich before sliding onto the stool next to hers. Min watched everything with a rapt eye.

"So," she said. "You two are really together now? Not just bullshitting yourselves?"

Brittany and Gus made eye contact, slowly smiling.

"We're really together," he said. He slid his hand to her thigh and squeezed.

"And Robbie?"

"He knows."

"And he's fine with it?"

"He'll get over it."

Hayden nodded from where he was leaning next to Min, diving into his French toast while Min asked a thousand questions about the night before. Brittany did her best to answer, because lord knows if Min had been the one to be attacked she would want the same details. But by the time Brittany was finishing her coffee, she was tired, as if she had just worked a full day instead of just having breakfast with friends.

"So I have to tell you something." The nerves in Min's voice were enough to put Brittany on high alert.

"What?"

"Your mother called me. She heard from your security company what happened and she wanted more details."

Brittany sat up straight, seeing exactly where this disaster was headed and not liking it one bit.

"And you told her I was fine and that I'd just sleep it off."

Min bit her lip and Brittany let her head fall into her hands.

"She was concerned! I couldn't lie to her!"

"Min, tell me she's not on her way here."

Hayden snickered, and Brittany glared at him. He took the hint and gathered the dishes to bring to the sink to wash, letting Brittany focus her anger on Min, who was looking more and more guilty.

"She was just worried about you. I can't blame her. I was scared as hell, Brittany."

Brittany felt herself give in, knowing it was useless to be mad. If Kathleen decided she needed to be somewhere, she would be there.

"Did she at least give you an arrival time?"

A knock sounded at the door, and everyone in the kitchen froze. Then Hayden looked at his phone.

"We should head out, anyway. We have a panel for the game."

Min was already nodding, eager to get out of here before Brittany blew a gasket.

"Yup, sure thing, you're totally right."

She grabbed Brittany in a hug, the diamond on her ring finger glinting in the light.

"I'm really, really sorry."

"Just for that, I'm not going to show you the lingerie I've been sketching for you."

Min gasped and pulled away, excited.

"Really?! A Brittany original just for me?"

"Always. Although now it's going to be made out of itchy fabric. Ever had a wool teddy?"

Min laughed. "Knowing you, it'd still be sexy as fuck."

Gus, meanwhile, went to the front door and opened it, revealing Brittany's mom. She looked exactly the same, how Brittany knew she would look when she was older—same stick straight blonde hair, same disdainful expression on her face. Min nervously glanced back and forth between them all before grabbing Hayden's hand and pulling him toward the door.

"SogoodtoseeyouagainMsJenssen," she got out in a rush, the door shutting behind her before anyone could have replied. Kathleen ignored her to level Brittany with a look.

"It seems I should've hired a better security company for you."

Gus stiffened, and Brittany immediately went to his defense.

"Mom, chill. Gus was the one that saved me. I'd say you picked pretty damn well."

Kathleen sniffed, clearly unimpressed.

"The point of security was to prevent you from being attacked in the first place."

Brittany opened her mouth to probably say something rude, but Gus stepped in, a hand on her arm to stop her.

"Ms. Jenssen, I get that you're upset. You hired us to protect your daughter and she was attacked in my home, where she was presumably safe. But trust me when I say if it hadn't been here, it would've been somewhere else, somewhere she was alone and unprotected in a way that her security couldn't get to her, which possibly could've ended much, much worse. Now we have the guy in custody, your daughter will press charges, and we'll get him off the streets where he can't hurt anyone ever again. Brittany is safe now. This clearly isn't the way I wanted it to go down, but the outcome is still positive."

Brittany's mom eyed Gus, not used to being contradicted or spoken to in such a way. Brittany tensed, not sure what her mom would do. In the past, Kathleen had treated Brittany's boyfriends as speed bumps on the road to her real life, never more important than a quick dinner to meet before she promptly forgot their name. When Brittany had brought Robbie home, Kathleen had given him the once over and then proceeded to ignore him for the night, which was rude but still not the worst thing she had done. One time in high school, she had drilled so hard into Brittany's prom date about his plans after graduation that he had left crying. Kathleen could sense weakness, and once she did, she wouldn't stop until the threat was destroyed.

And now her shark eyes were focused on Gus, who waited patiently for her to respond, not appearing intimidated.

"By the way, feel free to ask your daughter how she's feeling after being attacked," Gus said in a mild tone of voice.

Whoa, that was some sass, which Brittany wasn't expecting but in retrospect shouldn't be surprised about. Kathleen's eyes narrowed, and then she looked to Brittany.

"You are okay?" It was almost a statement but had enough of a lilt at the end to disguise itself as a question. Brittany nodded.

"I am. A little sore, but grateful Gus got to me when he did." Her tone was pointed, but she was tired of her mom blaming the attack on Gus. After all, the asshole in jail was the one who had actually attacked her.

"Have you done any work on the Champagne sketches?"

Brittany rolled her eyes. Of course that was all her mom cared about—the damn deal with Champagne. She felt Gus stiffen next to her, and she put a hand on his arm.

"I did, but I went in a different direction from what we had talked about."

"Different than high end?"

Without answering, Brittany grabbed her nearby sketchbook and handed it over to her mom. Kathleen flipped through, silent, the sounds of the thick pages turning filling the room, and Brittany started to fidget.

Finally, Kathleen closed the book and looked up.

"Underwear?"

"Lingerie. All of my audience is constantly looking for good bras, underwear, anything that looks good under their outfits and makes them feel sexy with their partner. It feels right."

"Champagne has never done a lingerie line."

"Don't you often tell me that people don't know what they want until you tell them?"

Kathleen nodded, somehow her own words being the best argument against her, which Brittany had anticipated. She handed the sketchbook back.

"Send me some digital files, and I'll see what I can sell them on."

Brittany blew out a breath, tense. She knew what she wanted to say, and also knew this could go really, really poorly.

"Actually, Mom, I want to talk about that."

"About what?"

"About you stepping back as my manager."

Kathleen visibly froze in her perusal of the condo, turning with the elegance of a predator to eye Brittany. It was one of her most intimidating looks, but Brittany had had a lot of time to think about this at the hospital, and she knew it was the right move.

Even if this conversation was going to suck.

"What do you mean?" Kathleen asked, not blinking. Brittany set her shoulders.

"I mean, I don't think this is working. We're always tense, always on the verge of a fight. I'm tired of not feeling good enough for you when all I'm trying to do is something I love. Plus, frankly, I miss my mom. I want to keep business out of our relationship."

"You're firing me." It wasn't a question.

"Yes."

They stared at each other then, and Brittany put every

emotion she could in her eyes, willing her mother to understand what she was trying to say.

"I only wanted what was best," she said. "I wanted to be sure you would be set up and that no one would take advantage of you."

"You did. I promise. If I need anything, I'll ask. But you're still fired."

Finally, Kathleen nodded. "Fine. But you still have to answer my phone calls."

"Always, Mom."

Kathleen wasn't a hugger, so she merely nodded again and fiddled with her purse. But Brittany was happy. The relief that she could untangle their relationship, remove the business component and instead focus on being a family, was palpable. She felt Gus put an arm around her, squeezing her shoulder.

"Now, you can take me to breakfast and explain exactly why you thought it was a good idea to sleep with your bodyguard."

Okay, maybe they weren't all the way out of the woods. But they were getting there.

CHAPTER 27

GUS

Brittany's mom was out for blood, and really, Gus couldn't blame her. She had done what she could to keep her only daughter safe, and still Brittany had been attacked on Gus's watch. She wouldn't trust him anytime soon. They all talked for over an hour, explaining how Gus had come to be assigned to Brittany, the lead up to the attack, and the details of the aftermath. Kathleen asked many questions, blunt but clearly concerned about her daughter's safety. When she was finally satisfied with the details, Kathleen went to settle into her hotel room, warning Brittany that she wanted to have dinner to discuss the Champagne sketches further. Brittany agreed, seeming relieved that her mom was willing to go the underwear route with her.

After Kathleen left, Gus knew Brittany needed a break and took her to the Polka Dot for a coffee and terrible scone. They had just settled into their table when a voice called his name.

He turned to find Robbie standing there, holding up his hands as if to ward off attack.

"Don't yell at me. I was getting coffee and saw you here. I heard what happened."

Gus wasn't sure where Robbie was going with this, but this was his brother. He had to give him a chance. He met Robbie's eyes and gave him a small nod.

"You two are okay?" Robbie looked back and forth between Gus and Brittany.

"We're fine," Brittany told him. Her voice was tight, and Gus suddenly remembered that the last time they saw each other Robbie had been a drunken ass that had to be dragged out of the party.

Robbie shuffled his feet.

"Look, I just wanted to say I'm sorry. I didn't take the news well when you two got together, and that was after I had been an ass about our breakup. I think part of me always knew you two belonged together, and I couldn't stop myself from being a jerk. But I'm sorry. You both deserve happiness, especially after everything I put you through. And I'm going to be less of an ass about it from now on."

Gus waited. He appreciated the apology, but he knew it wasn't necessarily for him to accept—it was Brittany's. She stared at Robbie for a minute, then nodded.

"Apology accepted. I'd like to put all that crap behind us, especially since I'm with your brother now. You're important to him, and I don't want there to be a rift because of me."

At that, Gus stood up and pulled his brother into a hug. "Thank you."

Robbie hugged him, hard, and Gus felt a little proud of

how much he seemed to have grown up. It was a big step. When Gus stepped back, Robbie slapped his back.

"I'll see you around?" Robbie asked, his voice gruff.

"Damn straight."

Robbie nodded and, with a wave, headed out the door, leaving them alone. Brittany turned and looked at him.

"I don't know about you, but I am having the weirdest morning."

He scooted his chair closer and put his arm around her.

"I don't know, mine's going pretty well."

"Yeah? This is real?" She said it lightly, but there was something in her eyes that told Gus she needed validation.

"This is real, killer."

He pulled her in for a kiss, sweet and soft.

"Tell me we're not running off to some panel or something."

She snorted. "Nope. But I was going to stop by Randall's booth and do another stream. Which means I need to get dressed."

"Aren't your followers going to have questions about your bruises?"

"Yes. And I'm going to tell them, because I don't want this to happen again."

"Then let's go."

Gus pulled her out of the restaurant, and they ambled back to his condo. He helped Brittany set up her area for streaming and then ducked back to the kitchen, close enough to help if she needed it but out of her way so she could focus. She was so strong and capable, it was hard to watch her struggle with the bruises she was carrying thanks to that asshole.

When she hit the button to go live, she had a smile on her face.

"Hey everyone, thanks for joining. I had something happen yesterday that I want to address…"

GUS

"You can't propose to me." Brittany tapped her heeled toe against the hardwood floors of the event space, glaring up at Gus where he was simply grinning down at her.

"Good, because I'm not going to."

Her eyes narrowed in disbelief. Her very first collection was about to debut in a small loft in Los Angeles. Champagne had flipped for the lingerie designs and had immediately signed on to invest. Now, Brittany was part of a larger showcase featuring new and upcoming designers, and she was nervous as fuck. She was overloaded on caffeine and jitters, had a thousand loose threads to snip and adjust and didn't have time for whatever sweet gesture Gus had in mind.

Shortly after Kickoff, Brittany had relocated to Kimball, figuring she could design and stream anywhere. Gus had offered to move to LA, but Brittany decided she needed a new start, and something about living in Kimball where her life had completely changed felt right. The two of them had been together ever since, with Gus occasionally traveling for a job and Brittany often driving to LA for meetings or to see Min. It had been a rocky start, but they made it work, and Brittany couldn't be happier.

Except in this moment when her manicure was destroyed, her mascara was giving feral raccoon, and her stress was at an eleven.

"Then why do you keep fiddling with something in your pocket?"

"It's a pen, see." He pulled his hand out, revealed the click pen he was carrying.

"Gus, I mean it. I really can't handle one more surprise tonight."

"Killer, I promise. No proposal. Tonight is about celebrating you and your designs and your debut as a designer. No way am I stealing the spotlight."

She glared at him for another second, but then a PA came running up to her, harried.

"Ariel says the corset isn't fitting anymore, Georgina ripped her strap, and we're missing three shoes."

Brittany's eyes closed and she took a deep breath. When she opened them, her old fire was back, and she was ready to kick some ass. She stuck her finger in her boyfriend's face.

"You behave yourself."

He grabbed her finger and pulled her into him, kissing the daylights out of her until he felt her body melt against his.

"You're going to be amazing. Go show the world what you can do."

She grinned at him, then stormed off toward the main dressing room, ready to solve problems. Gus watched her go and felt more than saw Robbie join him.

"She doesn't know?"

"She knows, but she's too stressed to figure it out."

"So you're still waiting to do it at brunch?"

"Damn straight."

The next morning, Brittany, her mom, Min and Hayden and Dev and Iris, and Robbie and Gus's mom were going to a celebratory brunch in honor of Brittany's achievements. Theo had grumbled at the idea, complaining about all the people insisting on getting engaged, but Gus convinced him. So tomorrow, in a more intimate setting, he would finally propose with the ring he had purchased the day after Brittany had moved in with him.

He glanced at Robbie.

"Shall we find our seats?"

Robbie nodded, and Gus headed into the audience to watch the love of his life achieve her dreams.

ACKNOWLEDGMENTS

This book made me work for it. I wrote two previous versions of it that just didn't work before I accepted that Gus wasn't as outgoing as I thought he was. I had heard in the past from writers I admire that the second book is harder than the first, and that was certainly my experience with Brittany and Gus.

So thank you Daphne, once again, for patiently listening to my incoherent rants about story and for always being a great cheerleader.

Thanks to Kristine, for offering to read another book from me, and giving me the feedback I always desperately need.

Thanks to my loyal friends and family who read my first book and "didn't realize how much sex was in it" lol (I tried to warn you).

Thanks to booktok for all the recommendations, the support, and the inspiration. You are truly magic.

Thank you to Ellie at My Brother's Editor for helping me clean this monster up.

Thank you to Okay Creations for yet another gorgeous cover.

And thanks to you, for reading this book. I hope you're having the absolute best day.

🤍Ayla

ABOUT THE AUTHOR

Ayla Chandler is the pen name for an introverted ball of anxiety attempting to make it as a romance author. She lives in California with two cats and an insatiable love of Tiktok.